THE HAWTHORNE PROJECT

edited by tara caribou

Raw Earth Ink

2021

"In its purest form, an act of retribution provides symmetry. The rendering payment of crimes against the innocent. But a danger on retaliation lies on the furthering cycle of violence. Still, it's a risk that must be met; and the greater offense is to allow the guilty to go unpunished."

— *Emily Thorne*

"If you want to transition from your lower self to your higher self, a sacrifice is demanded. Everything has a cost. The greatest things have the greatest cost. Most people will never pay the price, hence they never become great."

— *Thomas Stark*

Table of Contents

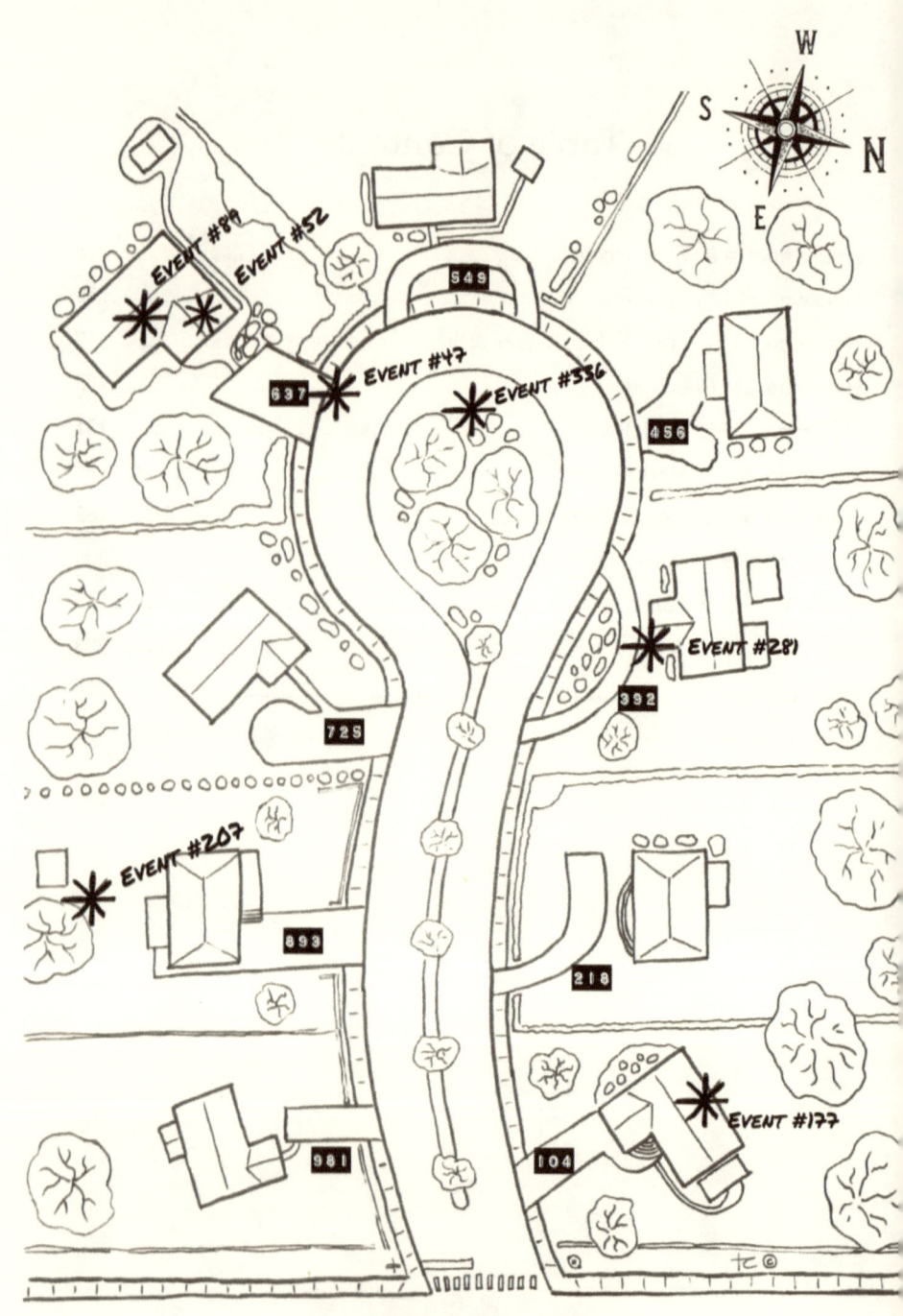

"Okay and sign here, here, initials, and... here."

"To be clear, once I've done my part, the land is free and clear? No strings attached?"

"Eventually it will need to be annexed, you understand?"

"Certainly that could be some time down the road?"

"Certainly."

A steady hand reached forward and picked up the pen then began the simple signatures. Across the desk, the other leaned forward and folded his manicured hands carefully before adding, "I understand you're to be a married man soon."

The signature faltered then finished with a slightly wobbly flourish. "Yes... though I can't for the life of me ascertain how you've come to this knowledge."

"Oh, I always take a keen interest in my... investments. It's good business. I trust she's a quiet one?"

The pen was returned to its holder. A throat cleared. "Prissy is a... simple, private woman. She adores me. But she never asks prying questions. Not about my work. Not about how I make my money. Nor will she ask about the land. You have my guarantee, just as I have yours."

"I believe our business is concluded, Jim. Do see yourself out."

104 W. HAWTHORNE DRIVE

104 W. HAWTHORNE DRIVE

by River Dixon

The members of the Terrance family sat around their dining room table, hands joined, and heads bowed. Jacob Terrance, who would turn eleven-years-old this November, had been delegated the honor of saying grace for the first time this evening. He pulled in a deep breath as the final words of thanks trembled from his young lips.

"Amen," the family sang out in unison.

Simon Terrance, husband, father, devoted follower of The Law, ruffled his son's hair with pride.

"That was a fine blessing, boy. A fine blessing. Your nerves didn't show through one bit." Simon smiled and winked at his wife, Anna. "Now, let's thank your mother for all she did preparing this fine meal before us."

"Thanks, mom," Jacob nodded.

"Thank you, Anna." Simon reached over and took her hand in his. Bringing it up to his lips to kiss the top of her hand.

"You're all more than welcome." Anna grinned as Simon released her hand so she could place her napkin in her lap. "Everybody dig in while it's still warm."

Simon generously spread honey butter on his biscuit before dipping it into the creamed spinach. "Oh," he closed his eyes and savored the onslaught of flavors. "This is so good. You really outdid yourself this time, Anna."

"Are you sure it's okay? I changed the recipe up a bit."

"Okay? It's better than okay. This is amazing. There's a little heat—some kick. Is that cayenne?"

"Just red pepper flakes. I used it instead of the paprika. I thought it would be a nice balance with the cream cheese."

"Well, let me tell you one thing, this is definitely—"

All three jumped at the sound of breaking glass coming from the living room.

Simon took pause, his eyes darting back and forth between Anna and Jacob. "Where's the cat?"

"He's right here, dad. Under my chair." Jacob pushed his plate forward and nervously folded his hands on the table in front of him.

Anna, clearly annoyed, wiped her mouth and threw down her napkin. "It's *him* again, I know it. I'm done playing games. Just who does he think he is, coming into our home and disturbing our family dinner?" The woman lit up with a rage unbecoming of her as she scooted back in her chair, attempting to stand but being swayed by Simon's gentle, controlling hand on her shoulder.

"Anna, let's take a moment. We don't want to be brash. We may do something we could regret." He got up from his chair and hiked up his pants. "Let's all three go out there together. Calm, cool, collected. Maybe this time he'll tell us what he wants."

"Wants? That's just it. He never tells us what he wants. This is all just a sick game to him." Anna's voice quivered as she forced herself to straighten in her chair.

Simon stopped and sat back down, "You know we have to have faith. The Lord will help us through this."

This time, from the kitchen, the sound of running water and slamming cabinet doors sent a chill through each member of the Terrance family that froze them in place. A blood-curdling scream reverberated off the surrounding walls, shaking the hanging light fixture above their heads.

"Join hands," Simon instructed, and the family followed. "Gracious Lord, You are our Loving Father who grants our protection and guides our actions."

The table shook beneath their joined hands, guttural screams rose from the cracks in the floorboards under their feet.

"I come before You to ask for my family's safekeeping. I pray You will guard our physical, mental, emotional, and spiritual well-being at all times."

Simon's plate flew from the table, shattering to pieces against the wall. He could feel his son's hand growing limp in his own. "Hold onto me, boy!" He shouted over the wailing cries and howling moans. "Keep the faith!"

Jacob felt the warmth of his mother, and the resolve of his father spread up each of his arms. This is the worst it's ever been, but he committed not to give in to fear.

"Let not the enemy gain a foothold in any aspect of our lives. Help each of us to keep trusting You, recognizing Your victory over the devil and acknowledging the strength you give us to resist him."

The air grew still as a calmness settled over the room. The family portrait fell from the wall, fracturing the glass and splitting the frame. A final scream grew faint, fading to a whisper.

"Amen," Simon conceded.

"Amen," Anna squeezed her son's hand. "It's okay, Jacob. It's over."

"Aye... a-men," the young boy fell into his mother's waiting arms, pressing his face against her shoulder, trying to stifle the tears but failing.

Simon let out a sigh as he brushed his fingers through his thinning hair and rose from the table. He picked up the broken picture, running his thumb along the length of the cracked glass. Three smiling faces stared back at him, with a fourth distorted, now unrecognizable. Anna met his eyes as he slowly turned, holding out the portrait.

"Oh no," she gasped as the crack in the glass drew her now frightened gaze.

"What's this mean, Anna?" Simon shook the picture, pleading. "What's he done?"

Anna darted from the dining room, not slowing a step as she navigated the debris-strewn living room and bound up the stairs to a second-floor bedroom. Her hand gingerly turning the brass knob and her other, making the sign of the cross on her chest. She whispered a short prayer as the door creaked open and the frigid, stale air pressed against her body.

"Abigail?"

Shortly after the birth of their second child, Simon and Anna Terrance decided they absolutely needed to leave the city. There was something about having a little girl that kicked their protective instincts into high gear. While they were dating, and even during the early years of their marriage, the city had a lot to offer them. A plethora of restaurants and bodegas provided endless food options. Shows and almost any genre of live music were available any night of the week. It was a magical place if one was single or a young couple exploring love. Having both grown up in the city, it was all they had ever known.

As is the case, with all the positive, there was the negative to contend with. All around them, crime was increasing on a seemingly daily basis. Even the nicer parts of the city were not spared. Murder, rape, armed robbery, car-jacking—all the usual suspects. When their first child, Jacob, was born, they naturally felt themselves moving in a more conservative direction. Priorities changed. It was no longer just about themselves or having a good time. For the first time in either of their lives, they felt the call to escape the chaotic urban center. They were drawn to the idea of small-town living. A sense of community, knowing the names of your neighbors, a house instead of an apartment, and doing all your shopping at local mom and pop stores increasingly appealed to them. They would spend their evenings browsing photos online of charming Cape Cod and towering Victorian homes. They would laugh together every time they came across a perfectly manicured lawn with a white picket fence. Never short of surprise at the fact that storybook places like that really exist.

Unfortunately, at that time, leaving the city would be nothing more than a dream—a fantasy to pass the time between the everyday grind. Money was tight, of course, and there is never a shortage of excuses as to why one cannot do something. But two years after Jacob was born, along came Abigail. That is when things changed.

Simon loved his son more than anything, but there was something about Abigail. During the long nights when she couldn't sleep, Simon would hold her tiny, swaddled body and lose himself in the innocence of her big, brown eyes. The little girl would look up at him with a fascination that seemed to hold answers to questions that Simon had never realized he was searching for. For the first time in his life, he felt that there may actually be a God, and he was staring into the face of undeniable proof that there is something beyond this man-made world. It was a spiritual awakening that wouldn't come to full fruition until a few years later.

The floor creaked under Anna's bare feet as she crossed the room and sat on the edge of a child's bed. Her breath danced before her in wisping strands of blue and gray. Chest pounding with the familiar anticipation of uncertainty that came each time she entered the bedroom. After a moment of smoothing out creases in the comforter, she folded her hands into her lap and bowed her head.

"Father, if it pleases You, I ask that You bless me with the knowledge of what needs be done. I come to You, Your humble servant, with an open heart, ready to receive what You have deemed. Without expectation, without pride, and without fear."

Simon put a finger to his lips and directed Jacob against the wall next to the room's entrance. They remained in the hallway, quietly reciting prayers of their own.

"If she has finally returned to Your arms, then I shall rejoice. I will welcome the peace You have ruled me worthy of receiving." Anna felt the pangs of guilt as she acknowledged that she did not truly believe all the words she was saying. "I know I am not without sin. And in my hollow words, I continue to sin. But please, Lord, she is innocent. Let me be punished and let her finally know Your Kingdom of Heaven. Let her be free from the evil that lurks in this place and in our hearts."

A strangely welcoming chill pierced Anna from head to toe. She was unable to move, frozen in place as eyes watched her from the corner of the bedroom. The darkness took a shadowy form, giving way to a defined shape that stepped forward, dropping to its knees at Anna's feet. The form shifted again, and a little girl in a button-down, flannel shirt and blue jeans crossed her legs and rocked back and forth as she smiled up at her mother.

A tear fell from Anna's red-rimmed eyes and hung for a moment off her chin before splashing onto her whitening knuckles.

"Abbie, you're okay. Thank You, blessed Father. I thank You. She's okay. My little girl is still here."

"Anna, I found it!" Simon burst into the kitchen, clutching his laptop. "It's perfect. I've found it!"

She shut off the water and dried her hands with a dishtowel. "What in the world are you yelling about? Found what?"

"One-zero-four Hawthorne. This is it. This is what we've been looking for." Simon handed her the laptop. Grinning like a Cheshire cat as she scrolled through the images.

"Oh my, just look at this place," Anna beamed. "It's incredible. Oh, so beautiful. It's huge! Four bedrooms, double car garage... and a basement."

"Did you see the price?"

"No, hold on a sec, let me go back." She almost dropped the computer as her eyes widened and mouth gaped. "You have got to be kidding me!"

"I know, right? I couldn't believe it either. We definitely have enough for a down payment. Anna, honey, this is it. I feel it in every fiber of my being. This is *our* house."

"Oh, my goodness, look, is that what I think it is?" Anna let out a squeal as she tapped the screen to zoom in on the image of the back yard.

"Holy moly, I didn't notice that before. You gotta be kidding me! A freakin' tire swing hanging from an oak tree. How could this place be any more perfect? That's it. That seals the deal for me. I'm emailing the realtor right now. We can't wait. I'll call off work tomorrow, and we'll drive out to see it. I guarantee that place won't be on the market for long."

In the living room, Jacob watched cartoons and tore pages from a coloring book as Abigail slept in her hand-me-down bassinet.

"I have a really good feeling about this, Simon." She set the laptop on the table and embraced her husband. "This is meant to be. No other explanation for it."

"We're gonna be like one of those Norman Rockwell paintings. Can you imagine?"

Upon hearing Anna's declaration that Abigail was okay, Simon braced an arm around his son's shoulder, and they both slid their backs down the wall to a seated position. Jacob picked at the skin around his thumbnail, and Simon held his breath, waiting for the next words to come out of Anna's mouth. The perspiration trickled down the back of his neck, adding to the growing dampness between himself and the wall. It was always cold in this part of the house. No matter how high the thermostat was set.

Simon squirmed and hated himself for not being strong enough to sit by his wife's side in Abigail's bedroom. He had tried once but was overcome with a brain-searing headache, nausea, and diarrhea as soon as he entered the bedroom. The sickness propelled him from the room before he ever caught a glimpse of Abbie. He had prayed on this and concluded that he was being punished for doubting his wife. His faith was weak, and he needed to prove himself worthy of receiving the Lord's gift. After that failure, Simon determined to entirely give himself to God in the hope that one day he would earn the opportunity to see his little girl again.

It was true that initially, he had doubted his wife when she came to him with stories of seeing Abigail. Simon didn't judge her, for he understood, but internally dismissed her declarations. A coping mechanism, he assumed. Perfectly normal. Trying to come to terms with the death of their little girl was tearing them apart. Anna had completely closed herself off from everyone around her. She didn't sleep, couldn't eat. Simon could do nothing but sit back and watch his wife spiral into darkness as he himself teetered on the same.

That is, until the morning he was awoken by the smell of fresh coffee, buttered toast, and crisp bacon. The sun was still teasing its rise as his ears perked to the sound of singing radiating up the stairs from the kitchen. It was a strange and welcoming start to a day otherwise weighed down with the burden of knowing. Knowing his little girl was gone. Knowing that she was never coming back. Knowing that life could never return to the way it was. Knowing that some things, once broken, can never be fixed.

Simon lay still, clutching the comforter under his chin, afraid to move until he was confident that the sounds and smells were not merely a dream, cruel in its offering of a smatter of hope. His eyes fluttered at the sound of clanking dishes, and he shot up in bed when he heard his wife sing out a good morning salutation to their son. Still cautious to the cruel trick that this may all be nothing more than a dream, Simon slid himself out of bed and found the robe hanging on the back of the closet door. The floor creaked beneath the weight of his hopeful footsteps.

In the doorway of the kitchen, he stood, stopped by Anna's warm embrace. Simon hadn't felt his wife's hands on him in such a long time. Her breath against his neck was warm and alive. Watery joy rimmed his eyes as he squeezed her tighter, afraid to let go.

"Good morning, Simon," her soft lips whispered into his ear. "I made breakfast. Are you hungry?"

Simon absorbed the words but gave no response. His hand slid as best it could under the tight braid on the back of her head; his forehead pressed against her shoulder. Overwhelmed by the weight of sensation tied to flooding memories, he rocked his head back and forth as his other hand searched for a place to rest, but nowhere felt right. He needed to touch her everywhere, all at once.

"I love you," his voice cracked, muffled against her over-sized flannel shirt.

"I love you too, Simon." Her voice had a surreal quality. Echoing in Simon's head as if from far away.

"I missed you... so much."

"I know; me too. I'm sorry. I'm sorry I left you and Jacob. I didn't know what to do. It was too much for me." She felt her husband tremble in her arms. "But it's okay now. Everything is going to be okay. He has brought me back."

"No, it's my fault. I was too weak. I couldn't find a way to hold us together. The pieces kept slipping further away. It was like I was watching you drown, but I was too afraid to jump in and try to save you. I've failed all of us."

"Simon, stop. Look at me." She put a hand under his chin and tried to lift his face toward hers, but he refused and buried his face harder against her chest. "Don't, please. Look at me. Trust me."

Jacob stood quietly, leaning against the counter, watching his parents with the eyes of a child. There seemed an aura radiating from his mother, spreading over his father, who himself was cocooned in a darkness that thrashed against the coming light. It was almost like a sunrise that rivaled the unstoppable morning that illuminated from the east. He could see the dark forces which have held his father for so long begin to retreat as the weakened man reluctantly lifted his gaze to meet that of his wife.

Her eyes smiled back at him. Devastating everything Simon clung to. They held something that hadn't been seen, hadn't been felt for longer than Simon cared to remember. There was peace in her eyes that gave birth to something Simon had been too afraid to ever recognize again. It was hope. That stinging possibility that a place beyond this tortured present could exist.

"Let's eat something," she smiled. "It's getting cold."

The shared reluctance was thick around the table. Plates were bountiful—looked and smelled delicious. Simon was well-aware of what Anna waited for. He wasn't sure if he was ready. It had been quite some time since they offered their thanks or even shared a meal together.

"Go ahead, Simon." Anna cupped her hands and bowed her head. "There is but a single path. We have strayed, but it welcomes us back."

"I... umm..." Simon nervously picked at his thumb and fidgeted in his chair, searching for the comfort this ritual once brought him.

"Hang on," Jacob reached to each side, taking a hand from his father and mother in each of his. Anna nodded and, squeezing Jacob's soft palm, leaned to her left and met Simon's hand across the table.

Recognizing the circle once broken again rejoined, Simon cleared his throat and found the words he had held suppressed for far too long.

"Father, We have gathered to share a meal in Your honor. Thank You for putting us together as family, and thank You for this food. Bless it to our bodies, Lord. We thank You for all of the gifts You've given to those around this table. Help each member of our family use these gifts to your glory. Guide our thoughts and actions and steer our hearts to Your purpose for our lives. In Jesus' Name, Amen."

"Amen." Anna lifted Jacob's hand and pressed it to her lips.

"Amen." Jacob's eyes searched his father up and down, hoping to once again see the strength and light that once covered the elder Terrance in an impenetrable shroud.

"Amen," Simon repeated.

Everyone was quiet throughout the meal. The struggle between the nostalgia of the past and their current situation was apparent, but each processed the flurry of emotion in their own way, in silence, trying to reconcile the illusion of normalcy that had abruptly returned. Simon was the first to break the reticence.

"This is really nice, Anna. Thank you."

She smiled warmly, "You are welcome."

"It's been so long, you know, since we were all," Simon remembered the empty fourth chair at the table, "together like this." The words weighed heavy on the appreciation that he tried to maintain his focus on. A darkness began to creep its way back over him.

"I know, Simon. It's been so hard—for all of us. But it's okay now. We've been given a great gift."

A crust from the piece of toast he was holding fell from his fingers and onto the drying egg yolk that painted the plate. Simon paused, holding back the words that threatened to blurt from his mouth. Collecting himself, he took a deep breath and proceeded cautiously.

"And what is this "gift" of which you speak?" Simon successfully fought back the condescending tone that threatened to coat his words.

Anna wiped her mouth with a napkin and straightened herself in the chair. Her eyes caught him with a confidence set in stone. "The Lord has blessed us with an incredible gift. He has heard my prayers, *our prayers*, and shown us mercy. His compassion has brought light back to these once hallowed halls."

"I don't understand."

"You will," Anna stood from the table and patted Jacob on the shoulder.

"Here, please help me clear the table, and then I would like you to go up to your room and play for a while. Your father and I need to discuss something amongst just the two of us. We'll explain everything to you once we've talked. Promise."

Jacob stacked his plate on top of his father's and took them to the sink.

"Just run some water over them and let them soak for a bit," Anna instructed the child. "Now go along up to your room. We'll be up shortly."

"Okay, mom. I'm gonna go read." Jacob turned as he walked from the kitchen, "I love you."

"I love you too. Have fun."

"Love you, dad," Jacob added.

"I love you too, kiddo." Simon rubbed the palms of his hands along the top of his thighs and watched his son disappear through the living room. Anna sat down across from him, picking off some fuzz from the sleeve of her shirt.

"Alright, Anna. Please, explain this to me."

"Promise me you'll hear me out with an open mind before you say anything."

"Yes, of course. Just tell me what's going on. Honestly, you're being kind of weird right now."

"There is nothing weird about a miracle. This is God's work. Nothing happens unless He wills it to happen. You know that. Or at least you did."

"Anna, yes, of course. I agree. You know me, and you know my faith, but what is this miracle?"

In the adjoining room, Jacob pressed his ear to the wall, struggling to make out what his parents were saying. The guilt he felt for sneaking far outweighed by his curiosity. At the words he heard his mother speak next, his eyes widened, and the book in his hand fell to the floor as a warm wetness trickled down his leg.

"It's Abigail. She's back."

The Hawthorne cul-de-sac was on full autumnal display. One of the highlights of moving to this area, Simon would often reiterate, was the generous population of old-growth trees. Dotting the neighborhood was a mix of maple, elm, and oak, but the most impressive was a massive sugar maple in their own front yard. Simon had no idea how old or tall the tree actually was, but he guessed it to be over sixty feet tall and easily as many years old. Truth be told, Simon didn't know much about trees other than the fact he loved to look at them and respected them as one of God's most wondrous creations.

Jacob and Abigail had been having a great time all week playing in the fallen leaves. A favored pastime for Jacob was collecting the helicopter seeds of the sugar maple and tossing them into the air, admiring the whirlybird motion as they spun, carried by the slightest of breeze, back down to the Earth. The hours of the day easily melted away on their flattened, paper-like wings. Abigail liked to peel the helicopter pods open, exposing the soft green seed that she would squeeze between her tiny thumb and forefinger, and if done just right, would send the seed projecting from its thin membrane through the air, hitting her brother. Most often, though, it would merely smash between her digits, and she would tenaciously begin the process again.

This day, however, Simon had given them a project to work on. He had produced two rakes from the shed and instructed them to start raking the leaves in the front yard into piles on the street along the curb for burning. He reminded them that there was nothing in the world like the smell of burning leaves on a chilly fall day. He promised to make hot cocoa as a reward if they did a good job.

The kids took on this duty with a sense of pride. They concluded that they would make the biggest pile of leaves anyone had ever seen. And they would do it together. For being siblings, they got along remarkably well. Sure, they had their moments, as all kids do, but overwhelmingly they rarely, if ever, fought over anything. They were close. Wherever Jacob went, Abigail followed, and vice-versa. Obviously, Abigail looked up to her big brother and wanted to impress him, but just as intensely, Jacob loved his little sister and felt it his obligation to look out for her and teach her the ways of the world.

Jacob hoisted the rake onto his shoulder, playfully slapped Abigail on the arm, and grinned a wide, tooth-sparse grin, gesturing her to follow him. The little girl adjusted the over-sized knit beanie just above her eyes and trailed after him, dragging her own rake behind her.

The colors burst forth from beneath their frantic rakes. Gleaming yellows, fiery reds, and burnt oranges danced along the ground and fluttered around their feet. They kept a steady pace to their work as best they could. Singing goofy songs and exaggerating the loot they would acquire on the fast-approaching Halloween night. They couldn't wait to make the rounds in the cul-de-sac. Their neighbors were incredibly generous when it came to handing out candy. Well, most of them, that is.

Across the street, a man sat on his porch watching the children with curiosity. The old man made it his responsibility to keep his sights set on the goings-on of the cul-de-sac. Not that he had much else to do or that there was really anything to keep an eye on, but he found it passed the time anyway. At one point, Jacob had noticed the man watching them and offered an enthusiastic, mittened wave. The old man raised a flat, open hand in the boy's direction and gave a quick, stoic flick of the wrist in acknowledgment. Abigail, observing what was going on and wanting to be part of it, yelled her own hello. Again, the man gave an open-handed flick of his wrist, but this time accompanied by a nod. Abigail laughed at the seriousness of the old man's interaction. Some of the people in the neighborhood thought he was an old grump, but she thought he was just silly.

The main pile of leaves on the street had grown to an impressive girth. Jacob stopped raking and stood with a wide stance and admired their work. Abigail dropped her own tool and joined at his side.

"Dang, Abbie. Now that is a pile of leaves," Jacob exclaimed with equal parts pride and astonishment.

Abigail stomped her feet and rubbed her gloved hands together in excitement. "Bury me!"

"Yeah?" he gave his sister an impish grin.

"Do it, do it, *dooo, iiit!*"

Laughter echoed down the street as Abigail dove face-first into the pile. She rolled onto her back and, barely visible, began to pump her arms legs up and down, in and out, as if making a snow angel.

"Hold still, I'm gonna cover you up." Jacob scooped a pile of leaves onto the rake, carefully balancing to not lose too much of the scarlet and ginger foliage. She lay stiff as a plank, arms across her chest, giggling through pursed lips as Jacob dumped the fall bounty over top of her. It only took a few piles to cover everything but her tiny, red face.

Her brother disappeared out of sight for only a moment, then quickly returned, fighting to stabilize another mound of leaves across the tines of the rake. "Okay, you ready? Here we go. Remember, keep your eyes and mouth closed." He tipped the rake, and the leaves cascaded down around and across Abigail's face. Burying any sign that the little girl was hidden within.

He paced the edge of the pile, ensuring he had done a thorough job of covering her. Once convinced the job was done to satisfaction, he took a long step back with his right foot and prepared to leap into the pile with her, belly-flop style. But before he could enact the graceful maneuver, he was struck with the sudden need to urinate. He didn't want to ruin the moment, so he tugged and squeezed at his crotch in a vain attempt to stifle nature's call, but it was too late. If he jumped into that pile of leaves now, he would surely pee his pants on impact.

"Dang, Abbie. Stay right there. I'll be right back. I gotta pee. Seriously, don't move. I've got a really funny idea for something to do when I get back. Okay?"

Ever so slowly, her little gloved thumb poked up out of the leaves, careful as to not disturb the leafy swaddling.

"Good. Be right back." Leaves crunched beneath his boots as he bound to the house.

The old man across the way had been keeping tabs on the entire spectacle. He chuckled to himself and tried to recall childhood memories of his own playing in the leaves. The warming nostalgia came to an abrupt halt at the sound of a roaring engine and tires shrieking around the corner onto Hawthorne. Before the old man could utter a word or call out in warning, the brown delivery truck plowed through the pile of leaves and came to a screeching stop in front of the Terrance house. Disturbed leaves showered down around the driver as he hopped from his truck to the street, a package under one arm. As the old man struggled from his chair, the high-pitched scream of a frantic child carried across and down the block. The moment took everything from him, and he fell to his knees, able to do nothing more than watch, frozen, as young Jacob ran from his porch to what was left of the pile of leaves behind the idling truck. The package slipped from under the driver's arm and crashed to the ground as he rounded the back of the towering vehicle to where Jacob was on his knees, begging his sister to be okay. At that moment, Anna Terrance stepped out onto the porch to see what all the yelling was about. Her heart stopped when she saw her son dragging her little girl's body from the street up onto the sidewalk.

Abigail's sunken chest hitched in shallow attempts to take in a breath. She could see, hear her mother and brother shouting down at her, but try as she might, could not form a word. Within seconds, the shouting gave way to a burning silence. Through her tears, Abigail caught a fleeting glimpse of her father, and then she was gone.

The pit of his stomach churned, and Simon was overcome with a dizzying hot flash. "Anna, honey, what do you mean Abigail is back?"

"Listen to me carefully, Simon. With an open heart. Don't let judgment or doubt cloud what I'm about to tell you. You know me. I'm not crazy, and I would never make something like this up. It would be blasphemy."

Simon conceded. "I'm listening," his insides twisted into knots.

"Last night, I was in Abigail's bedroom. Sitting on her bed and talking to God. I pleaded for some sort of direction. Understanding as to why he would give us such a test. Prayed for the strength to hold onto what was left of the tattered remnants of my faith. And I prayed for you and Jacob. Prayed for the words to say to you. It had been so long since we even looked at one another. Spoke a kind word or held each other."

Overcome with guilt and shame as he acknowledged the truth in her words, every fiber of Simon's being screamed at him to reach out and take her hand in his, but he couldn't. He was stuck in place—palms sweating with the tension of where this conversation was heading.

"It was then that God blessed me with the clarity of my own behavior. He opened my heart to the understanding that I resented you. Not that I blamed you for her death, no, but that I couldn't understand how you were able to keep going. Working, cooking, taking care of things—it angered me. It felt like you weren't hurting in the way that I was. Like you had left me to suffer and then moved on."

"Anna, I—"

"Please," she interrupted, "just listen to me."

Simon nodded, and she continued. "In that clarity, I found that His love was still with me. It always had been. And you, I had been hurting you to try and make myself feel better, feel normal. And that was so wrong of me. I know you hurt just as deeply as I do. You're just as lost as I am. I'm sorry, Simon."

The momentary relief Simon felt from her confession was erased by his own feelings of guilt. He carried his own burden of blame in all this. The disdain he had felt seeing her wallowing in despair day after day. He had judged her for that. He had found it easier to busy himself with things than to try and reach her. He had given up on her, it's true. The woman he had sworn to always love, honor, and cherish. He had felt hatred toward her.

Anna scooted her chair around the table next to Simon. She took his hand and lifted his chin so that their watery eyes met. "Simon, I'm sorry."

"I'm sorry too. I'm so, so sorry. The things I felt, things I thought, they were horrible. Anna, I—"

"Shhh, don't," she cut him off. "I have already forgiven you. You don't need to confess to me, you need to confide in God. You need to forgive yourself, and the only way to do that is through Him."

"Yes," he nodded in agreement. "I will. Thank you." Simon choked on the words remembering what had initiated this conversation. "Now, please, tell me about Abbie."

"You remember the song I always sang to her when she was a baby?"

"Of course. James Taylor, *You Can Close Your Eyes*. I love that song."

"For the first time in so long, I was feeling at peace. I sat back on her bed, closed my eyes, and began singing that song. I can't explain what happened next, but the room grew cold, colder than normal. Something passed over me like an icy feather tickling my skin. The melody continued from my lips, and I felt something in the room with me. A soft glow radiated up from the floor at the side of the bed. Somehow, I knew that I had to keep singing. Whatever was happening depended on that."

Simon watched his wife with intent eyes. He knew where this was going but wasn't sure if he could believe it once the words had been spoken. The firmness of her lips and unwavering voice told him that in her mind, there was no question as to what had happened last night. He fought the urge to interrupt and surrendered to remain quiet and let her finish.

"As I hummed the final bars of the song, I rolled to my side. The light from moments before was now gone. But in its place was Abigail. Praise Jesus, I'm telling you, right there, sitting cross-legged on the floor, was little Abbie. Oh, Simon, I don't know how to put into words the way that felt."

Anna began to shake violently, tears erupting; she threw her arms around Simon. He held her, rocking gently, trying to calm his awestricken wife. When the trembling subsided, Anna broke free from his embrace and gently put a hand on each side of his face. She pressed her forehead to his, the intensity of her warm breath giving Simon goosebumps.

"I don't know how or why, but she's back, Simon. The Lord has blessed us with more time. Tell me you won't question this. Tell me you will accept this with unquestionable faith in what the Lord has planned for us. You have to trust Him. Promise me. I'm afraid of what may happen if we allow our faith to waiver again."

Simon promised her at that moment that he fully accepted what she told him. But in his heart, he didn't believe her—couldn't believe her. What she spoke of was impossible. He believed that she believed, but certainly, there was no way. The only thing, though, was Anna's eyes. They never lied, and right now, against all odds, they were reflecting a truth in everything she said.

"Did she say anything to you?"

"No, she did not. She just sat there, smiling up at me with her big, beautiful brown eyes. I wanted so badly to hear her little voice but was content to simply be near her again."

"So, she just sat there? For how long?"

"I don't know. I don't remember doing it, but I must have fallen asleep. One minute I was there, sitting on the edge of the bed telling her how much I love her, and it seemed the next I was waking early this morning. I jumped up and looked everywhere for her, but she was gone."

Things were starting to make sense to Simon now. Obviously, she had fallen asleep, and the whole ordeal was a dream. He considered asking if she thought that was a possibility but decided against it. No, right now, that would be the wrong thing to do. It was best to go along with her story, at least outwardly. To support her and help her work through this. He had failed her for months. Now was the time to be there for her.

"I'm going to try again tonight. I'll do the exact same routine. Now, please, don't be mad at me, but I want to do it alone. I think it's best that I don't deviate from even the tiniest of details. Then maybe after a few nights of seeing her on my own, we'll try it together."

Simon felt a tinge of relief. "Yeah, that makes sense. I understand. Try it again just how you did it last night and see what happens. But please, promise me that if you start to feel out of control, or scared — anything, that you'll come get me. Or yell for me. Whatever you need to do. I'll be there, I promise."

"Thank you. I knew you'd understand." Anna let out a heavy sigh, "This is a lot to take in, isn't it?"

"That's putting it mildly." They both laughed at his quip but stopped in tandem as the sober realization weighed down on them that neither could remember the last time they laughed.

Simon scooted back in his chair and slapped a hand down on his knee. "Well, I think we'd better go talk to Jacob. The poor kid has got to be confused about what's going on."

Hearing this, Jacob, who still had his ear attentively pressed to the living room wall, broke into an awkward run/walk through the living room and up the stairs to his bedroom. He leaped onto his bed and pulled the comforter over top of him, remembering with sudden panic that he had peed his pants.

Not long after Abigail's appearance, something else began happening in the Terrance house. At first, the occurrences, while somewhat odd in nature, were easily rationalized and dismissed as absent-mindedness, the house settling, or even the wind. The cat also frequently finding itself on the receiving end of blame. Lights left on that Simon was certain he had turned off. Doors left open, others normally open mysteriously closed and locked, seemingly on their own. A broken dish here and there; objects being knocked to the floor. Nothing too disruptive, that is, until one mid-October evening exactly one year after Abigail's death. That was the first time they saw *him*.

The family was in the living room. Simon reading the newspaper, Anna reading a book, and Jacob on the floor working a puzzle. Setting down the newspaper, Simon noted with confusion the ice-cold state of his coffee. That was strange, considering he had poured it only moments before. Anna placed the book in her lap, watching her husband with curiosity as he examined his coffee mug from every angle. Abruptly, the book flew from Anna's lap, landing and skidding through the pile of puzzle pieces in front of Jacob. All three jumped and stared in wonder at one another. And then, a deep, raspy chortle came from somewhere in the living room, soaking everyone in a wave of panic. Jacob ran to his mother and hid behind her chair.

"Okay, so, I know we all heard that." Simon stuttered, feigning stoicism. "Just everybody stay where they are. There's got to be some sort of an explanation."

One by one, pieces of the puzzle tossed from the original, scattered pile to a new stack. Grumbling was heard by each of them, although none of them were making a sound.

"Hmmph, start with the edge pieces, boy. Didn't nobody ever teach you nothin'?" The deep male voice sent shivers across the family.

"Who's there?" Anna offered, reaching her arm around the back of her chair, grasping Jacob's hand.

There was no response, only continued sorting of the puzzle pieces.

Simon studied his wife, unsure of what to do next. "Please," she whimpered, "sir, what do you want?"

A blood-curdling scream rose from depths unknown, and Simon's heart skipped a beat as a deep split formed in the drywall in the corner of the living room. A burst of frigid, bitter air rushed forth from the crack, causing a chill that penetrated them to their very core. Anna leaped from her chair and around behind, throwing herself over Jacob. She peeked around the side, and her eyes met the same thing that held Simon entranced. A swirling, dark form hovered three or four feet off the ground with protrusions resembling arms, outstretched.

Nobody moved or made a sound. Then, as quickly as it had appeared, it was gone. Simon collapsed from his chair and crawled to his wife and son. Together, they huddled and prayed. It was a long night for the three of them as no one was able to sleep a wink. Although Anna found some level of comfort in her now nightly visit with Abigail.

Jacob bit his bottom lip as his father's arm tightened around him. There was something he had been needing to tell him but has been too afraid. With what happened at dinner, he knew that he could wait no longer, no matter the consequence.

"Dad?"

Simon loosened his grip on Jacob and leaned to the side, giving them some space to breathe. "I know, son. I know. This is all very confusing. I'm trying to understand it myself. Just keep praying for guidance; it's the best we can do."

"Umm, it's not that. I have to tell you something."

The seriousness in his young son's voice gave Simon concern. "Okay, I'm listening. What is it?"

"You know how mom always says she can hear God speaking to her when she's with Abigail?"

"Yeah," Simon nodded.

"What if," the boy swallowed hard and clicked his tongue, "it isn't God that's whispering in her ear?"

His father stared, dumbfounded at the boy. "Wh—, what are you talking about? Of course it's God. Only He could produce the miracle that is Abigail's return. Only He can give the mercy that our family so desperately needed. You need to check your faith, boy. You're bordering on blasphemy here."

Jacob scooted farther from his father. "Please, dad, don't be mad."

"I'm not angry, son. It's just that you have to understand that powerful forces are at work here. Danger comes when we doubt the Lord."

"I know, dad. I don't doubt Him, promise. But I have to tell you something."

Simon warmed to the fear in his son's eyes and recognized that he needed to approach the boy with a soft heart. "It's okay, Jacob. Tell me. I'll listen, and I promise not to be angry." He leaned in and tousled his son's hair. "Go on, tell me."

"I remember what you said about my sneaking, but last week I couldn't help myself. It was late, and mom's voice coming from Abigail's bedroom woke me up. There were some strange sounds too, besides the talking. I know you and mom told me I couldn't see Abigail, that it would be too much for me, but I just had to see what was going on. I couldn't help myself. I'm sorry, dad, but I snuck down there and peeked into the room."

A tinge of jealousy struck a chord in Simon. "What? You saw her? You saw Abigail?"

"That's the thing, dad. I saw something, but it sure wasn't Abigail."

Ice ran through Simon's veins as the words pressed down upon him. "What are you saying?"

"It was him, dad. Black, smokey, floating in front of her. Mom was talking to him like she was talking to Abbie."

"That's not funny, Jacob. The things you're saying are nothing to joke about. The Devil will use our own tongues to trick us," Simon lashed out, affirming his denial.

"That's exactly what he's doing, dad. He's tricking mom, and I think he's trying to take her."

"Wait, shhh," Simon jerked as he heard Anna's voice raise to a high-pitched squeal. He pulled Jacob closer.

"Oh, praise Jesus. Do you really mean it? You're ready?" Anna's jubilation rang from the bedroom. "Yes, yes, of course. I've waited for this for so long. I'm ready too."

Simon's heart pounded as he reached for the door.

"Certainly, they want to see you too. They've missed you so much. What? You need my help? Of course. I'll do anything. Oh, thank the Lord. Praise be in His name for all to see."

The doorknob turned slowly; Simon cracked the door ever so slightly.

"Of course, I understand. You can use me. We'll be together again. We'll play like we used to. All of us—together."

Through the doorway, Simon could see Anna lying on the bed, the dark form rising up and enveloping her from head to toe. Her body seized as the smokey tendrils penetrated her flesh. Simon rose to his feet and burst through the door.

"*NO, ANNA!*" he screamed as he slipped, stumbled, and fell to the frost-covered floor. "*STOP! WHAT ARE YOU DOING TO HER?*"

"It's okay, Simon. She's ready for you. She's ready for all of us. We're going to be a family again." Anna slid herself from the bed and crossed the room, dismissively stepping over Simon's sprawled, trembling form. Mechanically, she pulled the door fully open and disappeared down the stairway.

Simon scurried out of the room and found Jacob, still in the hallway, curled into the fetal position. Tears strewed down his reddened face.

"I need you to get to your room and hide. You hear me? Under the bed, closet, anywhere. And don't come out until I come to get you. Just me, nobody else, understand? Look at me... *JACOB!*" The young boy looked to his father with horror in his eyes. "Do it, *NOW*," Simon commanded.

Once confident Jacob was in his bedroom, Simon made his way slowly, methodically down the stairs. When he reached the living room, he could hear Anna singing from the kitchen.

"we gonna have a good time... and no one's gonna take that time away..."

He passed into the kitchen and was greeted by Anna turning from the counter, smiling, her over-sized flannel shirt crisp and covered with frost. It made a crackling sound as she brought her arm from behind her back and showed him the butcher's knife she held. A raspy, guttural laugh escaped from her twisted mouth.

"so close your eyes, you can close your eyes, it's al – right..."

WHAT THE SNOW BRINGS

981 W. HAWTHORNE DRIVE

by Christo Healy

Sunday. October 25th. 8:30pm

The air held a chill but it wasn't cold for the area. A gentle fall breeze rustled the leaves of the oak and elm trees that lined the sidewalk of the Hawthorne Drive cul-de-sac. Just past the old stop sign that wasn't so much cemented in anymore and creaked when the wind blew, the first house on the left side of the street was 981. The old man in the rocking chair coated in chipping white paint on the front porch of the beige house with white trim that didn't fare much better than the chair, was as much of a fixture as the trees. At this moment he was chewing on a toothpick and staring across the street at house number 104. His brow was furrowed and his eyes hard.

The screen door slammed open behind him, caught by the wind and banging into the siding of the house. A young man in his early twenties stepped out of the house with a frown. He inspected the hinges before facing the old man rocking gently in his chair who had yet to so much as look his way. The young man sighed. He walked forward and rested his elbows on the porch banister and faced the old man whose eyes were still glued to the house across the street. "It's supposed to snow this weekend, Pop-pop. Maybe you should get some practice sitting inside the house before then."

The old man waved him off. He spoke to the boy without looking at him. "I'm telling you Aaron, I seen it again."

Aaron McCallister rubbed at the tension in his face. "Come on Pop, don't do this."

Finally the old man looked over at the man who could have been a younger version of himself. He glared at him, as if his eyes held stingers. "I know what I saw, boy. Listen. You know them folks over there are religious zealots and whatnot. I bet they're in a cult. Maybe they used their voodoo or whatever to call forth a demon from Hell or something other."

Aaron reached into his pocket and dug out a pack of cigarettes. "I just can't even..." he said, lighting one. "They're just people, Pop-pop, our neighbors. You should try leaving the porch and talking to them one day instead of sitting here spouting cultural inaccuracies."

"Don't patronize me. I'm not too old to kick your ass. It came from down the road at the end of the cul-de-sac. It had no face. Just a shadow thing it was and it walked right through the wall into their house."

Aaron opened his mouth to discourage his grandfather again, but he couldn't help looking at the wall of the house across the way. He swallowed a lump in his throat and then shook his head. "No. Nope. I'm not doing this. Come inside. Have you even eaten dinner?"

"I'll eat when I'm hungry. Don't try to parent me, young man. I came out here from Alabama to raise you when your Daddy took ill. Your momma was long gone and I foot the bill. You talk to me with respect."

"I appreciate all you've done, Pops. That's why I want you to eat and not catch cold out here. I'd like to keep you around for a while." He took a long drag off of his cigarette to calm his nerves.

The old man pushed himself up from the chair on trembling arms. Aaron watched him, ready to catch him if his unsteady legs couldn't hold him but the younger man knew better than to offer him help. He stubbed his cigarette out on the porch railing where the paint had already chipped away and then set the unsmoked half down on the ledge for later.

"Don't look at me like that. I'm not handicapped. I'm just old for God's sake."

Aaron frowned but offered no rebuttal. He just stepped aside to let his grandfather have room to pass by. Aaron watched as he hobbled his way into the house. "I know what I saw," he said as he crossed the threshold.

Aaron bit down into his lip to lock the protest inside the cage of his mouth. He waited for his grandfather to make it fully inside and then he stepped in and gently shut the door, turning the lock on the knob.

Aaron's grandfather, known to the rest of the world as Wilson, shakily took a seat in a recliner in front of the TV. He reached over and opened a mini-fridge beside it and withdrew a beer. Then he grabbed the remote from the arm of the chair and turned the television on.

"Seriously Pop-pop, is that your dinner?" Aaron asked.

"I said I'll eat when I'm hungry. I ain't hungry."

Aaron looked at the screen and took a long, slow, deep breath. When he exhaled, he mumbled, "They just had to reboot Walker Texas Ranger, huh?"

Despite the mumble, Wilson heard what his grandson said and replied without taking his eyes off of the television. "Well, this boy ain't no Chuck Norris, that's for damned sure, but I like him."

Aaron just nodded and headed into the kitchen. He grabbed a stainless steel pot and filled it with water and then set it on the stove, turning the burner on. Then he retrieved a package of hot dogs from the full size refrigerator nearby and set it beside the oven. While he waited for the water to boil, he took out his phone and made a call. When the person picked up, Aaron said, "He's still not eating. I don't know what to do."

"You just keep doing the best you can. That's all you can do," a woman's voice said back. "He's old and stubborn, set in his ways."

"That's for sure," Aaron said, glancing through the doorway towards the living room where the man sat in his chair staring at what lay before him, just as he had outside, just as he did every day. "I'm just afraid of losing him. He's all I've got left."

"If he was all you had left, Aaron, you wouldn't have had someone to call and tell that to."

Aaron laughed and rubbed at his eyes. "You are pretty great, Nat. I don't know what I would do without you. You want to come by this weekend?"

"Sure, but it's supposed to snow at some point so we'll see what happens. No promises."

"Fair enough," Aaron said with a smile. He saw the water boil over the edge of his pot with a loud sizzle and he hurried to it, telling Natalie that he had to go and would talk later.

"What in the hell is going on in there?" his grandfather called from his chair.

"Nothing, Pop-pop, I got it." He blew on the foam billowing from the pot until it died down and then he tossed the hot dogs in and set a timer on the stove. Then he reopened the fridge and grabbed a beer for himself, sitting down at the kitchen table with it. He sipped on it while he waited for the hot dogs to boil. The beer was done before the dogs were. At last, he was putting them in buns and topping them with ketchup and mustard. Then he carried the plate into the living room.

His grandfather looked at the plate and then looked up at him. "You're right stubborn, ain't ya?"

"I learned it from you. Now eat."

"Just set it down. I'll get to it."

Aaron stared at him for a moment. Then he set the plate down on the nearby coffee table with a huff. "I'm going to bed," he said as he headed towards the staircase at the back of the room. "I have work in the morning."

"Night."

"Night." Aaron stopped halfway up the stairs and looked back at the old man, his heart heavy. Then he turned and finished his ascent.

Monday. October 26th. 6:05am

Aaron came bounding down the stairs, freshly clean and smelling like aftershave. He was already dressed in his work clothes and he hurried into the kitchen where the timer on the coffee pot had a fresh pot ready for him. He poured a cup and took it with him to the front door. He stopped, the coffee in one hand and the doorknob in the other. Aaron turned and looked over at his grandfather. He was sound asleep in his chair, the plate of hot dogs on the coffee table before him as untouched as they were when Aaron had set them there. With a frown, Aaron opened the door and headed out to work.

5:30pm

Aaron pulled into the driveway and cut the car off. He stepped out and looked up at his grandfather who had moved enough to make it from the recliner to the rocking chair. The old man's eyes were still glued to the house across the street. Aaron couldn't help turning and looking over his shoulder at it. A chill danced over his spine that had nothing to do with the weather. The thing that freaked him out was the fact that his grandfather wasn't the only one to claim to see the faceless shadow figure. Other people on Hawthorne had mentioned it going as far back as Aaron could remember. He used to wonder if it was his father, if he had hung around after he passed to look after him. But if that were true, why would he be going to the neighbors instead of coming to see his son?

Aaron forced himself to pull his gaze away from house 104. He turned back towards his own and climbed the steps to the porch. His grandfather actually looked up at him and smiled. It raised his brows. "What?" Aaron asked.

"I was just thinking... it's almost Halloween. I remember how much you used to love Halloween when you were younger. You'd always dress up and make me drive you to some spot you heard had the best candy."

Aaron couldn't help but share the smile on his grandfather's face. "That was a long time ago, Pop, but I did love it."

"Well, I was thinking, why don't you have that gal you've been talking to come over and help you decorate. You can make the house look all Halloween, try to have some fun for a change."

"I have fun," Aaron said, but it was less than convincing. He sighed. "I mean, what's the point? No one is gonna come here. Even the kids that live here will probably go somewhere else."

His grandfather was just staring at him, speaking with his eyes more than he ever could with his mouth. Aaron threw his hands up. "Alright. I get it. I'll call her. Have you eaten anything today?"

"Worry about yourself, alright? How was work at that overpriced supermarket?"

"Long. I'm definitely ready for a beer. Pays the bills though."

"There's more to life than that," his grandfather said with a groan before getting up and heading into the house without being told to. When Aaron followed him inside, he added, "When I'm gone you'll have plenty of money to pay the bills for a long time. Do something you love. Live."

Aaron just looked at him silently. His heart felt like it was being squeezed by a giant fist. Was that what this was all about? Was he forfeiting his own life because he thought it would improve Aaron's? "What have you eaten today?" he asked.

"I had some toast. Happy? Thought we were going to drink beer."

Aaron sighed with frustration. He grabbed two stouts from the refrigerator and brought them back, handing one to his grandfather. "At least this is close to food," he said. "You're getting so thin, Pop-pop. You're scaring me."

"I'm trying to look like one of them zombies before the holiday," the old man said with a grin as he plopped down in his recliner. "Someone's gotta get in the spirit around here."

Aaron grit his teeth and nodded. He took his phone out and called Natalie. "How would you like to come help me decorate for Halloween?"

"I'm at the hospital all night. Tomorrow?"

"Sounds good. It's a date."

"Is it?"

Aaron blushed and bit his lip. "Is that okay, Nurse Natalie?"

The sound of her laughter warmed him like a shot of whiskey. "Yeah. I think so. I'll see you tomorrow."

When Aaron hung up his grandfather was sipping his beer and chuckling behind the glass. "Oh hush," Aaron told him. "She's coming by tomorrow and maybe this weekend if the snow doesn't ruin it. No faceless spirit talk."

"Snow is gonna be bad. I can smell it, feel it in my bones."

Aaron sighed and plopped down on the nearby couch, sipping his beer. "It's not supposed to hit us until the weekend. They say it's going to be in the sixties the next few days."

"It's not the snow that you need to worry about. It's what the snow brings to this town. Maybe you should go spend Halloween with your girlfriend."

Aaron set his empty bottle on the coffee table. He let out an exasperated exhale and looked over at his grandfather who was turning on the television. "She's not my girlfriend yet, and what do you think the snow is going to bring? More shadow people?"

Wilson McCallister grumbled and opened his mini fridge for another beer. "I guess you never know since it'll be Halloween and all, but no. Greenfield is a commuter town for Milwaukee, boy. If folks are passing through on their commute and can't go any further due to the snow, then all kinds of folks are going to be needing places to stay in our little town. There will be a lot of no good around here until it passes."

Aaron chewed on his lip and thought about what his grandfather was saying. "It's snowed before," he said then. "Nothing bad came of it. We're in our own little world over here on Hawthorne. I'm sure it will be fine."

His grandfather didn't answer. He just leaned back in his chair and pinned his eyes to the fight scene portrayed on the television.

Tuesday. October 27th. 6:09pm

Aaron stood on the porch smoking a cigarette. He was facing the house across the street and he felt the urge to go knock on their door, to get to know them, to ask them if they've seen any ghosts lately, but he didn't feel like listening to their religious talk. After losing his father and his mom walking out, then his grandmother passing, he had lost too much to want to hear about God's mysterious ways, true or not.

He heard the screen door open and was glad to hear that it didn't bang against the house. It seemed his tightening the screws on the hinges worked. The sound of the door was followed by the scraping shuffle of his grandfather's footsteps. "She's not coming is she?" Wilson said from behind him.

Aaron took a drag off of his cigarette, and exhaled smoke with a sigh. "Nope. She called and cancelled. She got called into work."

His grandfather sighed. "That's the life of a nurse. You need to be ready for that and accept it if you really like this girl."

"I do, but what good is it if I never get to see her."

"Depends on how good it is when you do get to see her."

Aaron stubbed out his cigarette and walked past his grandfather into the house for a change. He plopped down on the couch, feeling defeated and down. He wished his grandfather had never given him the idea to invite Natalie over. He wouldn't have done it on his own and then he wouldn't have been disappointed.

He looked up and saw his grandfather in the doorway. The old man had his hands on his hips and he was scowling. "What are you doing moping?"

"It's what I feel like doing, okay?"

"Nope." The old man crossed the threshold into the house, shuffling along as he did. "If that gal is coming by this weekend for the holiday the house should still be festive and whatnot so get up off your ass and help me decorate."

Aaron raised his brows. "*You're* going to decorate?" he asked with a chuckle.

"Why not? ...Watch what you answer now."

"I'm not trying to be offensive. I just didn't see you decorating."

"Well you're not going to see it if you don't get up off your crying ass and help me."

Aaron laughed and shook his head. He huffed and stood up. "Alright. Let's do it."

Together they went to the storage room and retrieved all the boxes of Halloween stuff from when Aaron was a child. They hung up black and orange streamers on the trees outside and put witches and mummies in the windows of the beige house. They inflated a skeleton and let him sway in the gentle breeze from the center of the front lawn. Plastic skulls were placed on the railing to the porch and more decorations were hung up inside the house.

When they were finished, they stood beside each other and sighed contentedly. "Looks pretty good if I don't say so myself," Wilson remarked.

Aaron nodded. "You know what? Tomorrow, I'm going to bring some pumpkins home with me when I come home from work. We sell them at the store. You and I are gonna carve some jack o'lanterns to put the finishing touch on the atmosphere."

"You should get some candy too, just in case the neighbor kids come looking."

"Only if you eat some."

"Well then you better get something good like spice drops or circus peanuts."

Aaron shook his head vigorously. "What?! Who thinks those are good? Next thing you'll ask for black licorice."

"Oh yeah. That too. I love it. Grew up on that stuff."

"Gross, Pop-pop. Candy has gotten much better since then."

"Nothing better than the classics," his grandfather told him as he worked to lower himself into his chair.

"You're just holding onto that belief because you *are* one of the classics," Aaron said with a laugh.

"You're damn right I am," his grandfather answered, as he picked up the remote and turned on the TV. Aaron decided with a shrug to go join him, taking his own seat on the couch.

After a few minutes of campy crime drama, Aaron said, "Thanks Pop-pop. You really helped me out tonight, got me out of my funk. I appreciate you."

"I know."

After that, they just sat in silence and watched TV together for hours. Aaron didn't even cook dinner. He decided to splurge and ordered a pizza to the house. He ate half of it and the other half sat in the open box on the coffee table. He looked at his grandfather and frowned but he didn't voice his feelings. He didn't know the last time the man ate a meal. He was going to die if he didn't. Aaron knew that. And what a terrible way to go, he thought. Who would willfully starve themselves? It had to be painful. There was no way the old man wasn't hungry. His gut had to be screaming to be fed at this point but his stubborn nature just overrode it. For whatever reason, he had just put his foot down and decided that he wasn't going to eat. Aaron knew that he couldn't force feed him. He was going to do what he was going to do.

He looked over at him and sighed when he saw that the old man had fallen asleep in his chair again. He had a bed. He just chose to never use it. Something about chairs that man just seemed to love. Aaron took a deep breath to steady his nerves and he turned the television off. Then he stood and walked past the sleeping man en route for the staircase to his own bed. He stopped at the foot of the stairs when his phone vibrated in his pocket.

Aaron took his phone out and looked to see what it was. He had gotten a text message from Natalie. She said she was sorry and she would make it up to him this weekend. Then she punctuated it with a flurry of emojis. Aaron found himself smiling. Pop-pop was right. He needed to look at how good the times were when they were together and focus on that. "It's okay," he typed back and sent.

When he saw the red heart emoji appear on his screen, he went up the staircase to bed with a skip in his step. When he got to his bedroom, he looked out the window beside his bed and stared at the sky that was dimly lit by the moon's glow. "You better not snow too much and make it so that she can't get to me this weekend," he said. "If you do, I'll ask the neighbors to use their Christian voodoo on you."

Aaron collapsed on his bed and laughed at his own joke. Then he leaned over and stretched for his clock, set his alarm for work in the morning and went to sleep. Before he did, he said a prayer for his Pop-pop, just in case someone was listening. He didn't know if it would really do any good, but he knew that it wouldn't hurt to try. He was afraid. He wasn't ready to lose anyone else. Before long he was immersed in dreams of spending Halloween with Natalie, holding hands and walking through streets full of kids in costumes trick or treating. They stopped by that rickety old stop sign and kissed passionately. When his alarm went off, Aaron didn't want to get up. He wished he could lay there all day, to abandon the grocery store and spend the day under his covers, snug and happy in a make believe world where he could spend all the time he wanted to with Natalie, kissing her, holding her, and cherishing every moment.

Wednesday. October 28th. 8:53pm.

Aaron was so tired when he got home from work that he didn't even go inside. He just sat down on the steps of the porch, rubbed his face, and dug a cigarette out of the pack in his pocket.

"You know those things will send you to an early grave," his grandfather said from his rocking chair. "You should quit while you're young, keep your health, live as much as you can."

Aaron sighed out a big plume of smoke. "I know you're right, but I can't think about it today. Maybe tomorrow when I've not spent a day from hell at a grocery store in what felt like the apocalypse. I have no idea why it was so insanely busy. People were acting crazy. It was all day. I'm just so stressed and so tired."

"They know what's coming," his grandfather said, his voice forlorn. Aaron turned to glance up at him and saw him staring at 104 again.

"Please tell me you're referring to the snow," Aaron said after another drag off of his cigarette.

"Not the snow. I told you. What it brings." Wilson struggled to stand from his chair. "It's already getting late for me. I'm going to go in."

Aaron turned back towards the street. He looked towards the sky. It looked normal. It wasn't even that cold for Wisconsin. He had no idea how his grandfather could tell snow was coming. After the way people were at work today though, everyone seemed to know something that he didn't.

His eyes fell on the Halloween decorations and he realized that he had forgotten to bring home the pumpkins. He huffed, coughed on smoke, and then cursed under his breath. There was still time, he told himself.

Aaron thought he saw someone walking towards him from the end of the cul-de-sac. It was out of the corner of his eye and he couldn't make out details so he turned that direction for a better look. No one was there but the trees.

"Great," he said. "Fantastic."

When he turned away, he could swear he saw the person out of the corner of his eye once more. He didn't bother turning to look again. Something in his gut told him that he wouldn't see anything if he did, but eventually they would have to walk past him and he would see them then.

He lit another cigarette and looked straight forward towards the house across the street, the muddled image of the walking man in the corner of his vision. He blinked and they were gone. They never crossed in front of him. Then he noticed he could see someone out of the corner of his other eye, walking away from him. He gasped and turned that direction but saw no one. The stop sign creaked and wavered all alone.

"Time to go in," Aaron said. He stubbed out his cigarette and hurried up the steps on sore legs. When he went into the house his grandfather was already asleep in his chair. Aaron sighed and made his way to the kitchen. He was so tired but he didn't want to take a page out of the old man's book and go to sleep without eating.

"God, I don't feel like cooking," he said to no one as he popped open a beer, the metal lid falling with a clatter to the floor at his feet. He decided on cereal and fixed a bowl. Then he went into the living room and sat on the couch with his cereal and his beer. He didn't know why he didn't just eat at the table in the kitchen. For some reason he just wanted to be near his grandfather, even if he wasn't awake. Even when Aaron's father was alive, he was sick. He was just another person for Pop-pop to take care of. The old man was a little rough around the edges but he took care of all of them. He raised Aaron while his father looked on with tearful eyes from an in-home hospital bed. Wilson McCallister never complained about his role either. He took it all in stride.

"I could only hope to be half the man you are," Aaron said quietly to the sleeping man. He took the thin frail hand that rested on the arm of the recliner and he held it in his own for a bit. Then with a deep exhale of resignation, he replaced it and got to his feet. He took his empty bowl to the dishwasher and then headed up to bed. As much as he hated the thought, he had work again in the morning.

Before he climbed into his bed, he looked out his bedroom window at the street below. Hawthorne was quiet and ordinary, almost too much so. Would the snow really bring crazy people to their door? It seemed like such a surreal concept. It was hard to fathom but Pop-pop seemed so convinced.

The truth was that he didn't know what was normal, what the rest of the world knew. The grocery store had taken over Aaron's life all but completely. He used to wear comic book t-shirts or a Green Bay Packers jersey, things that showed his interests, his personality. Now it was just his work uniform, day in and day out. He didn't change out of it when he got home. There was no point. He didn't go anywhere. He had to go back to the store in the morning.

Other twenty-somethings were hanging out at the bar or the club, living it up, going to college. His grandfather told him regularly that he should be doing those things too but he had to work. It was important and not something he could just stop doing. It was, wasn't it?

Aaron sighed and left the window to climb into bed.

Thursday. October 29th. 12:14pm

Aaron was pacing the backroom of the grocery store, wishing he had drunk a second cup of coffee today. He looked at his work apron and realized how filthy it was. He needed to remember to take it home and wash it. What was the point of getting all clean and smelling good just to come to work and don a filthy apron?

"You can go," a voice said from behind him. Aaron turned around to see his manager standing there.

"Home?" he asked. It was such a foreign concept. They never let anyone go home. They didn't even act like people had homes.

"Seems the snow has already started elsewhere. The distribution center got hit. Trucks aren't coming. We've got enough people on the front. We can't pay you to do nothing."

"Am I gonna lose my day off tomorrow?" Aaron asked nervously, thinking about Natalie.

"Snow should be on us then. Store probably won't even be open. But expect to come in here for a long day on Saturday to get this place put back together."

Aaron huffed. "But Saturday is Halloween."

"You got kids I didn't know about?"

"No, sir. See you Saturday," Aaron said, hoping his irritation didn't show in his tone. He went to the time clock and punched out and then headed out to the car, carrying his apron over his shoulder. He tossed it onto the passenger seat and started the car. *Screw it*, he thought.

Then, instead of driving home, he made his way over to the hospital where he was sure Natalie was working. She was always there, not that his job was any better. The hospital was a good thirty minutes away. He had doubts of her being able to make it to him tomorrow if the snow really did hit as hard as everyone seemed to think it would. He had a rare opportunity to see her now so he had to take it.

He smiled as he passed by the houses decorated for the holiday. He really did love Halloween. He had a fondness for all things spooky. It was a way to escape the actual dark things from reality, like his father slowly dying in the other room. His grandfather always helped him make the best costumes and took him trick or treating. Even when he got older he made sure to still dress up and find a party to go to. That was over now.

It took forever for him to find parking. When he got inside he asked one of the nurses at the front desk where Natalie was. They called around and he waited for what felt like forever before they finally gave him a floor and directions on how to get there. Apparently only certain elevators went to certain places to make sick and injured people struggle to find where they were going or for their families to have a hard time reaching them. Aaron felt frustrated. It made him feel glad that his father was given the opportunity to pass at home.

When he was on the right floor, he was walking down the hallway and he thought he saw something out of the corner of his eye. He turned to look and saw nothing but white walls, white tiles. He nodded and took a deep breath. When he turned back he was face to face with a smiling Natalie.

Aaron couldn't help but smile back. Pop-pop was right. He was really smitten. He told her what happened with work and she thanked him for coming by. He waited around for a while and talked to Natalie and her coworkers until she had a break to grab lunch. Then they ate together at a small table in the hospital cafeteria. They talked and laughed and to Aaron's surprise the food actually wasn't half bad.

"Not much of a date," she said to him with a crooked smile, her brown hair falling in front of her right eye.

"It was perfect," Aaron told her with a big grin. "Will I see you tomorrow?"

"If the snow permits it, and then we won't be at my job and we can kiss a lot."

"Then it better not snow," he said. They shared a laugh. He gave her a small kiss on the lips and then let her get back to work.

When Aaron got home his grandfather wasn't on the porch. It was strange to see the rocking chair empty. There was enough of a breeze to move it anyway, and something about the image of the empty chair rocking on its own got under his skin and sent a chill scurrying up his spine like the tiny walking legs of a beetle.

"Pop-pop," Aaron called as he walked up the steps towards the house. "Pop-pop?"

He unlocked the front door and went inside. Aaron sighed with relief when his grandfather was seated in his recliner looking up at him with a curious expression. "You're home early," he said.

Aaron sat next to him and grabbed one of the beers from the mini-fridge between them. "Trucks never came because of the snow," he said. "Apparently it's already coming down at the distribution center."

"You remember how to use my gun?" Wilson asked his grandson.

Aaron looked at him like he'd lost his mind. "Do you want me to shoot the snow?"

"I just want to know that you're safe, Aaron. The snow brings bad things. I've already got it loaded for you. I just want to know if you remember what I taught you to make sure you ain't gonna blow your damn head off with it if you try to use it."

Aaron frowned. "I know how to use it. I doubt I'll need to, but I know how to use it." Then he changed the subject. "I went and saw Natalie today since I was out early. She's gonna come by tomorrow if she can beat the snow."

"Why don't you go see her instead? It's much safer that way."

"I really do like her, Pops. So please keep the doom talk to a minimum when she's here."

"Don't worry about me. I won't say a word. You just go ahead and make that gal your girlfriend before someone else does."

"Yes, sir," Aaron said, punctuating it with a laugh. Then he took a sip of his beer and clanged the bottle against the one in his grandfather's hand.

Friday. October 30th. 1:47pm

Aaron looked out the window, his mouth agape. He couldn't see enough of house number 104 to know if there were faceless entities having a picnic on the lawn or not. The storm was raging and the snow met with the wind to reduce visibility to next to nothing. Natalie had said that she was on the way, but he hadn't seen or heard from her yet.

Her apartment was about a thirty minute drive past the hospital so it was an hour drive in good weather. When he couldn't see as far as the house across the street, he couldn't imagine driving in this. He wouldn't have blamed her if she cancelled on him again. In fact, he wished she had, but she had told him she was going to try to make it and he hadn't heard from her since. That was at noon.

"Be patient," his grandfather said from his recliner behind him. "She'll get here. Just give her time."

"I'm just worried about her," Aaron said, his shoulders slumping. "Hell of a Halloween, huh?"

"Maybe exactly that. Come sit for now, watch some TV; try to take your mind off things."

"Maybe in a little bit," Aaron told him. He tugged open the front door and immediately recoiled from the blast of cold that hit him. His grandfather just frowned at him. Aaron pushed against the wind to fight his way outside and then tugged the door shut to keep anymore cold from getting into the house. If his grandfather got sick he wouldn't forgive himself.

Aaron's nerves were on the fritz. He couldn't breathe. He was frightened. He wasn't worried about the snow. He was worried about what it would bring. He didn't think it would bring what Pop-pop thought it would. He feared it would leave Natalie stranded, or worse, that it would cause a power outage and his grandfather would be without heat; that they would run out of food before the roads were clear. He had kicked himself for forgetting the pumpkins and he hadn't even thought about bringing home extra food and being prepared for this thing, despite his grandfather's warnings. If he lost his grandfather, he didn't know what he would do. He couldn't even think about it.

Aaron shivered as he dug a cigarette out of the pack he pulled from his pants pocket. He struggled to light it as the wind howled and beat against the lighter's small flame. When it finally caught, he hugged himself and pulled at it, breathing smoke out of his nose. He turned and tried to look down towards the end of the cul-de-sac but Hawthorne was a blanket of white, like it was a drawing that had been erased from the paper.

Aaron trembled from the cold. He turned to look the other way, to stare past the stop sign that rattled and squealed even more than usual in the wind of the storm. He couldn't even see the road beyond. All he saw was snow. He shook his head and dragged on his cigarette. There was no way that Natalie could make it to him. He just wanted her to be okay. He fished his phone from his pocket and frowned at it. It seemed the storm had taken its toll on his signal too.

When he turned back to face the snow covered house 104, there was a man standing in front of him, blonde hair blowing about from under the hood of his winter coat. Aaron yelped with a start and jumped backwards, dropping his cigarette onto the snow covered porch. When it met the wet whiteness the red tip sizzled and faded to black.

The stranger laughed. "Sorry to scare you. I'm a driver. I do long hauls. This is a commuter town right? So you understand what it's like to have to go back and forth to make your living. Seems most of the commuters didn't bother today, but the ones that did are all stuck. There are abandoned cars all over the roads. Visibility is terrible. I can't get through and I can't go back. I just need somewhere to stay warm until this blows through."

Aaron looked the man over with obvious suspicion. His mind was going back to the things Pop-pop had said about the snow. "If you are a long haul driver, don't you have a rig that you can stay in? Don't drivers do that all the time?"

The stranger nodded his big hooded head. He hugged himself against the cold. "You're right. Unfortunately my heater is out. I might as well stay in a freezer. I can't call for help because my phone doesn't have any signal, and even if I could, it would take them forever to get to me with the state of the road out there."

Aaron frowned. Everything the man said made sense. Was he just being paranoid because of his grandfather's warning? He didn't want to leave someone to freeze to death because of an old man's paranoia. "I suppose you can at least come in and get warm. Grab a cup of coffee or something."

"That would be fantastic," the man said, flashing a smile. "I'm Charles."

"Aaron. My grandfather is Wilson. He's also a bit southern and a bit paranoid of strangers so be forewarned."

"Got it," Charles said, showing his smile again.

Aaron led the way back into the house. Charles didn't need to be told to shut the door behind them. Aaron felt a tug of guilt when he saw the empty recliner. His grandfather must have seen him talking to the stranger outside and taken his leave. Aaron just hoped he wasn't going to hobble back into the room with a gun in his hand. He thought about calling to him but decided to leave him be. Maybe he was actually lying in his bed. He hadn't done so in what felt like months, maybe more. It couldn't have been good on his tired old bones to sleep in that chair all the time.

"Not to be a bother, but how about that coffee," Charles said. "Sorry, but I walked for a while before I found your road. The cold has seeped into my bones, even with this big old coat."

"Of course. Sorry," Aaron said. He started towards the kitchen and then looked back. "Have a seat. Relax a minute. Watch some TV. You can put on whatever you want. I'll be back in a minute."

"Sounds good," Charles told him, adding a wave for good measure.

Aaron hurried into the kitchen. He put just enough for a couple of cups into the pot so it would brew faster. Then he grabbed a cup from the cabinet above the pot and set it in front. Thinking for a moment, he went back to the doorway. "Cream or sugar?" he asked, leaning his head out to look towards the living room.

He didn't see Charles on the couch or anywhere else for that matter. That's strange, he thought. Abandoning the coffee that was loudly percolating, Aaron headed back to the living room. He noticed that the front door was locked from the inside so the man hadn't left, but he was nowhere to be seen.

"Charles?"

"Right here," the man said from behind him, causing Aaron to jump again. He whirled around and saw the driver's hands were raised defensively, palms out. "I just went to find your bathroom. I was about to burst. You okay?"

"Right. Yeah. Sorry," Aaron said, working to steady his heart with slow breaths. "Coffee should be about done. Why don't you come into the kitchen and make the cup how you want it?"

Charles gave a thumbs-up and let Aaron lead the way. Aaron took the cream out of the fridge and set it next to the empty cup. Then he pointed out the sugar canister. As Charles went to work, fixing his beverage, Aaron went to find his grandfather.

Wilson had retired to his bedroom, but he was sitting in a chair next to his bed watching a small television that stood atop his dresser. "I can't believe you let him in here," he said, "and I can't believe you're smoking those things even in a snowstorm. You of all people know how sick they make you and what it does, how painful it is."

Aaron closed his eyes and sighed at the images that passed behind his eyes. When he opened them, he frowned. "I know. You're right. I'm sorry. But it's an addiction, Pops. It's not that easy to quit."

"I remember hearing my son say those same words."

Aaron looked at the ground feeling the weight of those words. Without looking up, he said, "He's just warming up for the walk back to his truck."

His grandfather gestured to his gun, but Aaron shook his head. He turned and left the room, heading back to the kitchen. When he found it empty he felt nervous, but he turned towards the living room and saw the man's hood over the top of the couch. Sighing with relief, he scurried into the kitchen and fixed himself a cup of black coffee and then he took it to the living room. He sat in his grandfather's recliner and looked at the television. It was still off.

Aaron glanced over towards the man on the couch. He was sipping his coffee and staring towards the blank screen like there was something mesmerizing playing on it that Aaron failed to see. "Should I turn it on?" Aaron asked him.

"If you'd like," Charles answered.

Aaron frowned. There was something strange about the long haul driver, but Aaron didn't know what else to do so he lifted the remote and turned the power on. "So where were you driving to?"

"I'm supposed to pick a load in Whitefish Bay and then take it to Chicago. I'm not off to a great start. What do you do?"

"I'm the stock manager at a grocery store that is thankfully closed today, but I'm not looking forward to tomorrow."

"I bet not. That coffee went right through me. I'm going to use the restroom again."

"Sure. Do you want me to brew some more?"

"That would be great. Thank you."

They both stood and walked across the room. Charles went to the bathroom and Aaron kept walking to the kitchen. He set the machine for a full pot of coffee this time and then started it. When he came out of the kitchen, he noticed that Charles had not returned to the couch yet. He turned to look at the bathroom and found the door open, light shining through the crack. Curious, Aaron walked over to it.

He didn't want to assume the man wasn't inside just because the door was open so he knocked on the door. When there was no response, he knocked again and this time he called, "Charles?"

There was still no answer.

Aaron put his hand on the door and gently pushed it open completely. The small bathroom was empty with nowhere for the stranger to hide. Aaron felt suddenly nervous. He ran across the living room to the front door. He looked out the window and saw that his grandfather was now in his rocking chair. Charles wasn't with him. Aaron thought about opening the door and telling his grandfather not to be out there in this storm, but it felt more pertinent to find Charles first.

He turned back and went to the storage room. The man wasn't there though it did look like he rummaged through some things, unless that was just from when they got the Halloween decorations out and Aaron just couldn't remember. He didn't waste the time to think about it.

He ran to his grandfather's bedroom. It was the only other room on the first floor. It used to be his father's room, the room where he lay dying, and his grandfather's room had been upstairs, beside Aaron's own room back then, but once it got too hard for him to navigate the stairs so often, he moved rooms. His father was long gone by then.

Aaron found the room to be just as empty as the others on the first floor which meant that the man had gone upstairs. At least he knew that his grandfather was safe outside, on the snow covered porch. Aaron noticed that his grandfather's gun was gone. He froze. Had the old man taken it outside with him or did Charles have it with him on the second floor?

His gut told him it was the latter. He took his phone out to call the police and found he was still without signal. He didn't know what to do. Maybe he should just let the man do what he wanted and get his grandfather and go. How far would they make it in this storm though? Trudging through this level of snow would likely cause his grandfather a heart attack. It was just as dangerous if not more so than staying here with Charles, if that was even his real name.

Now Aaron was praying that Natalie didn't show up. He would hate for her to get here and wind up in danger. Aaron knew he needed to go up those stairs but he was pretty sure the stranger was armed and he didn't want to go up being quite the opposite. He hurried to the kitchen and tore a draw open, grabbing the biggest knife they owned. Then he headed back. He glanced towards the front windows and saw his grandfather still rocking away on the porch. With a deep breath, he gripped the knife and moved to the stairs.

Aaron ascended slowly. He stepped carefully, trying to avoid the spots that creaked in the old steps. His heart was pounding like a drum in his chest. When he reached the top he nervously looked around. He was trembling. His palm was sweating and he adjusted his grip on the handle of the knife.

Aaron looked down the hall. There were three rooms the man could be in; his grandfather's old bedroom, the master bath, and his own room. He decided to take them in order, starting with his own room. He pushed the door open, breath catching in his chest. He cringed when it creaked loudly.

He didn't see Charles within, but he stepped over the threshold to be sure. Just to be thorough, he checked his closet. The room had obviously been ransacked but the man who had done it was no longer there. Aaron kept his ears open, listening for footsteps that were not his own. He didn't want Charles to head down towards his grandfather while he was up here searching for him.

Aaron turned back towards the hall when he heard a click behind him. It was a familiar sound, the hammer of his grandfather's gun. He stopped where he was. "What do you want?" he asked.

"For starters, I want you to drop that knife," Charles said from behind him. "I was hiding under your bed forever. What kept you?"

"I was looking for you," Aaron said as he dropped the knife to the rug at his feet. "Now tell me what you want."

"Just to have a fun Halloween," Charles said with a menacing laugh. "Don't scream or I'll shoot you."

"As opposed to what?" Aaron asked.

Charles gave another sinister sounding laugh. "Walk to the other bedroom."

"Fine. I'll do what you say. Just leave my grandfather alone. Don't hurt him."

"Whatever you say."

Aaron walked to the unused bedroom and then turned to face the man whose hood was now down. His eyes shone with madness under the wisps of blonde hair that fell over his face. Charles reached into his coat pocket with the hand not holding a gun and came out with a pair of handcuffs. He threw them to Aaron. "Lay down on the bed and cuff yourself to the headboard. Now."

Aaron hesitated. He stared at the man before him. Charles jammed the gun towards him like a metal index finger. "Do it. Now."

Aaron took a deep breath. He moved towards the bed but he froze when he heard someone call his name. The voice was Natalie's. Somehow she must have made it there in the storm. He needed her to get out of the house. Why hadn't his grandfather warned her?

Aaron stared at the gun wielding man before him. "Now who might that be?" Charles said, his smile returning. He turned towards the doorway when she called again. Natalie's feet were pounding their way up the stairs. "Aaron? Aaron, you up here?"

Aaron knew that he only had a split second to act. He moved before Charles could, jumping onto his back. The man went down to his knees under his weight. He tried to flip Aaron over him but he held on tight. Charles swung the gun, trying to get a shot, and Aaron wrapped his hands around the man's throat.

Natalie appeared in the doorway and screamed at what she saw. Charles pointed the gun at her and pulled the trigger. Aaron screamed but Natalie ducked out of the doorway before the bullet came her way, leaving it to tear plaster from the wall. The thought of Natalie being hurt sent a surge of adrenaline through Aaron and he swung a fist into the side of Charles' head.

Charles worked hard to try to buck him off again, but again it was to no avail. Aaron landed another punch and another. Natalie was there and then gone again but not before Charles fired another blast tearing through sheetrock and leaving a cloud of white dust in the air.

"No!" Aaron yelled, fearing for Natalie. Below him, Charles was laughing, even as Aaron resumed choking him. He coughed and laughed in unison. Then the laughing stopped and he slumped to the ground.

It took Aaron a minute to realize that Natalie had stabbed Charles with the knife he had dropped in the other room. He sighed with relief and pried the gun from the man's hand. Then he climbed off of his back and stood next to Natalie, pointing the gun at the man on the floor. "Are you okay?" he asked Natalie. "You're not hurt are you?"

"I'm alright," she said. "Are you?"

"I'm okay," he said. He looked down at Charles' unmoving form. "Is he dead?"

"He should be," Natalie said. "I'm a nurse. I went straight for the carotid artery."

Aaron passed her the gun to be sure that Charles didn't try to take it if he happened to still live. Then he knelt beside the man and checked his pulse. "He's gone."

He stood and took the gun back from her. "We're going to have to wait until phones are working to call the police."

"Hopefully that won't be too long," Natalie said back. "The snow has slowed down a lot. It seems the worst of the storm is over now."

They didn't want to stay there with the dead man while they waited so they made their way downstairs. "I'm glad to see you," Aaron told her as they walked. "I was so afraid that something had happened to you out there."

"It was pretty crazy. I'm not gonna lie," Natalie told him. "I just took it slow and pulled over when I couldn't see."

Aaron leaned over and kissed her lips when they reached the bottom of the stairs. "Who was that?" she asked afterwards.

"I don't know. Someone evil that came with the snow. Pop-pop tried to warn me that the storm would bring the crazies but I didn't believe him."

Natalie paid him a curious look. "Hey. Where is your grandfather?" she asked.

"What do you mean? He was outside on the porch in his rocking chair. You should have walked past him when you came in." Aaron felt a surge of panic.

Natalie frowned and shook her head. "There was no one there."

Scared, Aaron hurried to the front of the house. He undid the lock on the door and tore it open. His grandfather was sitting in his chair just like always. Aaron closed his eyes and sighed with relief. "See," Natalie said from behind him. "There's no one there."

Aaron opened his eyes and his grandfather was still there. He was pushing himself up, his frail arms trembling. "Pop-pop? What is going on?" Aaron asked him.

His grandfather touched the side of his face. His fingers were warm despite the snowstorm. "You weren't ready to let me go," he said. "Now take that insurance money and do something you love. Be with this great gal. Be happy. And for God's sake, quit smoking."

Aaron watched with tearful eyes as his grandfather walked down the steps and towards the road. He suddenly realized why the old man never needed to eat. As he watched his grandfather gracefully navigate the snow, heading towards the stop sign that was now blowing wildly on the corner, tears were running down Aaron's cheeks. His grandfather had reached the corner and then he was just gone. In a blink, he went from being there, to being nowhere. Aaron hurried after him, looking to see where he went. He stopped by the loudly creaking stop sign, blowing back and forth beside him.

He saw nothing, no one. His grandfather was gone. It was as if he vanished into thin air. Aaron turned to head back to the house and when he did, he saw someone out of the corner of his eye, walking away from him down the road. He whirled around quickly and found only an empty street. Then he finally understood.

"Goodbye, Pop-pop," he said. "Thank you for everything. I love you." He walked up the path to the porch where Natalie was waiting for him, looking at him with sympathetic eyes as if she already understood.

"The veil is thinner this month," she told him as he approached. "I've seen them at the hospital too. I'm glad you got to be with him a little longer."

Aaron smiled up at that magical woman, tears spilling over his eyelids to career down his pink frozen cheeks. "And he's glad I get to be with you. We both are."

Natalie smiled, tears in her own eyes. "I got signal back and called the police. They said they're on the way but it's gonna be a while."

Aaron nodded. "Okay," he said, taking her into his arms. "Hell of a date, huh?"

Natalie chuckled. She took his face in her hands and kissed him like she meant it and he returned the favor.

"So how would you like to officially be my girlfriend?" Aaron asked when their lips parted.

"I just killed a man in your house," she said back. "I think we're way past that."

"Fair enough," he said with a laugh. Then their lips found their way back to each other and they kissed again.

THE HOLE TRUTH IN THE YELLOW HOUSE
893 W. HAWTHORNE DRIVE

by Tristan Drue Rogers & Sarah Anne Rogers

Sunday. October 25th.

Debbie was unpacking boxes again before bed when she caught sight of the fading Lone Star tattoo peaking out of the sleeve of her shirt. This was her ex-husband's idea many years ago that they both get an enormous star on the right side of their chests and, even though she loved her time in Texas, she moved all the way to Wisconsin in order to find some semblance of peace and quiet from all that bull. It reminded her of too many false starts and too much day to day minutia that would get in the way of actual living. And now that she moved her family to this smaller town of Greenfield—a place where everyone gets a chance to go to work in the big city—it was ironic that time still eluded her, especially since she wouldn't start work until next week.

Debbie shook her head. It had been a long day and an even longer month spent unpacking. She hadn't even found her box of Halloween decorations and that is one big no-no when only a handful of days from it. Her son would definitely be missing out on a few things until she put her butt into high gear. Her room was a mess compared to the rooms of her children, yet she knew that with each second spent not sleeping, the bags under her eyes would continue to grow. A few hours rest on and off would be magic, if she were so lucky. Her anxieties haven't allowed her a decent-sized slumber in a long while. She tried to remember what Dr. Pleasanton always said in her books, of which Debbie had an entire library shelf dedicated to, which was: *Don't let your shadows of the past cast darkness upon the light sprouting from your present.*

"Allow it instead to rise into sunshine upon your future," said Debbie, finishing her thought by saying the rest of it out loud.

She nodded her head, adjusting her short-sleeve shirt to cover the point sticking out from her tattoo. In short time, it snuck back out. Doing a quick scan of the dozens of boxes that she had left to unload into her room or around the house, she wondered if they even needed or missed what was inside. It had been a month already without them. Debbie told her kids during the move that they were going to get rid of things. However, besides gaining a backyard, their new house was starting to look a lot like their old apartment.

Right as she started to picture herself floating to her bed for the night, she heard the screams of her daughter. The fight or flight mode of a parent is a special thing for Debbie didn't even remember reacting or entering her daughter's room. She was simply already there, having flipped the light on.

"June, what's wrong?!" asked Debbie.

Her daughter pointed her finger at the edge of her bed in the middle of the room. She was curled up on the other side, under her blankets, looking no older than six right now, even though she was already coming up on fourteen years old.

Debbie ran over to her bed and sat next to her. She was shivering. "Honey," said Debbie. "What happened? Did you have a bad dream?"

June screamed one more time, just as loud as before. Debbie panicked, grabbing her daughter and holding her tight.

"Mom," said June, screaming. "Look! Look in the corner!"

"What?!"

"He's still in here!"

Debbie turned around quickly, perusing the room like a concerned mother would. The room was immaculate. Not a single thing seemed out of place. Debbie's eyes bounced to June. Beside her bed held a framed photograph of the entire family, including her father. The double wide window was cracked open, overlooking the backyard. Debbie had yet to go out and buy curtains that fit. Next to it was a rocking chair and lurking right beside it was a man.

A chill went up Debbie's spine and her eye began to twitch. Debbie's vision began to blur for but a second until it became crisper than she had ever seen before. The man was wearing pantyhose on his face. His face was distorted down inside it. He was enjoying every minute, grinning from ear to ear like a half moon bleeding through the fabric.

Debbie's heart started racing from on empty to a full tank of gas as if someone had slammed their foot onto the accelerator. Instincts kicked in. Debbie pushed her daughter out of the bed and onto the other side. "Move, now!"

"Mom!"

"Go get your brother!"

Debbie knew that the door was only a few feet away from the rocking chair and closer still to the intruder. She lunged at him quickly, sloppily, but thankfully the man was not fit for the likes of a single mother protecting her children.

After June had escaped to her little brother's room, Debbie ran out and slammed the door shut. She immediately found her phone and called the police. She waited for the police to arrive, pacing back and forth in her son's room, while checking the window as her kids were held up in the closet. She told them not to make a sound.

By the time the police came and found the family standing on the side of the road, the intruder had already left. Apparently, there was no forced entry and no sign of a rushed escape. One of the officers offhandedly said that it was likely one of her neighbors before their partner scolded them for making up stories without evidence. They offered to escort Debbie and the kids to a family or friend's house, but when Debbie told them they just moved here and didn't know anyone, the officers simply nodded and handed her their cards with both a badge and phone number printed on them.

Debbie watched them drive off, thanking the Lord that none of her neighbors stepped out to see what was going on. Under the sugar maple tree, the moonlight shown through the orange and red leaves as Debbie remembered when her dad offered to give her a gun the day before the move. She was regretting her decision. She wrapped her arm around June and called for her son, whom June had left behind when walking back inside, "Choice, come on. Don't dillydally." They were both shivering and if it weren't for Debbie's adrenaline still kicking in, she was sure that she'd be, too.

June insisted that they check each and every window and door, for good reason, so they did. Even a few times climbing out of bed to see if anything changed. They slept in Debbie's room, sharing the bed that night. Debbie didn't get an ounce of sleep and she suspected none of her children did, either. She wouldn't really know it, though, since none of them moved a muscle until the morning.

Monday. October 26th.

Choice's eyes shot open at the sound of a motorcycle engine revving in the street. It was their neighbors on the west side. They had a white house with red around their windows, red like a cool race car. At least one of the old couple would go on a drive, often in the morning, and Choice never missed a takeoff. Choice ran out of his mother's bedroom, darting off toward the window facing Hawthorne Drive. He jumped onto the couch, lifted the blinds, and put his head under. What he saw did not disappoint.

The old lady shot down the street and popped a wheelie. It was glorious.

"Vroom vroom," Choice said loudly through his bubbling lips. "Vroom vroom vroom!" He leapt off the couch, almost taking the blinds with him. He started pretending that his hands were over the handles of his own motorcycle, revving it up around the room, drifting in and out of dangerous corners.

In the midst of all this fun, Choice's stomach growled.

June popped her head out of the door frame of her mother's room.

She saw Choice holding his stomach, now lying on the floor, murmuring ever so faintly, a remnant of tires pealing out onto the pavement. "Mom," she said with her teeth clamped down. "The monster needs a feeding." June walked over to the couch and sat down, phone in her hand.

"Mom!" Choice repeated his sister's call.

Their mother popped out, her hair all pushed to one side and her eyes barely lifted from the ground. "Yes, children?"

Choice sat up and smiled. "Did you know that sharks have, like, three hundred or even four hundred teeth?"

Debbie walked into the kitchen, passing them both for the sweet imagery of the coffee pot. "I didn't know that, baby," she said. "Why don't you go play outside while mommy makes breakfast, okay?"

"Can I be a shark for Halloween?"

"If we have time to go to the store, otherwise we can do that ghost costume again from a few years ago. How does that sound?"

Choice shot up, shaking his head and running to the backdoor. "No way," he said. "I want to eat people." Practically flying out of the door frame, leaving it opened, he drifted into the grass and dirt, screeching with each jerky movement. While the sunlight popped through the shelter of the oak tree's branches, Choice was pretending to drive on the old Route 66 Highway that he heard so much about in his daddy's favorite song. The loud smack of the backdoor closing did nothing to deter the boy. "Get your kicks," sang Choice, struggling with the exact rhythm of the melody. "On route —"

He was interrupted by a gust of wind. Only it didn't sound the way one normally would. The way it would brush against the eardrum, whistling, showing itself only slightly and never heard again. This was different. It was a line pulling Choice to its origin. The hook firmly in his skin, reeling him in farther until he found himself behind the tree in the backyard beside the tool shed.

A man drenched in darkness like a living shadow and as tall as his daddy stood there, holding his hand out. Choice froze as the sunlight kissed the top of his forehead and nothing more. He watched the shadowy man's hand turn from shape to shape until becoming less of a shadow and more of this world. For a moment, Choice thought he was in a movie with magic in it. The shadowy man transformed his hand into a fishing lure with faded red and green stripes and little bells attached. Choice looked up to the shadowy man's eyes, or where they normally should be, and asked a question. "Where's the hook?"

The shadowy man made a sound of soft confusion, "Uh-uh?"

"Can't catch a fish without a hook," said Choice, putting his finger inside his mouth, pretending to hook his own cheek before lifting both of his hands into the air. "Like that. Don't you know anything?"

The backdoor opened up, causing Choice to take a step back from the oak tree and turned away from the shadowy man. At first he saw the house itself: a bright yellow home with grey trim. The yellow paint was fading in certain spots, but practically matched the sun in others.

Eventually, his eyes went to the opened backdoor of the house. It was his sister, tapping her feet against the concrete stairs. "Come in and eat, dude," she said.

Choice, now realizing the oddity in his situation, turned slower than before to face the shadowy man. He took an exaggerated gulp from his throat and felt a bead of sweat fall down his armpit onto the side of his stomach. Eventually, his face was in the same direction as his body. No one was there. All that remained was the wooden fishing lure with bells and no hook.

"Dude, come on or it will get cold," said June.

Choice grabbed the lure and bolted toward the door.

Before he could open the screen door and walk inside, he could tell by the sound of his mother's voice that things were about to get serious. He stashed the lure inside his pajama pocket.

"Choice, June," she said. "Could y'all listen to me for a second?"

Finally inside, June pointed to the table where Choice's food was cooling. His mother made a plate of scrambled eggs and jelly toast with a cup of orange juice to wash it down. The green salsa from back home was next to his plate. Once he sat down, he poured the salsa atop his eggs and started to eat.

"We need to talk about what happened last night, okay?" She took a sip of her coffee. "Since y'all aren't going to school right now, I need us to all stick together. If any strangers try to even talk to you, both of you have to tell me."

Choice's eyes widened. He started nodding.

"It doesn't matter how innocent it seems, I need to know about it!" She yelled that last part, setting her coffee mug down, banging it loudly against the counter.

"Mom," said June. "We get it. I'll keep an eye out." June was equal parts inside the living room and kitchen with her face in her phone. The clicks that her thumb made onto the touch screen created a musical score representing her disinterest.

"I mean it!"

Choice finished his eggs and started to eat his jelly toast. "Could I have more orange juice?" His mom opened the fridge, taking the jug out to refill his cup. She left the jug on the table and sat across from him.

"Son," she said, tenderly and filled with concern. "Do you understand what happened last night?"

Choice spoke with the chewed toast in his mouth. "A bad man was in sissy's room."

"That's right. And how do we know that he's a bad man?"

He swallowed his toast and took a sip of his juice. "...Because he wasn't supposed to be there?" He said his answer as a question.

"Yes. That man is still out there—" Debbie stopped herself and Choice could tell that she was going to say more, but wasn't sure how to go about it.

Something hit the floor directly below his chair at the table and Choice's eyes widened again.

June, being far enough away from the two to easily view what was under the table, spoke first. "You want to go fishing?"

Debbie ducked her head to see what her daughter was talking about. "I don't remember your dad giving you this. Where did you get that lure?"

Her question seemed innocent enough, without a real care or prodding, yet Choice lied anyway. "I found it in the backyard," he said. "Thought it looked cool." It wasn't a *full on* lie, he thought. Only a little one.

Debbie shrugged her shoulders and sighed. "We really need to clean this place up."

There was a quiet that blanketed the room before it was urgently unraveled by June. "Mom, could I have some money to buy headphones?"

"And candy," said Choice.

Tuesday. October 27th.

June was in her room, not having left it since sneaking out from her mother's earlier this morning. Her mother hadn't woken up to make breakfast yet and Choice was busy doing his own thing. Perhaps June should have made him food, but she didn't.

The night before June thought she was quite clever by asking her mother about her college years and how she met dad, only to find each of them drifting off into slumber land within the master bedroom a few hours later. June wasn't sure she could ever fall asleep in her own room again.

She also couldn't take her eyes off that chair. If that chair so much as made a creaky noise against the wooden floor, she'd be two seconds from hightailing it to Texas, enjoying tacos, and wouldn't have to worry about anything else ever again.

When June's phone started to vibrate against the windowsill, however, her heart sunk into the pit of her stomach, her feet became one with the wooden flooring, her skin became greener, and she was still stuck in this stupid state that no one in their right mind ever dreamed of moving to. It wasn't right that she was imprisoned here, June told herself. She had been threatened before at school back home and even at the gas station, but never by a stranger in her room in the brisk cold night while she was sleeping. This was crazy.

After dozens of minutes filled with silent deliberating and more than a few too many deep breaths, she decided that it was already time to rearrange her room. June was the first one of the household to be nearly finished with unpacking and setting up her room anyway, yet it didn't feel right. She didn't have to wonder why. Not really.

First, she moved her bed opposite the window, as far away from it as possible and completely unobstructed whenever she'd go to sleep.

June's phone vibrated again. She ran to it this time instead of avoiding it. She knew that she needed the distraction. Whoever it was and whatever it was about, no pressure to the sender.

It was a text from her friend back home. "Cassie," she said. Cassie was replying to her freak out message from the other night. It started with an OMG and later detailed how sorry she was for texting back so late. It was fine, really. June knew that she'd been busy with school. June heard from Daniela that Cassie had a boyfriend now, too, so of course she was too busy to talk with little old Junebug, right?

Cassie asked if she was okay and if they caught the creeper who broke in. June answered her and sent a few GIFs to illustrate her emotional distress right now, all in good humor. June asked if anything new had been going on with her. She watched as the three dots in the corner where Cassie's message would appear were stuck in a rhythmic loop. Time went on without receiving a message and then the dots disappeared.

June didn't like this, but, really, like, who does?

"How you doing, honey," June's mom popped her head in, not really saying the sentence as a question.

June turned to look at her. "I'm fine," she said, setting her phone down onto the floor beside her feet. She then walked over to the closet, pulling out her last unopened box, unfolding the opening to reveal her old stuffed animals, relegated to a forever box until now. She wasn't going to pull these out before because she was a serious adult and adults didn't need the safety net of having animal friends by your side.

Her mom watched her walk back and forth from one section of the room to the next for a moment, placing stuffed animals atop furniture here and there, before asking a real question this time, "Why are you moving your room around already?"

"I didn't like it the way it was." She shrugged, or more like shrunk down to the floor, pulling a bright pink pig and a mallard duck out of the box. Each hand held a wealth of memories. Suddenly, she felt warm, not realizing that she was cold before.

June's mother tilted her head, resting it against the frame of the doorway. "All right, honey," she said. "I'm about to fix lunch. If you need anything, just let me know. And please spend some time with your brother today. He's just as lonely as any of us, even if he doesn't act like it."

June stood at attention, placing her hand to her forehead in a faux-salute, and smacking her heels and thighs together. "Yessir!" She threw her hand out from her head and into the air before getting back to work. Her mother was halfway down the hallway and June already regretted her response.

Another vibration was heard against the wooden floor. It shot a shockwave of emotional dread into June's spine, although she really didn't understand why. She was certainly a little tense, but she knew Cassie would text her back eventually, so what gives?

She put the mallard and pig up against the pillows atop her bed and jolted toward the phone, crouching down to pick it up. It kept vibrating.

Her eyes opened in a fiercely excited manner at the realization of who it was. It wasn't Cassie, but her father instead, calling from back home.

She put the phone to her ear and listened to the vibration for a few seconds before she figured out that she hadn't slid the green icon yet to answer.

Finally landing back on earth and answering the call, she went to say hello, but her father spoke first. "Heya, Junebug! How's my little princess doing?"

"Hiya, daddy," said June, practically transported. "Are you off today?"

"Yeah, I don't work on Tuesdays anymore. Things are getting a little easier nowadays."

"At the oil rigs?"

"Yeah, I'm still here. Living in a trailer right now with two other guys until my three weeks are up. I met a lady at the bar here, she's really nice. You'd like her. Might introduce y'all."

"Oh," said June, not meaning to be any type of way, but couldn't really help it, either.

"So, uh…what have y'all been up to? How're the new digs? Mom and Choice taking care of each other? Any new friends at school?"

June started walking to the window. She needed the sunlight, but that giant tree in the backyard was blocking it again. The natural lighting in her room was awful so far.

"Junebug," said her dad. "You still there?"

"Yeah, I'm here. We haven't started school yet." June looked into the backyard and saw her little brother by the tree, seemingly talking to someone that wasn't there. June couldn't see anyone, but it looked like he was handed something, probably pretending, before he turned around. Looking all over the back of the house, scanning everything he could, and that was when June watched Choice reveal the pocket knife, stabbing at the wind and smiling the entire time. Without a partner to play with, it was a sad sight to behold, even if Choice was honestly looking like he was enjoying himself. He was engulfed in fall leaves. The vision of so many different colors of orange and more than a few stubborn greens did made her smile, even if for a second.

"What do you mean you haven't started school?"

"I don't know," said June. "Ask mom."

"Hey, baby," said a woman's voice, sounding sleepy through the speaker. "Just a minute," said June's dad. "Junebug, tell your mom to call me and let Choice know that I love him, okay? I'll talk to you later."

"I love you, dadd—" The receiver cut off. He hung up.

June put her back against the wall beside the window, sliding her body down onto the floor. She closed her eyes, wondering on and on forever as the tears started to burn her eyes. Eventually, wishing it was all a dream, June fell asleep with the sun piercing through the branches of the tree, into the window, and onto her cheek.

Awakening a half hour later, during what seemed like a month long hibernation, to the sound of a creaky chair, it rocking with no one in it, June rediscovered that her nightmare was indeed still reality. She ran to her bed, leaping onto it, and began to tightly squeeze her two stuffed animals. June's heart was racing.

Her mom called for her to come to eat lunch. She couldn't find the strength to run until being called a third time, at which point she busted out of there, still holding that stuffed pig and mallard.

The sound of that chair rocking back and forth echoed into the hallway and into her forsaken mind for the remainder of the day and night. When she later worked up the courage to ask her mother and even her little brother about that disrupting noise coming from the rocking chair, no one seemed to hear a thing. The calm only began when her mother surprised her with a set of headphones. She wore them with the intention of making her ears bleed.

It didn't work, but it was a nice try.

Wednesday. October 28th.

It was a thunderous night and yet the weather was just fine at a brisk 65 degrees, with the breeze coming and going, making it even cooler and more welcoming than one accustomed to the state could ever hope for. This was ridiculously cold for a few Texans, however. The thunder came when Debbie could hear the strangest sounds, possibly coming from her son somewhere in or around the house. She couldn't be sure. Immediately after walking out of the shower, rubbing lotion over her skin, and getting dressed in comfy sweat pants to match her favorite baggy shirt— the one with the old school UTPA Broncs logo—and still that boy managed to get himself into trouble. He was supposed to be asleep.

Her daughter had already passed out under the covers of Debbie's bed. June's phone was still in her hand, glowing from whatever video she was watching. Her headphones were wrapping around her neck, only slightly less tightly than a pair of knotted shoelaces. Debbie didn't have the heart to wake her up, but she did unravel the wire, placing them elsewhere. Her daughter turned over, blissfully unaware of any danger that wasn't presiding within her skull.

Pressing on, Debbie began searching for her son inside the house with nothing in her own hand but lotion. *Silky Smooth won't help in a fight*, she thought to herself. Of course, the realization that it was probably Choice just being a boy and being weird like most boys who grow up to be men act like anyway brought her to shake her head at the thought of violence and continued to listen further. The only little boy that she ever knew was her own brother when she was a little girl. He was a different kind of weird as a kid, but grew up to be a good man before he died in a car wreck. For a moment, Debbie lowered her head and thought what Choice would be like with her brother in their life. His influence would have surely done more than her ex-husband's ever did.

Debbie scanned through every room, unable to find Choice. That mix of movement and breathing kept scratching at her eardrum and her heart. She was starting to panic.

Swinging the door open into the backyard, she winced at her inability to sneak up on whatever was going on. *A strong and respected individual who bursts through the door, rather than knock, will garner the utmost respect in not just the workplace, but in the real world*, said Dr. Pleasanton in her newest book, Debbie remembered.

She recounted this statement to herself as she perused the shadows all around her. Debbie saw the old man next door in the beige house just standing there on his back porch, hardly moving at all, but definitely glaring at her. She tried to be friendly and waved at him, an action she immediately regretted. Dr. Pleasanton mentions that *friendliness in the realm of the inhospitable jungle is always perceived as a weakness.*

He doesn't wave back anyway. *Maybe he doesn't see me*, she thought to herself. Or just old and pilled-out or whatever. She was ashamed of that thought, but kept on pursuing her son. No reason to let manners, or lack of, get in the way of finding Choice.

Debbie turned her head back to her yard, still unable to see much of anything. She looked back at the old man, now realizing that he barely looked like himself. He was more a shadow now than her own silhouette against the pavement. She had seen the old man on many occasions with June, since she'd stare through the window to gander at the young man who lived with him. June thought the younger man was cute but was too shy to say hello across the fence. Debbie knew to let her work through this crush in her own way, so left her to it.

The old man seemed to frown while his sights were set on the tree on Debbie's side of the fence. He turned just then, stepping through the backdoor, and disappearing for the rest of the night. She didn't recall him opening the door, though, she thought, *the night can play tricks on people.*

Running to the tree — each footstep crunching into the dead leaves — Debbie tripped and fell onto the ground, but finally reached the other side as she slammed into the dirt through the piles of leaves where she discovered what those strange noises were and what they had to do with Choice.

Her son was digging rapidly. Silently, carefully. He created a hole that had gotten to be knee deep for any adult who stepped down into it, almost at the waist for Choice.

Debbie lay there on the dirt like a collection of chopped wood tossed about the yard. Her body was frozen, however, her intensions were to stand and hold her little boy. Nothing could stop that.

"Choice! What are you doing?"

She didn't receive any kind of answer or acknowledgement. Debbie tried to lift herself up. She fell back down due to the pain that her arms and wrists felt when holding the weight of her body. She hadn't thought her fall was that serious before, now she wasn't so sure. Realizing that she was running out of time before something crazy happened, even though she didn't know why her internal clock was counting down, or to what, the adrenaline kept her going enough to crawl into the hole.

Now that she was within arm's reach of her son, Debbie grabbed him and pulled him in close. Half of her body was hanging down into the deepening hole with her son in her grasp and the other was uncomfortably set onto the high ground.

"Baby," she said. "What are you doing?" Debbie saw little knickknacks and items that were lined up in a row from where she had pulled him. There was an old rusty pocket watch, a wooden fishing lure, and a knife with the blade out and ready to use.

She pulled Choice's face to hers, attempting to align their eyes. Choice didn't look like he was all there, more like sleep walking. Debbie had seen this exact face before on her brother, which is why she considered this likelihood, but that was so long ago and she wasn't positive how her parents handled it, if at all. The one thing she was aware of was that she shouldn't shake him awake or he could freak out.

"Mine," said Choice.

Debbie's heart sunk. "What—" She tried to ask a follow up question.

Choice interrupted. "My totems," he said. "They're mine. For safe keeping."

Debbie stumbled to find her words, but pressed on until she found them. This time, she lessened her grip on her son, allowing him to go about whatever his sleepwalking compelled him to do. "Safe keeping for what?"

He started to dig again, only now he simply covered the items with the dirt, packing the ground with his palms. "To hide from mommy," said Choice. "The Shadowy Man says she won't understand and might take me away from him."

Debbie was silent.

Choice kept going. "I'm scared that if I don't keep quiet, I'd stop getting to see The Shadowy Man and then no more stuff to play with."

The wind began blowing in the dead of night.

Debbie built up her strength, finally able to rise to a stand. "Choice," she said. "Where is this shadowy man?"

"He was at home," said her son, now climbing out of the hole.

"Where is he now?"

"He's with us behind the tree," he said.

Debbie's heart sunk once more as she turned to look at that tee. The wind blew even harder, nicely cooling the warmth of her face and dancing with her hair, while her body shook as if it was below freezing temperature.

When she focused enough, glaring into the darkness, Debbie realized that no one was there.

She grabbed her son's hand, quietly walking him through the backyard, occasionally scoping out the yard behind them. Choice followed her guiding touch without any resistance. When they reached the door,

Debbie heard a loud clinging off into the corner near the hole. Quickly turning back around, lifting Choice up into her arms, now dead weight, she saw the gate door banging back and forth against the fence from which it's connected. Debbie scanned the driveway and there it was. A figure in the night darting off into a more complete darkness.

The hairs on the back of her neck rose toward the stars peering down at them. Squeezing her son, she just appeared onto the other side of that door with Choice and no recollection of opening it or slamming it shut behind them.

Thursday. October 29th.

June shifted, waking up slowly to the feeling of dirt around her legs, scratching against her skin as she stretched out on her mother's bed. She opened her eyes to her mother's white sheets, now covered in dark streaks. June impulsively gasped, taking in the sight of her brother and mother painted in earth, sleeping beside her.

"What the…" she groaned. "Mom!" Angry and freaked out, she jumped away from the sheets when she felt her brother's arm fall against her skin. He was sleeping upside down with his head at the foot of the bed and his face planted into the mattress, his filthy feet sprawled out onto the pillow.

Her throat immediately felt dry as she attempted to swallow. The air thinned and June's sweat began to chill as visions of Choice lying there dead penetrated her mind.

Her eyes then jotted to her mother. June let out a bellowing cry as she called for her. "Mom!" And again. "Mom!" And again. "Mommy!" Back to her brother, "Choice!"

June felt her body rattling. Her mom was lying half in the bed with her eyes wide open. She didn't seem to be looking at anything. Her eyes just agape like a dried fish out of water.

She leapt onto her mother's body, onto the bed and over Choice, to find her mouth stuffed with dirt. "No!" She screamed and screamed. "No no no no no..."

Beginning now to scoop the dirt out, carefully with her index finger, hands shaking erratically all the while doing so, June opened her jaws, scraping out the bits of earth buried inside her mother. Screaming once more, she flung her head back, racing to Choice, twisting her body back around to his. June lifted him to her, raising his head from the sheets. She found dirt in his mouth, too, it spilling out from his lips and onto her chest.

Shrieking uncontrollably, she saw that Choice's eyes were replaced by two brightly covered objects. The heat of those eyes burned through her. Throwing his body off of her in panic, June's despair grew deeper and deeper until she fell off of the bed and onto the ground. Crawling to the door, she could not believe what she was seeing, trying to make sense of this terrible thing that had happened to her family. She thought, *Could this be a dream?*

She jolted awake. Her eyes wide open with fear until she realized that she was back in her bed yet again, next to her brother's feet, still covered in dirt.

June let out a high-pitched scream with all the energy that her body could muster, setting her mother off, who only laid right beside her. Quickly, her terror brought her to tears.

"June," said Debbie, whisper-yelling at her daughter. "Hush! The boy is sleeping." She then placed her entire hand over her face, massaging her temples with no real technique. "I've really had a night, okay, so please don't make this morning any worse."

June kept quiet, although she was still sobbing. She could feel her heart rushing to break down the doors of her chest as she attempted to understand that it was all just a dream and that her family was still whole, for the most part. She needs them just as much as they need her.

While lost in thought, her mother turned to look at her. "Gosh, honey," she said. "I'm sorry." Debbie rolled over near Choice, reaching her arm over him and to June. "Are you okay? Did you have a bad dream?"

June nodded.

"It must have been a real doozy, huh?" She brushed the stray hairs out of her daughter's face.

June felt at home for the first time since moving here. She hadn't been babied like that from her mother since back in Texas. They used to be so close. It wasn't anyone's fault. This is just how it is when you start growing up. She was real good at forgetting the world revolved around more than herself, yet June realized right then as her mother looked deep into her eyes, trying to console her, that her mother was doing all she could. *She really loves her kids*, June thought. She wondered how she could ever lose sight of that.

"I don't want to lose you two," said June with a stream of tears falling down the side of her face.

Her mother stood up, walked around the bed, and met her daughter's warmth. She wrapped her arms around June and told her it was all going to be all right. "You will never lose us," she said. "The devil himself would be too scared to get in the middle of me and my kids."

June sniffed, wiping away her tears with her mother's sheets. She asked her through the fabric "Do you mean it?" even though she knew the answer and felt like such a child needing to hear it anyway.

Debbie smiled at her, kissing her forehead. "I know that I say a lot of things and that they don't always come true, but you have my word, baby. I will always be here for you. Always and forever, Junebug."

Sitting up, June hugged her mother and for a brief moment all was right with the world. Yet, still, June put her free hand over her little brother's back. When her hand sunk in and then lifted due to Choice's breathing, she was finally back to her old self again. Everyone was alive, for sure this time.

"You are not going to believe what happened last night," Debbie said before kissing June's shoulder.

June tilted her head up to look at her mother, noticing a deep concern for more than she was letting on.

They stood there in silence below the broad daylight, the sun gleaming through the orange leaves of their oak tree. The backyard was in serious need of a raking; also Choice had apparently brought every single toy that he'd ever owned out here. It was a mess. Her dad used to rake the front yard of their old house and mom always tidied up their children's messes. Their dad just mowed down the backyard's leaves, since he did the front yard first, growing tired of it rather quickly. He always said that he had no idea how having a house would be this much work.

Spiders, thought June as she turned her head, inspecting the yard around them. *Spiders everywhere. Perfect home for the dang things. Choice better be careful.*

The hole was encircled by those random pieces of junk and knickknacks that Choice had been playing with the past few days, looking shinier than ever and almost brand new. An old timey metal John Deere toy tractor was there, too. That was a new one.

Her mother broke the silence, only echoed by the calm of the wind.

"The realtor who sold me the place," she said, "told me that this cul-de-sac was named Hawthorne Drive after the old couple who live two houses to the left of us. They used to be the only house on the block, I guess."

June turned to look at her mother now, listening intently, still unsure what she was brought out here for.

"Mrs. Hawthorne's husband died of mysterious circumstances," her mother continued, "and people who've lived in the homes on this street have all witnessed his ghost, or whatever, someway or somehow. The realtor told me that he's sort of the undead mascot around here."

"Mom," said June.

"Of course, the realtor laughed after saying that, so how was I to know that we'd be in danger..." She trailed off, muttering words that only she could hear.

June noticed the look in her eyes, that of a deer in the headlights or a mommy pit-bull blacking out in pure anger from the fight.

The sound of a motorcycle revving its engine went off throughout the neighborhood.

"That'll be Choice's cue," said June, banging an invisible gong in the still air with her hands.

Her mother didn't look away from the hole in the ground, but a grin did sneak out from the side of her cheek.

A gust of wind startled them both, crawling up through their shirts, brushing against their spines, and causing them to shiver, stepping closer to one another.

"Let's go inside, mom," said June. "It's going to be okay." She grabbed her mother by the waist and started to turn her toward the backdoor when they saw Choice standing there in the entrance, still covered in dirt. The door hadn't swung open, even with the wind picking up. Though, that didn't make sense why no one heard the latches squeak.

Startled once again, the two of them froze. June was the first to break the ice. "Good morning, sleepy-butt," she said to her brother.

"What are you doing here," he said to them both, but not really as a question.

June popped her head back, sinking her chin into her neck. "What's it to you, small-fry?"

Their mother stepped forward, cracking through the dead leaves. "You have to be honest with me about something, Choice, okay?" She kept on walking closer. "I know things have been hard here. We don't know anyone, we aren't going to school," she turned to look at June, "I haven't made life easier for y'all in the ways that I promised to before we drove over here. My friends haven't kept in touch with me, either. It's hard doing anything long distance. And dad, well, he'll get better at it—we should invite him over once we settle in more."

She mouthed "I'm sorry" to June, which meant the world to her. June fought the tears coming on. She was tired of crying. June knew it was okay to cry. It's been a crazy week. She knew her mother didn't mean for this stuff. This scary, boring place would get better as they made it a real home. All they needed was each other.

Turning back to Choice, Debbie continued. "I want you to tell me who's been giving you these things, Choice."

Choice shook his head.

"Please, baby," she said. "It's not okay if the man who broke into June's room, threatening your big sister's life, has been sneaking around my little boy. I'd have killed him if I could."

June couldn't hold back her tears any longer. *What the hell is happening?* she thought to herself, *please don't make Choice part of this. Please. Oh. Please.*

Choice tilted his head before speaking. "The Shadowy Man wouldn't have done that and besides June knows what he looks like."

"That shadow guy?" Their mother was close enough to pick her son up.

"No," he said. "The bad man, right?" He looked at his older sister, putting his hand out to her from a good few feet away. Debbie carried him to her.

"He was bald with a creepy smile, and he wore black everything except for his socks and the nude pantyhose on his head," June said this with an almost robotic, matter-of-fact rhythm.

Debbie and Choice together pulled her close to them, all three holding one another as the wind brushed against their bodies. The dead leaves flew into the air, escaping into other yards, while some pressed against the fence. Most of the leaves were floating in the air around them, waiting to fall back onto the ground as soon as the wind calmed again.

June realized that she hadn't spoken about that man since the police questioned her that night.

"So, yeah," said Choice. "You can't see The Shadowy Man. He doesn't really have a face."

Debbie asked, "Is he here now?"

June pulled away, looking all around just as before, only this time with purpose.

"I don't know," said Choice. "He usually comes when the wind blows like this. I have an ear for it." He drew a line from his ear to the wind with his hand.

Debbie snickered. "Oh, do you?" She put her face against his stomach, making weird baby noises that Choice was too old for, but made him laugh anyway. June joined in until they were both so tired from laughter that they had to put Choice down, each sitting in the leaves beside one another.

They breathed heavy and hard from the fun, but then a moment took hold of June that she couldn't ever describe in words, but that made her feel... maybe... sort of... perfect? If that was the right word, she wasn't sure. Regardless, it was a nice feeling to have bearing in mind everything that's happened.

"All right, kids," their mom said, "we've been cooped up in this house for long enough. What say y'all that we should go out and see a movie, maybe get some takeout or something?"

June would have made fun of Choice's reaction, sprouting up from the leaves with that big ol' smile on his face, practically bouncing for joy, if not for the fact that she did the exact same thing.

Choice turned to his mother. "Can we see a slasher flick?"

Their mother looked at June. "Let's go see something a little more... fun?"

"But those are fun," he said.

"How would you know?"

June answered her before her little brother had the chance. "Dad, obviously," she said, pronouncing those words like her old self again. "Because they're fun!" Repeating Choice's reply. Speaking her second language again: sarcasm with a side of despair. It was good to be back.

"Okay…" said Choice, deep in thought. "How about a superhero movie?"

Their mother looked over at June again, who nodded reluctantly.

"Yay!" Choice threw his hands up in the air, like he was announcing a field goal.

"We could all use a hero in our lives right now."

June agreed. It was truer than she'd like to admit, that the world had far more villains than heroes in it and if she were to protect her family, she'd have to start now, maybe not with super powers or with guns, but with making their lives easier day by day. Honestly, she thought to herself, she should have done it sooner. It was time to stop day dreaming about being a big girl and to actually grow up, take action, and to help around the house. Her mom was going to need all the help she could get, obviously.

Friday. October 30th.

The afternoon was calm and brisk as Debbie looked on through the window above the sink, overlooking the two greatest gifts in her life actually spending time together. Not to mention that they were both outside without having been told to — this was a miracle, especially for June. The dishes had piled up from the last few days. Though Debbie knew she could blow it off for even longer, starting work at her new job bright and early on Monday wouldn't be easy if she knew she had to tackle a pile of dirty plates that same night. Her first day would likely entail mostly meeting new people, introducing herself ad nauseam, and nothing more, but she was nervous anyway. Nervous to fit in with a new group of working people from an entirely different background than her. Nervous to leave her kids. She hadn't been apart from them for more than a month and it was truly a blessing to even have the option to do that. It seemed to Debbie that ever since June was born, their worlds were nothing but *go-go-go* until this moment.

Debbie had actually gotten to know her children in a way that she never could have if she stayed in Texas with her old job, near her ex-husband, and all their burnout, party friends. Texas as a whole was great, but where they specifically lived in Texas in the Rio Grande Valley, that was the problem. The joke was to call their town "quicksand" whenever someone had a chance to leave it and move onto something bigger and better, only to turn back around and stay put. It happened in front of her far too many times and as a mother, she wanted more for her children than simply working, drinking, smoking, and having kids to start the process all over again. They were meant to be something and in this world that far outweighed the need to be surrounded by old friends.

This is my purpose, she thought. It was to free her children from the shackles of her past, no matter how melodramatic that sounded.

Finally finishing up the dishes—making a mental note to purchase and install a dishwasher—Debbie downed her lukewarm cup of coffee and walked outside, meeting her children in the backyard.

"Hey, mom," said June, all smiles, wiping the sweat off her forehead. She was doing something unfathomable: June was raking the leaves in the backyard. She had one big pile in one of the corners and a smaller pile forming in the middle.

Debbie grinned back at her. "Wow," she said. "Am I going to have to pay you for this later?"

June kept busy while answering her mom. "No," she said. "I'm just doing it, okay?"

"All right," said Debbie, putting her hands up in the air toward June. "Don't let me spoil it, honey. You do what you gotta do." Debbie stood in awe at the organization skills in front of her. Even Choice was collecting his toys and lining them up against the house.

"I also covered the hole up," said June.

Debbie looked at the spot and saw that her daughter did a pretty good job collecting dirt without putting another hole in the ground to get it, seeing as it was haphazardly thrown every which way in order to dig it in the first place. "Thank you, baby. You're growing up so fast."

"Mom," groaned June.

Debbie became an onlooker again, watching her children clean up the place. It was a sight to see. "Soon as y'all finish up the good work you're doing, let's set up for tomorrow. We got all sorts of pumpkins to carve and whatnot."

Choice stopped what he was doing and darted for the bigger pile of leaves.

Debbie hollered at him to stop, but June interrupted.

"It's okay, mom," she said. "Let him have his fun. Besides, I already promised the little monster that he could do it anyway."

Debbie backed off, presenting the gathered leaves to Choice.

The two watched on as he barreled into those leaves like Wiley Coyote into a mountain. He screamed *"Geronimo!"* as he did it, too. For a moment, he was engulfed within the leaves, nowhere to be seen, but soon he popped out with his eyes wide open and his grin even bigger. "Again! Again!" Choice then saw a particularly gigantic spider crawling by his foot, instinct apparently set in and the boy lifted his leg into the air before stomping its guts out over the dirt. He wiped the bottom of his shoe onto the leaves. Looking back up to June, he repeated his last words before the execution.

"Hold on, loser," said June. "I need to gather up the leaves real quick."

Debbie snuck away, stepping back inside and poured herself one more cup of coffee, heating it up in the microwave first. She took her time before calling them in or doing any real work around the house, fiddling on her phone without interruption.

Sighing, she tapped open her audio book and took a gulp of her surprisingly hot coffee. Debbie occasionally checked on them through the window above the sink as she listened in on her new chapter titled *The Reflection in Your Eye*. It only took a few moments for her thoughts to be led away from her therapy and back to the sounds of her children laughing when it occurred to her. Grinning to herself, she stopped the female voice instructing and chanting at her and swiped for freedom.

Best thing I've done for myself, she thought. Her attention was now on just them. She was so happy to see that they got along the entire time before coming in. Debbie even noticed that June hopped into the pile of leaves at least once before the day was done. Rubbing her eyes, Debbie thought it could have all been a dream. She was relieved to discover that once her hands left her face that she hadn't woken up just yet. This was the real world and not some fantasy, at least until proven otherwise.

Three enormous jack o' lanterns down—two by June and one from Choice—and a single little pumpkin left for each member of the family was primed and ripe for carving.

Debbie had popcorn ready and was baking the pumpkin seeds as they came to her. They had already been through a few episodes of *Scooby-*

Doo when Debbie dropped down onto the floor in-between the two, sitting on the towels she set up so as to collect the gunk and juices, and readying an attack on her orange victim. Choice saw a flash of her tattoo as it popped out from her short sleeve shirt.

"When daddy sees his star," he said, "he thinks of you." Choice went back to stick poking his pumpkin, tracing the picture they stuck onto it. "I know it," he added.

Debbie gave a crooked smile. "I think of him when I see it, too…" she hesitated. "…sometimes." It wasn't that she was ashamed of it, but, honestly, Debbie had been wondering what it would be like if their father was here. Maybe things would have been less stressful. Then again, maybe not. She knew she had been suppressing the urgency to need him through all of this. "All right! No more *Scooby-Doo*," she said after letting out a theatrically heavy sigh. "Let's watch an oldie, but a goodie."

Choice, with a bit of a whine in his voice, replied, "But *Scooby-Doo* is already old."

June answered back, "Well, it's not a goodie."

Debbie asserted herself. "Okay, guys, we're talking classics. Your uncle and I used to watch this one all the time when we were kids." Debbie fluttered her hands in the air, attempting her most spooky voice, "And it's called… *The Invisible Man!*"

Debbie jammed a steak knife into her pumpkin. The kids had those serrated vegetable knives that come with carving kits. June had started carving freehand.

"Maybe tomorrow," Debbie started, "before the trick-or-treaters come we can go look at the schools I need to register y'all for. It's a new life for us, so let's not hold it back any longer. Deal?"

"Finally."

"Deal!"

"Well, all right," said Debbie. "Sounds like a plan to me."

"You're such a dork, mom."

"And don't you forget it!" Debbie grabbed her kids by the shoulders, pulling them in for a hug. These were the good times people always talk about missing when they're older. She really prayed her children would remember these days when they grew up and flew the coop.

After a while, Debbie gave up on the failings of her carving. She started to get sucked into the movie. It was almost like she was watching the movie for the first time. When the kids put their pumpkins down and rested against her, she knew that they were getting just as sucked in as her at the scene which entailed two of the characters searching Dr. Jack Griffin's laboratory for any details that may lead them to his whereabouts, only to find one little note left behind that catches their eye.

The timer went off from the oven, causing Debbie to jump. This, in turn, had the effect of startling her two kids as well. In unison, seconds after they collected themselves, they said, "Mom!"

June added, "It's not even at a scary part."

"It is kind of creepy, though," Choice replied.

"Sorry, y'all," she said. "I was, like, in it." She laughed it off as she stood up, heading toward the kitchen.

"I went too deep with my carving!"

June crawled over toward Choice. "Here," she said, "I can fix it and then you can keep going. That doesn't look so bad, bud."

Debbie overheard June helping Choice and even heard him say, "Thank you, sissy." Debbie's heart practically melted as she opened the oven and pulled out the current batch of pumpkin seeds.

Just then a surprise noise—a loud bang, perhaps the wind rattling the house. Debbie dropped the hot pan from the oven, startling the kids and herself even more. The temperature lowered, sending chills through each person's spine.

"What's happened, mom?" asked June.

Choice stood up. "Did mommy burn her hand?"

"Oh, I'm so sorry, kids," she said, practically out of breath. "I think the back door popped open. I got it. It just startled me, but I'm good."

Debbie, unharmed, left the pan, and ran to the backdoor, which had grown dark due to the sun being blocked by their house as it fell. Flipping the light switch on illuminated the entirety of her backyard. She held herself as the winter-like breeze sliced even more harshly against her skin.

Just when she was beginning to think that her nerves were too erratic once again, there it was. A body was face down in the grass. Many feet away from the door. Too far away to have hit the screen before bolting in the opposite direction.

It took a few seconds before Debbie realized that she was standing there in silence, her heart racing, and not acknowledging her children. She was someplace else, someplace horrible, losing hope.

June walked over to her, placing her hand over her mother's shoulder. "Mom," she said, "what's gotten into—" June turned her head and saw the body. She immediately slammed the door shut, locking it, staring at her mother with concern. "Mom."

Debbie snapped out of it in panic, guiding her daughter halfway toward the kitchen. "Grab my purse and find the officer's card from the other day. Tell them that we think our intruder is back." Debbie whispered the word *intruder*, so as to not freak out Choice.

It was obvious that June was regressing into the takeover that this event caused her. June was attempting to control her breathing, taking deep, deliberate gasps of air. "But... mom... he's..." June started to fiddle with the lock to the back door.

Debbie stopped her, looking into her daughter's eyes. "Don't worry," she said. "He is not coming in here. No one is going to hurt you."

Once the police were welcomed inside by Debbie, they found an empty living room. The officers walked through to the backyard, examining the body. To their knowledge, the suspect had taken a terrible fall, possibly from the hole in the yard or by getting hit in the face by a branch since his face was scratched up. This may have caused his neck to snap. However, when Debbie was asked to identify the man, she remarked that his neck looked like a pretzel. In fact, it looked like it was twisted around more than once. Further examination within the house uncovered that the upper window into June's room had been slightly pried open. Obvious scratch marks chipped away at the gray painted trim connecting to the window. Sloppily, a few thick gashes of the yellow painted siding were discovered as well. Satisfied with their investigation of the house, the police checked the crime scene and the man's dead body for weapons. They discovered a flattened metal pipe with gray and yellow pieces of wood stuck onto the end in his insert jacket pocket. Shaking the hand of the two officers, Debbie was told that the intruder obviously wouldn't be bothering them anymore and so she can rest easy for the night, but she will have to deal with a few visits by police and detectives, as well as appearances in court if necessary in the coming weeks. Thankfully, the body was picked up within the hour.

Waving at the police as they drove off, she stopped to look into the sky. The moon was about to take over.

Debbie turned to the view of her new house on Hawthorne Drive. There was a lot to soak in at that moment. Before she could allow herself to be engulfed by it all, she was compelled to check on her kids. Debbie saw two sets of eyes peeking through the blinds.

Choice's socks were slipping as he was standing on the lid of the toilet, adjusting himself to better see through the window that overlooked the backyard from the upstairs bathroom. He remembered to reach down and flush, hoping his sister believed that he was on the potty all this time. *I saw it. I saw the dead body,* he thought to himself. His eyes gaped open and mind ran wild as he replayed the images of the crime scene. Suddenly, the wind blew and Choice knew the shadowy man was coming for a visit. Only this time, it never died down. Choice could hear it through the window. The shadowy man was there, he had been there all night, watching them. He was looking up at Choice from the backyard and he put his finger up to where his mouth would be and said through the wind, *"Shush."*

"Don't worry," Choice whispered back. Just then he overheard the frantic footsteps of his older sister. "Choice?! What's taking you so long?" she said. He jumped, planting his feet onto the fluffy rug and downstairs into the living room joining her with eagerness to peep from a new view.

Choice and his sister backed away from the window when their mother saw them. He watched as June started to pace around the room. She was fiddling with her hands, terribly upset by what had been happening.

Opening the front door, but still standing outside on the porch, their mother looked too afraid to walk inside. June kept pacing. Choice shivered from the outside cold; fighting his chills, he ran up to his mother, prompting her to kneel before him as he embraced her tightly.

June suddenly stopped and turned to them. "How could he get knocked like that from something hitting him in the face and then falling face down onto the grass? Wouldn't he have been face up? Mom?"

"Yeah," their mother said. "That is weird."

Choice let go of his mother and pointed at June. "You filled that hole, too, sissy. Remember?"

Choice saw June's eyes widen and knew they matched his mother's. They both realized that Choice was right. June had covered the hole earlier that afternoon.

"It was *The Shadowy Man*," said Choice as he ran back into the living room, covering himself with a blanket left on the couch. It was getting too cold to handle.

"Mom, are they one-hundred percent sure that this was the guy who was in my room last time?"

"Baby, I am going to help in every way to figure that out. Believe me." Their mother grabbed onto June's shoulders, looked her in the eyes, and then pulled her close, embracing her. "I think this is the guy, but I'll be visiting the police soon enough to really figure that out."

Choice covered his mouth with the blanket and started to breathe into the fabric.

"Also I found this by the door," she mentioned. "Choice is this yours honey? It's odd, I don't remember seeing this there before," she mumbled to herself with confusion. Debbie held out a tiny wooden box covered in old withered stamps.

June pulled away from their mom. "Should we open it?"

"Okay," said their mom, leading them outside under the porch light. "Choice, come over here, baby."

He waddled over. The little guy was starting to get tired and cranky. It had been an eventful night. He really just wanted to go to sleep, but he fought the feeling anyway so that he wouldn't miss out.

Before Choice could ask what this was about, he saw all of his old knickknacks. A fishing lure with faded stripes and little bells attached, a vintage pocket knife, an old rusty pocket watch, and a toy tractor. "Wow, my stuff!" said Choice, barreling into the box to grab all of his things, dropping his blanket in the process. Choice looked up at his mother and sister, smiling, before setting his eyes back in the box. "Oh, look!"

June and their mother did as instructed.

Inside was a beautifully intricate music box with a tiny crank popped out of the side, while a tapered and silky red ribbon was coiled beside it.

Debbie grabbed her ribbon from the box and confiscated Choice's pocket knife from his collection.

Choice held onto his mother again, holding her close.

June pulled out the music box, inspecting its delicate craft, and began cranking it. A soft melody escaped the box and began to play an old familiar tune. Time stood still as snow started to fall outside, each snowflake dancing from the clouds down onto the earth around them. Neither of the kids had ever seen snow in their lives before. It was really something. June grabbed the blanket that Choice forgot and wrapped them both inside of it. Their eyes gleaming with wonder.

The song from the box ended its arrangement and June held onto

Choice tighter. He could feel her warmth against him and he felt safe with his sissy.

Choice wondered if the shadowy man was the one who made it snow. He thought the shadowy man could do anything. Choice hoped he'd remember to ask the shadowy man if he presented gifts to everyone else on the street. They didn't seem like bad people and some looked like they needed a friend. The shadowy man, however, wasn't going anywhere. This was just the beginning for his family on Hawthorne Drive and Choice knew it. He was sure they all did.

WHEN THE WALLS FALL DOWN
218 W. HAWTHORNE DRIVE

by Lou Rasmus

It's a ceramic pan. There are two raw chicken thighs inside of the pan. Some olive oil is pooling beneath the chicken and then I add salt, pepper, onion powder, a little cayenne, and I top it with some herbs. The oven is at 400 degrees. The rack is on the second rung from the bottom. Before I put the pan in the oven, I mix the seasonings and the oil and the two raw chicken thighs until everything is evenly spread. The chicken is icy between my fingers; my fingers are slimy between the chicken and the oil.

It's a ceramic pan. And there are two beating hearts inside of the pan. Ugly, vascular hearts. Going *buh-bump buh-bump buh-bump*. And *buh-bump buh-bump buh-bump*. My hands spasm and recoil. One heart beats faster and more erratically than the other. So much so that it beats over the edge of the ceramic pan and onto the floor. There's a heavy, viscous pool of red where it lands. And then the thing just goes on beating - *buh-bump buh-bump buh-bump* - around the kitchen. One of the cats comes down from on top of the refrigerator where he was sleeping to look at it. His head turns one way and then the other as he studies it. It's unfamiliar to him, a beating heart. He's never seen anything like it. And when it goes beating and jumping around the kitchen it startles him. He jerks backward from it. He springs straight up into the air. And then he swats at it, with his little white paw. He swats at it in the fast, repetitive way cats swat at things. Like quick sideways jabs. But he can't seem to get it. The heart is beating too fast and too erratically. It's headed for the door. *It's leaving*, I think to myself. I'm not sure where it's leaving to, but I can tell that it doesn't want to be here, so I let it go.

I look back down at the pan. It's a ceramic pan. There are two raw chicken thighs in the pan and they're mixed together with olive oil, salt, pepper, onion powder, cayenne, and some herbs. It's just a regular pan with regular chicken. The one cat is asleep on the refrigerator and the other is sleeping on the couch in the living room, I'm sure. She sleeps there most of the day and usually through the night, too. The oven is at 400 degrees and the rack is on the second rung from the bottom of the oven. I put the pan into the oven, set a timer for forty minutes, and wash my hands.

When Oxford comes into the kitchen he asks me what's for dinner.

The chicken thighs have been in the oven for ten minutes, I have vegetables sautéing on the stove, and some sweet potatoes are boiling in a pot.

"Your favorite," I say brightly.

Oxford steps closer. A smile sneaks up on his face and he sniffs at the air. He has a cute, pointed nose, I think.

Then he says, "salmon? Is it the lemon-parmesan crusted salmon?"

I back myself up against the stovetop to hide the vegetables and sweet potatoes.

"Um…"

He comes closer and smiles bigger and sniffs a few more times.

"Oh!" Oxford says. "It smells like asparagus, too. Ah! I love asparagus Teddy!"

I stutter out a soft "well…"

He strides up to me until his chest is pressed against mine. Just enough for me to feel the size of his chest on mine. His broad and heavy and strong chest. It takes over my deflated frame and bends me backwards over the stovetop until the heat of the burners starts to make me sweat. That's when he sees it. Over my shoulder he sees the sautéed vegetables and boiled sweet potatoes. His pointed little nose turns down.

"Wait," he says. He grabs me by the arms and moves me to the side away from the oven door. Then he opens the oven, sees the chicken, and drops his head. He doesn't slam the door shut, but he closes it hard enough to make it clear that what he was going to say next isn't going to be good.

And what he says next isn't good. The same way much of the conversations between Oxford and me haven't been good lately. Tonight it was the chicken thighs. We've had chicken thighs three times in the last week, Oxford tells me. Last Sunday, Tuesday, and now today, Friday. And it's not even that he doesn't like the chicken thighs, or the sautéed vegetables or the sweet potatoes, he's just upset that I've made this meal three times in the last week, when he said several times last week that we needed to start eating some new dishes. He tells me that we've been in a rut and he knows things have been difficult lately but having something different for dinner every now and then would be a good start. And that's all we have to do right now. We have to start to try harder to change things. At the time I had agreed with him. But then I got so busy with work, I explain, that last Friday night when I went to the store, I was so exhausted and feeling lost that I just got what I always get, which is mostly chicken thighs and vegetables and potatoes. I say all of this and I tell him that I'm sorry, too, but he's upset anyway because it's not just the chicken thighs that he's mad about. It's the routine all around. The sad, redundant routine of going to work and coming home and asking each other about how our days went and pretending like everything is fine when it's not. Everything is not fine, he tells me, and it's ok that things aren't fine but what's not good is doing nothing about it. And now there's this *dullness* between us, he says. That's what it is. Oxford tells me that there's a dullness that has come into our relationship and left everything with a bland taste. Like everything that once was exciting and still should be exciting is now coming out flat.

"Like what?" I ask.

"Like last week," he says. It doesn't take him even a moment to respond. "We went to dinner and it wasn't fun."

"What?"

"Yes," he says again. He folds his arms across his chest. His lips purse together. He breathes in sharply and theatrically. Then he goes on: "we went to dinner at *Siciliano's*, and you know that I had been wanting to go there for a while, and you know that I had been wanting for us to have a date night because I thought it would be good for us, and then we went and you were on your phone almost the whole time."

"I was work—"

"You were working," he says. "We know. We all know. You were working. You're always working. But the point was that you said that you were going to take a break so that we could have a nice night—"

"I had a nice night!" I say.

Oxford rolls his eyes and tucks his arms up into himself harder and higher towards the chin.

"Well I'm happy you did," he says.

"I thought you did too."

"I didn't."

And then I stop. I have nothing left to stay. We've had this fight before and I know that saying anything else isn't going to change what's about to come. And what's to come is this:

"I just don't know if I can do this anymore, Ted." His voice gets shaky here. "I'm just exhausted by all of this. The ups and downs. The fighting every day. The feeling that I've lost a part of you. Teddy," he says. "I love you, but you're pushing me to the breaking point." Tears start to form at this point; maybe one will slip out of the corner of his eye, but quietly and without much notice if it does. It all happens right when it's supposed to. He has it timed just right. Like a dancer to the beat to a song. "I keep telling you over and over again that I need more from you. And I know you're trying but I need you to try harder. I need you to want to get through this as badly as I want us to get through this." Tears roll in full stream now. Eyes are buggy and red from the activity. Upper lip is quivering. He's a firm, big man but tender too.

"Do you even care about me? About us?" He finishes. Fireworks. Applause. End scene.

Of course I do care about him. When he lets me talk I always tell him that I do care about him, and that I love him, and that I'm sorry that I work so much and that I haven't been the easiest to be around for the last few months, but that it will get better. I'm just doing really well at work right now. That's what I tell him. I say that I don't want to be so wrapped up with work but that my bosses have been really impressed with me lately and that if I keep showing up early, working late, and keep getting results, I could be in line for a raise in the next quarter.

"What does that even mean, Teddy? To 'get results?'" He puts 'get results' in air quotes when he says it.

"More clients more tests more money."

"Clients for what!"

"Oxford," I say. "You know what I do. I work for the hospital."

"Yeah, so what are clients for a hospital?"

"I've explained this before."

"Explain it again."

I let out a breath, and then I explain to him again that I handle client acquisition and retention for the research arm of the hospital. Our clients are often animal shelters, other hospitals with overrun psych wards, or prisons at population capacity. The hospital that I work for contracts these third parties - our clients - to supply our research team with test groups for our various experiments. The more clients we acquire, the more tests we can run, the larger our sample size, and the more results we can publish. And results demonstrate problems. Problems need medicines. The hospital sells the findings to companies who produce medicines. More clients, more tests, more money, I say again.

Oxford just stands across from me and listens to all of this like he's never heard it before. His face makes twists and flinches when I mention the experiments and test subjects. Like I haven't told him eighty-three times already what I do. He says that it all sounds cruel and not right. I tell him that I'm not the one doing the experiments. I tell him that I've never even seen the test subjects or even seen any tests being done. He says that he doesn't believe me.

"Why would you not?" I ask. "What reason would I have for wanting to be a part of the experiments?"

"I don't know."

"Well then believe me," I say. "I have seen a county jail bus pull into the parking lot, and I've seen empty wire cages in the hallway after one of the local animal shelters has came and went, but I've never witnessed any experiments and I have no reason to ever want to."

"I've just never understood why you work for that hospital in the first place," he says. "All of that sounds horrible and cruel and now you've burnt the vegetables anyway."

I turn around to the stovetop. I had forgotten about the vegetables, and the potatoes and the chicken. That's when the timer goes off. The chicken is done and so I grab an oven mitt and I open the oven and in the fury of the sudden commotion I grab the pan out from the second rung of the oven, have a handle on it for a second, and then don't have a handle on it a second later. The pan and the two chicken thighs with the salt, pepper, onion powder, cayenne, and herbs on top crash and clatter against the tile floor of the kitchen. My heart is going *buh-bump buh-bump buh-bump*. Really fast and without any steady rhythm.

Oxford throws his arms into the air.

"I can't be here right now."

The timer is going off and there's smoke coming up from the vegetables and the water is boiling in this rapid-fire kind of way that seems to add to the maddening feeling of the entire last few minutes. I grab a shard of the broken ceramic pan before I remember that the ceramic pan had just been in the oven at 400 degrees for the last forty minutes. I drop the shard and it cracks again against the ground. My finger and thumb where I grabbed it are numb and burning and icy feeling all at once. I want to cry out but I bite my lip and pinch my face into a hard point instead. I don't want to make Oxford more upset than he already is. So I pick up the chicken thighs and then I turn off the burners on the stove. When I turn around to tell Oxford not to go, he's putting on his coat and walking out through the front door.

Sometimes I feel like I don't know where I am. It's this feeling that comes on when I'm right where I'm supposed to be, but I feel like I shouldn't be there. Almost like if my life were a movie, and everyone else's lives were their own movie, and then one scene I suddenly showed up for a scene in someone else's movie instead of my own. That's how I feel sometimes. And when I feel like this I get this shortness of breath that makes everything staticky and dark around the edges. It can grab me pretty bad at times. Like at the grocery store last week, when I couldn't remember that Oxford had told me that he wanted something new to have for dinner. Or like right now, as I pick up pieces of chicken and the ceramic pan from the floor. I feel like there's a weight pressing against my temples and a pressure behind my eyes and everything looks fuzzy. Dark around the edges. My chest feels compressed, too. That's the shortness of breath. And I don't know why I feel like I don't know where I am right now, but I do. I'm right where I should be, but I feel lost.

"You're just tired," I say out loud to myself. "You have been working a lot lately and you haven't been sleeping well."

"And what about the things you've been seeing?" I counter myself.

"Those are nothing."

"They've been happening more lately."

"Hardly."

"And it has nothing to do with the experiments?"

"It's not the experiments."

"How do you know?"

"I'm just tired," I say again, and then I go back to cleaning up the kitchen.

Richard comes down from the refrigerator and sniffs at the spots where the chicken had fallen against the floor. His tail flicks one way and then the other, snapping quickly and in a jerky sort of way. He sniffs some more and his nose twitches. Then he starts licking.

"Rich," I say. "No." I kick him gently from the back. "Stop."

But he doesn't stop.

"Richard, you better stop licking the floor, I need to clean it up."

He's purring and licking and flicking his tail back and forth.

I kick him a little harder this time. He's a big, round cat and his hair is long and greying. He doesn't budge.

"I'm serious," I say. The static is heavy and my temples are hurting and my chest is tight and then the cat is dead. That's how quickly it happens. The cat was there and he was purring and he was licking and now he is on his side not making any sounds or moving at all. I don't know much else about how it happened, but I know that I'm back in my own movie now.

At first I don't know what to do with the cat. Whatever had happened, it evidently didn't happen easily. The mess on the floor is unpleasant, and when I look down at myself I see that my arms are all cut up from cat scratches and my shirt has a hole in it from where Richard landed a claw. *I really liked this shirt*, I say to myself.

The other cat comes in from the living room and sniffs at Richard.

My stomach turns.

"I'm sorry," I say.

"Meow," the other cat says.

"I didn't mean to, Christine."

"Meow," Christine says again.

"I'm just tired."

Christine looks back down at Richard and then walks over to the litter box.

I decide to bury Richard. He was a good cat. A handsome, white cat with one orange spot on his right shoulder. I didn't mean to kill him, I tell myself. And I'll give him a beautiful funeral and maybe a wake afterwards. That's what I'll do. I'll go to the store and buy a bottle of champagne and then after I bury Richard we'll have a nice wake. We'll celebrate his life, I tell Christine, and maybe Oxford will come back and we can all have a toast to his life. I won't tell Oxford how it happened, I think, but I'll have to tell him something. So I resolve to tell him that he went peacefully. He was an old enough cat for that to make sense. It would still be a surprise, but not impossible. I'll tell him that he was licking at the chicken thighs one second and then he was on his side the next. That was it. He went peacefully and happily. And his body is only laid out the way that it is just because he fell in a weird way. *That's a good plan*, I say to myself, and then I leave for the liquor store.

Only, on my way I realize that champagne isn't the right drink for the wake. We're going to need tequila, I think. Something nice, too. In honor of Richard. He would want us to have nice tequila at his wake, not champagne. He always hated the French. That's how I figure it, anyway. I can't remember if he ever said that explicitly, but I'm mostly sure he was against the French just as a rule of thumb. So at the store I get a bottle of silver tequila, and a bottle of strawberry margarita mix, too. If Oxford comes back, he'll want a margarita, I think. He and Richard always had a love for Mexican culture. Ever since Oxford got that job shooting a commercial in Cancun. He came back and wouldn't stop talking about it. It's nothing like Wisconsin, he would say. There's so much sun and water and margaritas. And there were hotel rooms with a pool that went right up to the patio. You could just walk outside, take two steps, and be up to your chest in the cool, blue water. That's what he would say. It was all simple and obvious but wonderful. And nothing like Wisconsin. Some days he would get to talking about it and he would talk for so long that I would eventually fall asleep, and so then he would just keep talking about it to the cats. That's how Richard came to like Mexican culture too, from Oxford's stories that he would stay up late listening to. Christine liked the stories, too, and she would stay up listening to them right along with Richard, but Oxford always said she was really more busy licking herself than paying attention.

At the register the cashier asks me if everything is okay. She says I had a far off look in my eye, like there was some conversation happening that only I could hear.

I tell her that I'm fine and I pay for the tequila and the margarita mix and then I walk out.

Oxford is already home when I get back. I wasn't expecting him to be back so soon. He's in the kitchen standing over the mess of chicken thighs and ceramic pieces and Richard's body. There's a bag of takeout food on the counter.

"Oh, what did you get to eat?" I ask as I walk in.

Oxford turns around to me.

"Ted!" His face is sagging and soft looking. It's normally tight and youthful and it's hard to see it become so different. "What happened to Richard?" He says. The words come out squealy and shaky and breathy through the saggy skin. His eyes are bubbling over.

"Richard!" I cry out.

I drop the bottle of tequila and its shattering echoes behind my scream. Tequila and glass crack and spill across the floor. I jump and scream again from the excitement of it all. To Oxford it looks like natural shock.

"Teddy!" He says, and then he covers his mouth as he starts to cry.

I run to him and wrap my arms around his neck.

"What happened?"

He wraps his heavy arms around me and pulls me in so that I can feel his bigness against me again. Only this time it is not to say that he is bigger and more powerful, but that he is big and warm and safe. It says that whatever happened to Richard was horrible but that it wasn't anyone's fault and that everything is going to be okay.

"What a horrible night," I say.

He rubs his hand up and down my back and soothes me until my breathing slows and my eyelids grow heavy. There's a change in him from how he was with me earlier when he was talking about the *dullness* between us. There's a warmth in him now and I don't know what made the warmth come about but I feel at home in it so I just hug him tighter and rest my head on his chest.

"Don't cry," he says to me. "Things happen. Richard was old..."

"Not that old," I say.

And then he tells me that walking in to see this was a surprise, but that Richard was an old cat and sometimes old cats just die.

"It has been a possibility for a long time now," he tells me. "There's nothing either of us could have done."

"I could have not gone to the store," I say.

"Don't say that."

"No, I could have stayed home, and then I could've saved his life, or at least been here so that he didn't have to die alone."

"Stop blaming yourself, Teddy. That's just a part of all of this. You keep blaming yourself. And I'm sorry about what I said earlier. I was just hungry and upset and I didn't mean what I said. And I know I said a lot of awful things and I said we need change and everything else but if you're not there right now then you're not there and that's ok and I'm sorry. This has been a hard last few months and whatever happened here tonight is only going to make it harder, I know, but we'll get through this. I promised myself that I would help us get through this and I'm sorry for making such a commotion earlier but I think I was just hungry and I didn't want the chicken thighs and I know that's not a good excuse to say all of the things I said but I can't take it back now. All I can do is try to make it right and I will. I don't need change. I don't need anything more from you. I just want us to be happy and good again like it was before all of this."

"Oxford," I say, looking up at him with big heavy eyes.

"Plus," he says. "Christine was here, so it's not like Richard was alone."

Christine is sitting on the kitchen table, smelling the bag of takeout food that Oxford brought home.

"I just feel terrible," I say. "What an awful night. I just wanted to get us some drinks so that we could put the chicken thighs behind us. He was fine when I left. Everyone was fine." And then I do my best to sound like I'm crying, even though there aren't any tears that come.

"It's not your fault," he says again.

I sniffle and push back from his hug.

"You know what we should do?" I ask.

He looks down at me and his face is solid and safe again.

"What?"

"We should have a funeral," I tell him. I say it as cheerfully as I can. "It'll be a celebration of his life!" I start to take off my coat. "With a proper burial and then even a wake, Oxford."

"What are all of those scratches on your arms, Ted?"

I had forgotten about the scratches. I think about putting the coat back on but it's too late.

"Christine and I were playing earlier," I say. But I waited a second too long to answer.

"Earlier you were at work and then you came home and made chicken and then you threw all of the chicken on the ground."

I laugh in a ditsy sort of way.

"Oh, well then it must've been yesterday."

"You worked until ten last night and when you came home you came straight to bed."

"Yeah, before—"

He doesn't let me finish.

"I thought it looked like something was off. The whole thing." He waves his arm across the kitchen and his tone changes again. "None of this makes any sense. Why did you leave halfway through picking up the chicken and the pan? How would our cat die out of nowhere? He was old but he was healthy. And why is he laid out in the twisted way that he is? Teddy did you do this?"

I stand silent and still for a minute, and then I say, "I know just the right place to bury him. By the trees. I'll dig a little hole and we'll put him in a little box and we'll decorate it with a little wreath made of things from whatever twigs and leaves we can find in the backyard."

"I have to go," Oxford says. "I'm sorry, Teddy, but I just can't be here with you right now. I went out and I came back feeling changed and sorry about what I had said earlier and I was ready to tell you that I was ready and willing again to do whatever I needed to do to help you but this is too far. I've been trying so hard and I know I slipped earlier about the chicken and the feeling dull but I don't know if I have it in me to support you after what you've done now." He sniffles and wipes his nose. "You killed Richard."

"And after the funeral we'll have a nice wake," I say. "It will be pleasant and respectful and a celebration of his life. And we'll have margaritas not champagne because of Richard's aversion to the French and admiration for Mexico."

Oxford stares blankly at me.

"Teddy," he says. He puts his coat on again and grabs his food from the counter. "You need to get some rest. You've been in a bad place and you've been working too much and I'm worried about you, but right now I can't help you. I don't know how to help with this. And so I'm going again and when I come back maybe I can help you. I hope that I can. But right now I don't know how and I don't know where to even start and so I'm going."

"We'll need some more tequila for the margaritas to make it an honest celebration of Richard's life, though. All of the other tequila is on the floor."

"Get some rest," Oxford says again, and he walks out.

A good funeral is somber but happy. It is not just a mourning, but a mourning and a celebration all at once. A good funeral has a powerful, moving speech, and friends and family members crying but smiling as they wipe their eyes, and a good soundtrack too. Music has a way of bringing out feeling, and the right soundtrack can make the funeral feel just the right way. Somewhere between sorrow and reverence. A good funeral also has an open bar.

So after Oxford leaves I find a bottle of wine that had been sitting on a shelf next to where we kept our wine glasses and martini glasses. It has been there for a long time and it's starting to collect dust and I vaguely remember a conversation between Oxford and myself where we discussed saving the bottle for a special occasion, but it's perfect for right now, I think, so I open it. This is a special occasion. Not in a good way but a big one. The cat has died. So I take the bottle and I grab the little speaker we keep in the bathroom and I go to work on giving Richard the best funeral there has ever been. Something grand and somber and happy and something that will do justice to the life Richard lived. The mess on the floor will just have to wait.

It doesn't turn out quite the way I hope.

At first the music isn't right. I try something low and western sounding. Something you drink to when you're by yourself on a cold night. But by the third cowboy song I remember that Richard hated western music. I had forgotten that when I turned it on, but now I remember that he didn't like country music, folk-americana music, or even classic cowboy songs to drink to. Richard loved Spanish music. He loved Mexican culture and tequila and Spanish music. Señor Richard is what he'd always asked to be called. It sounded more like 'meow' when he said it, but Oxford and I both knew he had always thought of himself as Señor Richard. So I put on some Spanish music and finish the wine. I don't mean to drink it as fast as I do, but the emotion of the night and the moving of Señor Richard's body from the floor where he laid twisted and disjointed and covered in the grease of the spilled chicken thighs was overwhelming and so I drank the bottle faster than I had meant to. I move his body from the floor to an old shoe box. The box is orange and there's a big swoosh symbol across the top of it. But when I close the lid and think of Richard's body being in there it seems wrong. He never liked the company with the big swoosh logo and to bury him in a box with the swoosh seems insensitive and rude.

I need a new box, I think to myself, the open bottle next to me on the floor and the chicken grease and broken ceramic pieces scattered in front of me. The room is starting to take on a terrible smell of meat and death and booze and I'm surprised by how unaffected I feel by all of it.

Señor Richard will need a proper casket, I decide. Something sturdy and proud. And it will need to be decorated just right for him. I envision his name carved into the lid. Señor Richard von Richard. That's his full name, anyway. Oxford thought it was ridiculous and perfect, and he explained to me that that was the only name that truly suited him. The Señor was because he loved Mexican culture, Oxford said, and the von Richard part was homage to his noble German heritage. Obviously. I remember asking Oxford how he knew Richard was so passionate about Mexican culture and how he knew Richard's lineage traced back to German royalty and he just said it was intuition. He could see it in Richard's eyes, these things. And after I got to know Richard better I learned to see it, too. He was Señor Richard von Richard and he liked tequila and Spanish music and, even though he didn't identify strongly with his German ancestry, he respected it and appreciated it being a part of his name. It was a silent badge of honor to him, the von Richard bit.

So I go to the garage of the house and find some pieces of wood that I think I could put together to make a coffin. It isn't a lot of wood, but it will have to work, I think. Only I know that I can't make a proper coffin without something more to drink so I put the wood pieces down and I leave the kitchen as it is and I leave Richard in the box with the swoosh on it and I go back to the liquor store.

The cashier behind the counter is the same one that was there before, and when she recognizes that it's me she asks again if everything is okay. I give her my credit card and tell her that things are starting to look up and she doesn't seem to know what I mean by that and so I tell her about a party that I'm having. That's why I needed to come back for more tequila. The party is going so well that we ran out of tequila, I tell her. And she laughs at this but it's a nervous and uncomfortable laugh and I don't understand why she laughs that way.

"They will likely be talking about it in the papers," I go on. "The grandest and most immaculate party Wisconsin has ever seen. Gatsby couldn't match a party like this," I say.

Only she looks back at me with unimpressed eyes and her one eyebrow is raised as if to say that she is confused, or she doesn't know who Gatsby is.

"You should come by," I say. "But dress nice. It's a high class event. Tuxedos and ballroom dresses."

Her eyes fall down to my button up shirt that has a few buttons undone and then to my pants that have chicken grease stains on the knees and then she squints back at me as if to say that none of what I'm saying makes any sense.

"218 Hawthorne Drive," I tell her. "Come by any time tonight, we'll be going until the morning." I pick up the bottle of tequila from the counter. "And we'll have plenty of tequila to go around."

On the drive home it starts to snow and the roads quickly get slippery and uncertain and I wonder where Oxford is. When he gets mad he sometimes just goes out driving rather than going anywhere in particular and I wonder if that's what he's doing now. *It's not a good night for a mad drive*, I think, but the thought doesn't last for long because my mind goes back to Richard and the coffin I still have to build and the grand funeral I still have to host.

Back in the house things are as they were. Richard is still dead and still in the box that he loathes and the chicken and the ceramic and the smells are all the same. Spanish music is still playing over the speaker but I'm not familiar with the song and the foreign words mean nothing to me. *At least it's a comfort to Richard*, I think. And I haven't seen Christine since earlier but she prides herself on her indifference to things so I'm not surprised to not see her when I return.

In one of the cabinets we have a cocktail shaker and a long stirring spoon and some other things used to make drinks. It's a cabinet just to the side of the oven and in front of the mess of things on the floor and I have to step over the pooled chicken juices and across the broken ceramic to get to it. My feet cut on the shards of the shattered pan that are sharp like glass but I don't mind. The red slips through my socks and onto the floor with everything else that is ugly and unsettling. It's turning into quite a disgusting masterpiece, I think, and the blood from the cuts in my feet runs over the tile.

I grab ice from the freezer and drop it into the cocktail shaker. It's a chrome cocktail shaker. There are two ice cubes in it and then I pour some of the tequila over the ice. They crack and hiss as the liquor spills over and through them. It's a chrome cocktail shaker and there are two eyeballs swimming in a gummy kind of clear liquid. The eyeballs have hard, crimson veins from where the liquid has irritated them. They come up to the top of the goopy whatever and look at me. It's an unnerving look. Glaring and critical. And they want to know what I'm doing. They want to know why I'm here, making a drink in this kitchen while everything seems to be on fire all around me, and why I feel so comfortable with all of it. I tell them that I don't know how I got here or how this all happened but that it's happening now and the only way to the other side is through.

It's a chrome cocktail shaker and I put the lid on it and shake it and then I pour the chilled tequila into a martini glass. In the garage I pick up the wood pieces again and I study them and I drink from the glass and then I put everything down. *I don't know how to make a coffin*, I think, and then I start to cry.

I think again about how I don't know how I got here or how this happened at all. It was Friday morning and I was at the hospital and after I made some calls and sat in on some meetings my assistant told me that the day's experiments were starting and I said that I'd like to watch. He told me that it was not going to be a pretty experiment and that I shouldn't watch. It was movie day, he said. And I know that movie day is the most gruesome experiment but the other experiments that I had been watching recently had started to bore me and so the thought of sitting in on movie day sent this electric feeling from my toes to my knees to my heart and then to everywhere else.

It was Friday and I was sitting outside of the testing room and the movie started to play. I hadn't seen it before but I was familiar with its purpose and so I knew what to expect and I thought that knowing what to expect would make it easy enough to watch and experience without being wholly affected by it in the way that it was meant to affect the test subjects.

In the testing room was a pet monkey with bald spots down its spine that had been taken in by animal control after it attacked the seven-year-old daughter of its owner, and a man who had been sentenced to life in prison after he had killed his entire family by suffocation, one after the other.

Through the glass behind them I sat and watched the movie the same way as them. Captivated and completely transfixed. I don't remember what flashed on the screen but I remember that it churned my stomach and at one point I vomited and then went right back to watching. One of the head doctor's conducting the experiment told me that I shouldn't watch it but I told him that there were no rules against watching it and that I wanted to. It was Friday afternoon and it was movie day and the other experiments hadn't been making me feel anything anymore and so I wanted to watch. That's all I could think. Movie day is a good day because it's better than the other days and the movie really is something to see. Movie day is violent and disturbing and the different parts of it are hard to remember exactly but the violence and gruesomeness of it all is still with me, I think, as I come back to the garage.

There are six pieces of wood and then for a second they're mismatched limbs of an animal and a human and then a moment later they're back to being six pieces of wood. I don't know exactly how to make a wood box out of them but I take a swig of the tequila and then I grab some nails and a hammer and I start to put it all together as good as I can.

It doesn't come out quite like I want it, but it'll work, I tell myself. It has to work. And anything is better than burying Richard in that shoebox. He would never forgive me if I buried him with that swoosh logo. So the wood pieces are now a box and I want to carve his name into the lid of it but the only knife I find is a dull knife that doesn't seem like it can carve into anything. The blade is bent and rounded. But there's a marker that I find in a box with some tools and it works so I just write his name on the box instead. I figure it's the thought that counts. But when I bring the box into the kitchen with the dead cat and the chicken and smells and Spanish music playing something that sounds like *La Cucaracha* I realize that the box I made is not big enough. As soon as I see the shoe box in comparison to the box I made I realize that there's no way that Richard is going to fit into the little coffin. But his name is on it and I'm proud of myself for making it and so I decide that the rational thing to do is to do what I have to do to the cat to make it work for the box. That's the only way, I think. The box is worth it. And so I go back to the garage and I find the hatchet that Oxford bought for the one camping trip that we went on five years ago and I bring it back to the kitchen where I do what I have to do to make the limp cat fit into the box. I don't feel good about doing it but there's no other way, I think. He couldn't be buried in the shoe box.

I wipe myself off with a towel and change my shirt when I'm done. I put on an old, oversized knit sweater that Oxford had gotten me a few years ago, and now that I have Señor Richard in the box and I feel good and accomplished about everything that I've done, it's time for the burial.

It happens sometimes that a person is born into such prosperous circumstances, and things are so good and prosperous from the beginning and always, that it seems possible that they could live their whole lives without ever having anything bad happen. These are the people who grow up to be prom queens and high school quarterbacks, or famous actors and actresses, or CEOs and CFOs and C-whatever elses, and not once realize that the life they live, without any problems or challenges, is in any way uncommon or unnatural. It seems possible to them, even, that the world only started when they entered it. That everything before then was so unimportant that it might as well have not even happened. And now that it's happening it's only happening to care for and entertain them. This explains why things are always so great and easy.

But it happens then, too, when this kind of person finally meets trauma of some sort, the same way everyone experiences trauma of some sort mostly every day, that he or she may have a more dramatic reaction to it than others. So much so that they may start to feel lost in the world, or feel that they may not be able to go on living, because everything they had thought they knew about how the world works and what the purpose of life is was shattered in that moment.

"That's what's happened to you," Oxford tells me. He's standing behind me as I dig at the ground with a rusted spade.

"I'm just glad you got home safe," I tell him. I dig while I say it. I'm digging hard and fervently but the ground is tough from the colder weather and the snow and so I'm not getting very far. "The roads were getting pretty bad out there."

"Teddy," he says. "Are you even listening to me? I left and I thought about it and I thought about everything I know about you and everything you've been through lately and I think that's what it is. You're going through trauma for the first time in your life and I think you are having a mental breakdown."

"I wanted to carve his name into the box," I say, "but the only knife we have is dull. Did you know that? We only have one dull knife that's good for nothing? What if something were to happen? How would we protect ourselves with that dinky thing?"

"We need to get you help," he says. But the energy has come out of his voice. "I know that it's been tough since your brother died and I know that you don't want to talk about it but, Teddy —" he grabs me by the shoulder and without thinking I turn and stab at his hand with the spade. "FUCK!" He screams, and he stumbles away from me.

"Don't be loud, Oxford," I tell him. "You'll get the neighbors out here and then they'll interrupt Richard's funeral."

"You just stabbed me!" He says. The energy is back now.

"I know and I'm sorry but I'm trying to bury Señor Richard von Richard and you keep getting in the way."

"Oh, I'm getting in the way, Teddy? I'm in the way? I've done nothing but try to help you through this. I went to your brother's funeral with you and we had margaritas until the sun came up the next day because your brother loved margaritas and that's what he would've wanted us to do. And I only ever referred to him as Señor Carl that whole night because you said that's what he would've wanted, too."

"Señor Carl von Carlsberg," I say.

"Yeah, the whole thing," Oxford says. "As stupid as I think it was I did it anyway because I wanted to be supportive of you. And since he died I know you've been feeling lost and I know you've been trying to fill that sad feeling with work and I know you've been sitting in on the experiments, too."

I stop digging for a minute.

"Yeah," he goes on. "Your assistant called me the other day and said you've been going to more and more of them. He said you've been going to so many of them that you haven't been getting your work done and that he's worried about you."

I don't look back at him but I sit still and quiet so that he knows that I'm listening and that I'm ready for him to keep going.

"Well I'm worried about you, too, Teddy. And I know you haven't ever really had to deal with anything like this and I know in your world it seemed like everything was always going to be good and prosperous, but things happen. People die every day. In freak accidents and every other way. But it's not your fault. And just because Carl died that doesn't mean that your life is over. And it doesn't mean that you have to torment yourself to make up for the pain you're going through. That's not going to make anything change. But this, tonight, this is too much. You killed our cat and now you've been calling him Señor Richard von Richard like he was your brother and I'm starting to think that you're losing your grip on reality."

"I'm not crazy."

"I didn't say you were crazy."

I get up and turn around and I look at Oxford and, behind Oxford, across the street in front of the house where the single mother and her children moved in recently, I see a dark, faceless, *something*. I don't know what it is but it's not a dog or a human or anything and it makes me stop for a second.

"Oxford, what is *that*?" I point out towards where the being is.

He looks over his shoulder for a second and then he looks back at me.

"What is what?" he asks.

"That," I say again, still pointing.

"I don't see anything Teddy."

"It's right there," I say one more time. "I think it's Carl."

"Teddy, stop."

"It's Carl," I say. "Hey Señor!" I call out. "Señor, it's me!"

"It's time for bed, Teddy."

"No, Oxford, it's really him."

Oxford puts his arm around me and starts to walk me back into the house. Out of the corner of my eye I see the woman who lives next door turn her light on and look out at us. I look back at Oxford to see if he sees her or if he can now see the thing across the street but he's not looking at anything besides the house. His face is sharp and stoic and his features are all firm and nice to look at. The cat is still in pieces in the wooden box and the hole is only half dug but the snow is falling and I think it will probably cover everything up and I can deal with the burial another time. When we get into the house the Spanish music is still playing and Christine is licking at the mess on the kitchen floor.

MANTEO
725 W. HAWTHORNE DRIVE
by Mark Ryan

Sunday. October 25th.
(BEFORE)

-1-

She stood back a little, trying to catch the painting in a different light. To no avail. The small little antique shop played out its Aladdin's cave quality by becoming darker and more cavernous the further in you went. It was at the back she had seen it: a picture that seemed to resonate something inside of her. The frame would never do, of course, but those eyes!

She cocked her head from side to side, trying to capture a different angle, a new composition. She squinted and moved closer, eye to eye with the portrait which seemed to have bewitched her. The shop owner joined her by her side, assessing the portrait which she had lifted up and rested on a Federal period writing desk.

"He really captures the spirit of the era, doesn't he?" the owner said, removing a small wispy tissue from her sleeve and dabbing it to her nose.

Olivia glanced at the woman, her smile lingering only for a moment.

"There's something about him, something in his eyes," she said, as if lost for words.

"Not a bad price either," the woman added, knowing the sale was made. Her experience had taught her that once the buyer was emotionally attached, the job was done.

"Pretty steep I'd say; knock thirty off and I'll take it," Olivia replied, facing the painting still. The woman bristled slightly, like that of a huge bird shaking off the rain.

"Well, um... it's a good price, I think; and is a respectful representation," she added, not really wanting to come down in price, nor lose the sale.

"Representation?" Olivia queried, turning to her. Then, as if understanding, she said, "Oh: Indians. No wait, you can't call them that any more. Native Americans. Yeah, I see what you mean."

"Indigenous people, I think," the older woman said in a sweet tone, trying not to be too patronizing.

"Sure. Well, it's this man's face, his construct. His eyes. They are just so alluring and familiar," Olivia said, her eyes drawn once more to the portrait.

The owner would've said alarming, but for the sake of the sale, she merely nodded to hurry things along.

"I'll ring the sale up on the register," she said, bustling back to the front of the store where an old cash register stood proudly on the counter.

Olivia picked up the painting and took it across to her, taking some money from her purse and handing it over. The owner rung the sale through, minus the $30, and wrapped the painting up in brown paper.

"Enjoy it dear," the woman said, and Olivia replied a thanks before leaving the store with her new purchase.

As she walked down the street, she jostled with the portrait trying to fit it into her backpack. It wasn't overly large, but the frame was about an inch too big for her bag. She walked over to a bench and put both the bag and her new painting down. She turned it around and flicked up the protective casings on the back. She had no nails, and her fingers dug painfully into the metal tacks that held the back on. Eventually she had freed the painting, sliding it away from the frame and snuggly into her bag. She threw the frame into the bin next to the bench and started off again down the main street.

It was busy, despite the wind which was whipping up and already rosying her cheeks. She saw the moms hurrying along with their strollers, the kids within looking up at the Halloween decorations in the store windows as they passed. Their town always made a big deal about Halloween, and this year looked no different. A huge spider loomed atop the candy store on the corner, its legs dangling down; brushing Olivia with one of them with her head as she passed by and turned onto Maple drive.

She jumped onto her motorcycle, a '95 Red Triumph which sported a huge crack in its left mirror. It was her runaround ride. She and her husband's pride was a Triumph Rocket III Roadster, but that was out of action at the moment, sadly. Thinking on this, she started her bike angrily, revving the engine more than it needed. She checked the street and then set off down the quiet road with the noise of the bike vibrating slightly on the thin glassed windows of the old stores.

Turning into Hawthorne Drive, she noticed the neighbors opposite had put up more Halloween decorations. A sign now pointed to the 'Crypt' and some skeletons had been placed along the side fence. She thought they looked like huge white teeth against the gummy colour of the fencing. As she pulled into her driveway, a white cat darted out from the bushes, startling her.

"Motherfucker!" Olivia exclaimed into her helmet, and cut her engine as the cat raced off back towards its house.

Olivia dismounted, taking her backpack off and carrying it in her hand, making her way inside her house. She knew just where the painting would go, and she made her way into the large den area where a blank piece of wall seemed to ache for something to be hung upon it. Inside the room was her husband, Jason, still in the chair he'd been in when she'd left, the ice-hockey game still playing.

"Hey, how's the game?" she asked, walking across to him and kissing his cheek.

"Don't ask," he said.

She patted down some of his hair which was sticking up, licking her hand, and running it over the cowlick.

"I don't know why you bother with them still," she said, going across to the wall and removing her portrait from the bag.

"Loyalty," he replied. "What's that you got?" he asked her, curiously.

"Isn't it amazing?" she said, holding up the painting into place. The headshot profile of a Native American man glared out into the room. The ceremonial headdress dominated the outer parts of the painting, with the desert pushed back even further in the scene, barely noticeable. It was the man's striking features that dominated and seemed to pour out from the center, almost reaching outwards from the space.

"Looks creepy," Jason said, returning back to his game.

"I love it," Olivia said. And indeed she did, looking on it at several times of that day as she bustled about doing chores, making dinner, or relaxing with Jason in front of his own artistic extension, the television.

Both she and her husband worked from home, and they had arranged their own working spaces accordingly. They each had their own study areas, but on different sides of the house. Jason managed a signage design company and took the small room on the left side by the guest room. He worked usual office hours, but with the benefit of working from home, made allowances for long lay-ins and early finishes. It helped being the boss too, after all. Olivia took the larger room on the other side of the house. The room got more light in the day, which she preferred, enjoying the natural light more than her husband. She managed a trucking company from her little outpost on Hawthorne Drive, and could be found mostly on the phone when in her work area.

They had both worked in their jobs for a number of years now, with varying stages of happiness. At the moment, Olivia was the more content; the extra staff they had taken on recently had made her job a little bit easier. It gave her more time to potter the house and spend more quality time with her husband, as opposed to just brief snatches as they passed each other getting a drink or food.

They had lived at 725 Hawthorne Drive only a few years now, marrying but two of them ago. Their little slice of suburbia was somewhat forced upon them, with Jason having been left the house in his aunt's will. His family history was a muddled and sad affair; the spoils of this painful war seemed to be the white painted house with the blood red trimming that they now called home.

Olivia liked the house, though it wouldn't have been something she'd have chosen. They had been living in a ground floor apartment over on Lakeside, and though this was certainly a step up, she didn't think they were at the stage to settle down so fully. They were both young and spirited, though they sped closer to their forties. Their adventurous nature still took them off on motorcycle trips, up to Door Country and their favorite: Fox River.

Olivia thought of those trips now, sighing to herself knowing it had all changed.

She picked up her cup, which sported a Marquette University badge, a gift from her sister, and made her way to the kitchen. Jason was in the den, the TV off this time, his work scattered over the dining table that edged out of the kitchen area.

Walking in, her eyes locked onto the painting she had bought the previous day. She had hung it up almost immediately, finding an appropriate frame to use that had been in one of the spare rooms. Now framed in its golden glory, the image resonated off the sandy colored wall. She smiled seeing it, the eyes of the man following across as she stepped.

"I'm loving that painting, you know; it fits so perfectly there," she said, going into the kitchen and grabbing some coffee from the shelf. Jason looked over to it, then quickly back to her.

"Looks like your cousin Clifford," Jason said, his glasses sliding down the bridge of his nose.

"What?! No, it doesn't!" she shot back. Having been somewhat captured by the painting, she would have been reluctant to admit she was attracted to the image; still she wanted to dispel any likeness to any family member.

"I wonder what his story is, I wonder if I can perhaps find out more," she said, spooning the dried instant coffee into her mug.

"You know that thing is probably cursed or something. Bringing it in here probably opened some sort of doorway or spiritual connection. Like that movie *Poltergeist*," Jason teased.

"What, oh don't be ridiculous. It was the only thing in there worth getting," she said, shaking her head. "There was nothing for Steve, I hunted high and low." Jason looked over to her, his expression caught between despondence and apathy.

"Why are you hunting around antique shops anyway? We'll just get them something from a regular store. Bed linen or something. Can't see the point in all this added work," he said, making it seem like a waste a time.

"They're your friends, and childhood buddy; you should take more of an interest in them getting married. Besides, I want them to actually like and use the gift." She went across to the pantry and retrieved two cinnamon buns. She placed these on plates and took them over to where her husband sat.

"Steve *is* my friend; I don't even know Alex that well," Jason added.

"Well, they both deserve something heartfelt and thoughtful. Not granny linen from some generic store," she said, sipping from her cup. It burnt her lip slightly.

"You could always give them old smiley over there," Jason said, indicating to her new painting.

Olivia eyed him sternly before taking a bite of her cinnamon bun.

"How's work going?" she asked, knowing he had a lot going on at the moment.

"Getting there, I'll be glad when Jane gets back though."

Jane was the manager of their main office over on Franklin Street. She was a one woman show, working nonstop and handling the day to day activities there in the office and shop. She rarely took any time off, but it really showed when she did. She had taken a few days to go and see her parents who lived in Buffalo, and she could tell that Jason was eager for her to return.

Olivia liked Jane. She was a no-nonsense woman and said it how it was. It's how she got so much done really. She remembered how good she'd been to them after the accident. Taking care of the major things at work whilst Jason was on the mend. She also would come over once in a while, with forms to sign and the like; but never empty handed, always something home baked joining her.

"Well, if I can help with any..." Olivia had begun, but she suddenly looked at the window that led to their backyard. The grey backdrop of the cloudy sky washed away behind the faceless image of something pushed up to the glass. It looked charcoal grey and blurry, as if the features had smudged away. It hovered there for a moment, facing inwards before disappearing backwards and out of view.

Olivia was frozen, not knowing if to move and investigate or to close her eyes and hope she had been seeing things. She extended a slow blink, and when no figure loomed at the window upon opening her eyes, she quietly put her plate on the table and left the room.

- 3 -

When she was young, around nine or ten, Olivia and her sister had begun to be looked after by a Mrs. Langford who lived around the block from them. Up to that time, their mother had been taking them to their grandparent's house when she needed to work. The life of a single mother gave her the added stress of holding down two jobs, and much of the time she would have to drop her kids off with her parents. This was only up to the time when her own father passed away, and her mother struggled both with his passing and then in being able to look after the kids. The demands of a nine and six-year-old were too much for her and the onset of dementia. Olivia loved her grandparents, and enjoyed staying with them with their giant yard, plentiful and delicious food, and the tender moments only a family could provide.

Mrs. Langford offered no tender moments, her food was minimal and foul, and she lived in a small unit that smelled of cat piss. Both she and her sister hated going to her house, as Mrs. Langford - though it was never known of a Mr. Langford - refused to come to theirs. In hindsight, Olivia was somewhat thankful of this as she had been a cruel and suspicious woman, and Olivia could only imagine her sniffing about her home and forcing the chores upon them. As it was, they did very little when they stayed with her, as she seemed not to care about her own surroundings. Being told to keep quiet and out of sight surprisingly worked for both parties when they would stay with her. Olivia and her sister Rachel would usually take to the only other bedroom in the unit, and were thankful for the wall and dividing door between them and the older woman, who would while away her time watching television and smoking away on her Camel cigarettes as the tiles above her caramelized.

It was rare, but sometimes they would have to sleep over when their mother worked, Olivia could recall only a handful of times, but one stood out more than any of the others. She and Rachel were in the small single bed that was pushed up to the wall beneath the tiny window. The cold air would seep in, but it gave them a sense of a world beyond the realm of Mrs. Langford and the smoke-filled unit. Rachel had fallen asleep, something Olivia struggled to do there. She had heard Mrs. Langford go to bed earlier, for once not spending the night on the couch with the tv blaring.

All was somewhat quiet when she heard a small sound coming from the other room. The cat usually went where Mrs. Langford went, but Olivia was sure she was in her own bedroom. Listening harder, she watched suddenly as the door of their room clicked open and slowly pushed itself ajar by an invisible hand. Olivia had sat up then, scared and unsure what to do. She wanted to wake her sister but was too scared to make a sound. She saw it then, a dark figure looming in the crack of the door. Its head started low and then moved upwardly as if independent from any body. It had no features, and even in the dead light she could see it was not human, the head was pulled back in an unnatural fashion. It hovered there, seeming to have noticed the girls in the bed.

She heard it then, a low breath, like steam out of a heated pipe. Not from the figure, but next to her, breathing in her ear like a dead tongue. Motionless she sat there; her hands gripped to the duvet. The door nudged open a tiny bit further and it seemed the figure were about to cross the threshold of their little protected sanctuary. Just then, she had seen a light go on in the other room, and she heard Mrs. Langford stumbling out to go to the bathroom. One of the only times Olivia was ever grateful for the old bag. Though the figure disappeared instantly, in the moment that the light was on she had seen the faceless image clearly; and with eyes that she knew weren't there, she knew it had looked deep within her and marked her for something.

The figure at the window had troubled her. She could not tell her husband, how could she! It had unsettled something within her, dredging up the past that was so long ago now. She had always felt something trailing her life, watching quietly but always absently. Now the figure had taken shape. She had heard stories about the neighborhood, silly yarns about a murder and ghostly sightings. She struggled to believe most of what she heard, even despite her own experiences before. She tried to rationalize things, she had been through a lot recently, maybe her mind was slowly cracking up the bits that weren't working properly and reordering them, like how a computer would defragment.

She felt in her bones that it wasn't over, but despite this; she planned to carry on as normal. How else could she show it that she didn't care? She knew these things could easily take hold of someone, and dominant their every moment. Best to put it down to stress or something. She left Jason to his tasks and went back to work herself, finding him later getting ready for bed. *Where had the day gone?* she had thought, with no other appearance of the faceless spectre to trouble her further.

Wednesday. October 28th.
(DURING)

- 4 -

Knock knock knock.

She heard the loud hammering on the door and made her way to see who was there. It was Wednesday, and she had forgotten the plumber was coming over that day to fix some pipes in the basement.

She called off to Jason to say she'd get the door, not hearing him reply. She made her way down the stairs, turning on the lights as it had suddenly gotten very dark. A storm had been threatening, and the ominous clouds seemed to have choked out the sun on and off today. She opened the door and saw a man and a younger girl waiting there, both in overalls.

"Afternoon, Miss... Madison, is it?" the man said. He carried a huge toolbox, as did the girl next to him.

"Yes, oh hi. Please come in," Olivia said, spotting the van in the driveway now which read Plumb Plumbing, with a huge purple wrench motif on the side. She welcomed them both in, spotting one of her neighbors out walking on the other side of the street. They saw her also and waved a hand as they carried on past the dangling hangmen that made up the decorations for the house. Olivia waved back to them, then shutting the door once they were inside.

"This is Jessica, my apprentice," the man said, not indicating if it were his daughter or not, though Olivia saw no family resemblance.

"Hi," Olivia said, leading them towards the basement door which was tucked behind the stairs. "It's this way, as my husband explained on the phone, it's the water pipes to the laundry; the water isn't coming through properly." She flicked a switch on the wall, illuminating the steps in a nasty dirty yellow light.

"See it all the time, with washers and houses of this kind. The pipes go out of whack," the man said, following her down.

"Well, it's not that old; but we've not been here too long really. This is the first issue we've had with any of the plumbing or anything," Olivia said, getting to the bottom of the stairs.

Despite the depressing light going down, the basement itself was quite nice and brightly lit. It was clean and ordered, with boxes stacked neatly on shelves and a little area made for the washer and the dryer. On brighter days, some light would snake in from the slim windows they had on the far wall. But not today, and it was cool down there. The girl shivered. Noticing this, Olivia turned on the heating by a small dial.

"We'll take a look and see what we can do and get it sorted, miss; don't you worry," he added, putting his box down and assessing the room.

Olivia felt reassured somewhat; his old-fashioned manners led her to believe he had an old-style work ethic and would not be done until they found the problem and fixed it.

"Perfect. Would either of you like a drink?" she asked, going back over to the stairs to leave them be.

"Cup of coffee would be great. Black, please," he said.

The girl spoke for the first time, and her voice surprised Olivia. "Same for me please, if it's not too much trouble," she said, almost sing-songy in a very gentle voice.

"No problem," Olivia answered and ascended the stairs leaving them both in a cloud of plumbing terms and ideas to get on with.

It had been a couple of hours, and Olivia had decided to go and check on them in the basement. She had heard them coming and going to the van, the front door banging shut every so often. She had left them to it. *Nothing worse than someone hovering over you as you worked*, she thought.

Going down the stairs, she saw the girl hurriedly going out of the front door, carrying the toolbox. Just as she reached the bottom, the man came around the corner leading from the basement door.

"Ah, I was just coming to see how you were getting on," Olivia said.

The man was carrying his toolbox also, and in his other hand he held the two coffee cups she had taken down to them earlier, now empty.

"All done, it was a simple fix in the end, thankfully." Though he said it casually, his face seemed pained by something.

"That's a relief. Let me grab my bag, won't be a second," Olivia said, starting forward to go and retrieve her bag from the kitchen to pay him.

"Well, your husband said he would pay next week; he seemed quite adamant about that," he said, handing her the cups.

"Oh, really?" Olivia said, surprised he had gone down there.

"Excuse me for asking, but is everything okay with him?"

"Why do you ask?" Olivia said, almost defensively.

"Well, look. We're just here to get the job done. And Jessica was feeling a bit unnerved down in your basement as it was. But then your husband came down yelling from the stairs. It wasn't polite, Miss Madison."

Something about him still calling her miss seemed to irk her.

"I'm sorry about that. He was in an accident recently, being around people can be difficult still for him. But I'm sorry she felt uneasy," Olivia added, hoping to smooth things over.

"Well, it was the darndest thing; she kept saying she felt as if someone was watching her," he said, going on. "'Course, it is a spooky old house and it's a spooky week."

"The house isn't that ol..."

"Well, you know some kids just scare easy. Eh."

"I'm sorry for my husband's behavior. I'll see to it you are paid now, and a little extra for the problems." She left him in the hallway for a moment before returning with her wallet.

She paid him the full amount, though he wouldn't take any more from her, shaking his head. He did accept the apology she offered and would pass it on to Jessica, who sat in the van and had not returned to the house. She closed the door as he made his way to the van, and she turned inside thinking over what he had said. She looked up then, hearing the basement door snap shut.

Thursday. October 29th.
(DURING)

- 5 -

Olivia stared at the portrait, once again drawn in by the eyes of the man encased in the painted prison. She had found it on the floor this morning, not below where she had hung it, but over to the side and turned around. Placed there by someone or something. She checked the wall, and there were no scratches or that the hook had fallen. It was as if someone had lifted the painting off and placed it carefully on the floor.

She was puzzled, and irritated.

The Native American in the frame mockingly seemed to demand justice for his removal upon high on the wall. She had seen the same outrage in his features in her husband's face, affronted many times by actions and accusations. She heard him now upstairs, moving around noisily from room to room. *What was he **doing** up there?* she wondered.

It was early in the day, and Olivia had a mounting of things to be doing. Tasks and errands to run, on top of her own work. She needed to get some groceries for sure, their pantry was pretty empty, and she knew she needed stuff still to put out for the trick-or-treaters. She had forgotten one year only to find bananas in their exhausts and mountains of toilet paper covering everything the following day. Jason had asked her to pick something up from his office too, which she knew was important, but would've preferred any other day.

She hung the painting back on the wall, hoping nothing further would happen to it. She began to walk away, and she caught herself eyeing it as she moved across the room. He did look more like her husband than she'd realized previously, she thought to herself now. Which was odd, Jason was from a long line of white as white Irish immigrants, something his family were proud of, though Olivia never knew why. They always made a theater and a show about everything, and she had found the times spent with them would always exhaust her. Jason was as Native American as John Wayne, but something in the composition, the structure seemed to pester her.

She left the house, jumping on her bike and backing down the drive. She could hear shouting coming from one of the houses across the street, but she paid it little mind and zoomed off down the small cul-de-sac road off into town.

Her errands were quick, and the tasks began to be ticked off her mental list easily. The trouble arose when she got to Jason's office however. She had pulled up outside the small ubiquitous building that sat at the end of an industrial row of seemingly dull businesses. The back area housed the workshop for the signs and was always a hum with noise and movement. The front sported the administration, with a small display section showing off the signs and capabilities of the business. There were many cars parked out front, and one she recognized right away. Jane's.

"Olivia, nice to see you. How have you been?" Jane asked, coming around from her desk.

"Oh, you know, the usual. Pulled here and there but getting through. How was your trip?" she asked in reply.

Jane looked around, repressing something it seemed.

"Well, it was fine, just cut short unfortunately," she said, almost accusatorially. It seemed Jane thought she must know the reason why she was here in the office, and not drinking herbal tea with her parents in Buffalo.

"That's a shame, hope everything is alright?" Olivia asked, not picking up on Jane's annoyance it seemed.

"Well, just work; as you know. Thought the place would be fine for a few days but seems not," she said, folding her arms.

"Wait, did Jason ask you to come back early?" Olivia asked her, her composure changing.

"Yeah, he did. I thought you would know. I'm pretty pissed off with it, to be honest. I know he's been through a lot since the accident, I was just surprised. He was acting odd on the phone," she said.

"It's the medication. Since the crash he has been on so much, he acts a bit out of character. But I'm sorry it forced you back early," Olivia said, understanding now and concluding any mystery as to why she was here it seemed.

"Well, it's not just the phone call. He has been acting a little erratic. But I suppose, like you say; he's been through a lot and is on a bunch of pills I suppose..." Jane trailed off, concerning lying in her eyes.

She was referring to the motorcycle accident that Jason had been involved in recently. He'd collided with a small truck on the interstate. A little farmer's van carrying pumpkins. It hadn't seemed serious, both drivers were fine, and the cycle would be repairable. But there were complications after it seemed with Jason, with some lingering tissue and joint damage. Everyone knew he was on a lot of pain relief, and Olivia told anyone who would listen about it all.

"That's it. But hopefully you can get away again soon," Olivia added, stroking Jane's arm like one would a child. "I've come to pick up some of the account forms for the Leader & Burke projects."

"Oh, yes they're due at the accountants, aren't they. I don't mind sorting them out you know," Jane offered, friendly.

"No, it's fine. Jason wanted to check some things over himself I think," Olivia said.

"Fair enough, I'll go get them." And with that she went off to a filing cabinet and retrieved the folders. As she handed them to her she said. "I might pop by and see him soon, if he's up to it. Our calls are scarce these days."

"I guess he's swamped, you guys seem to be doing well. Probably why he needed you back. But yes, that would be nice. Be sure to call before you come over. See if he's up for it... he tends to sleep a lot with these meds, too, at strange times."

"Oh, understandable. And I will."

"See you soon Jane, and thanks again for these," she said, waving the files in the air.

"Take care, Olivia," Jane replied and watched her hurriedly leave the office.

Friday. October 30th.
(DURING)

- 6 -

The night was cool and Olivia had woken suddenly. Looking at the clock, she saw it was still early, only 3.30am. Jason was next to her, lying in a state that she knew was unreachable. He'd always been able to sleep without any issue.

Olivia lay there, listening to the wind howling outside. But then came another noise.

She sat up now, searching the dark for something out of place. Nothing moved, and all was quiet again besides the wind. She was just about to settle down when she heard the noise once more, coming from downstairs. She pulled the sheets off of her and went to investigate, leaving Jason where he lay.

Moving stealthily down the stairs, Olivia was alert despite having just woken. She stepped determinedly down each step and was shocked to see a shadow flash quickly out of the hallway leading towards the den. Her heart beat a little faster, but she hurried down the stairs and after it into the room, throwing on the lights which illuminated the scene before her.

She was confronted with chaos.

The room had been attacked, ravaged even as things lay about all over the place. Papers were strewn about, coffee cups smashed, chairs upturned. The blinds were hanging precariously on one side, seemingly to have been slashed at. Nothing had escaped the sacking of the room, all except the painting which remained undamaged, unmoved in its place on the wall. But Olivia could see now an addition to the painting, something which frightened her more than anything else she saw broken. 'Remember', had been written along the bottom frame in white, in what looked like chalk. She could see the dust and messy prints on the wall, and clouds of it peppering the carpet all around.

She turned suddenly, feeling something on her shoulders. The little hairs prickling on her neck like that thrill of something exciting. But she knew it was not. Looking behind her, she felt something watching, lurking and looming in the space. She turned back to the portrait, the target of her suspicion since all of this had begun after it had arrived in the house. Idly it hung there, saying nothing but also shouting up a storm inside her head.

Closing her eyes, she tried to make sense of it all. The day she had brought it back, excited to put it on the wall. Jason, not caring, not wanting to share in her new joy. Jason, always complaining and mocking. The image, resembling him. Why had she not seen it before?

She opened her eyes and knew it would be there, standing in front of her, towering above with its head bobbing like a high hanging flower whose stem was too long for it. That image from her childhood that had lurked in the doorway at Mrs Langford's. It did not whisper this time; it didn't have to. Its voice was her own, pulled and contorted, as if stretched over ghostly ribs.

"You know it Olivia," the voice rasped, echoing slightly; like from under a shell.

Olivia tried to close her eyes, but terrible little fingers rushed to prize them open.

"Heavy, heavy is the soul which snatches another," it seemed to hiss. Olivia shook her head, but it continued. *"Heavy are the chains which squeeze you in your eternity. Remember, Olivia, remember this is all your fault."* It came closer to her now.

"Fuck off!" she managed to scream, a single act of defiance that was itching to break out of her, yet only half committed. She was surprised of her own strength there, a part of her cowering in fear over in the corner.

The dark faceless specter hesitated, hovering unsure in the spot before her.

"I said: fuck off. Leave me alone!" Olivia commanded, and with this it actually retreated backwards towards the painting. The form shifted and twisted, taking on the shape of the figure behind it before evaporating into the wall leaving the room in silence.

Olivia stood back; her hands cupped to her face as if to feel her own skin. To confirm she was there and that this was the place she could understand.

The room lay in its disarray still, the mess and the chaos had not vanished. The painting still hung there, if not skewed slightly, but as it was before. The word *'Remember'* still printed on the bottom, the eyes of the native American still searching outwardly.

Olivia sat down for a moment to take everything in. She noticed a light going on and off next door, the garden light signaling something active in the yard. She turned the coffee table up back into position, there were dried flecks of blood on the underside she had noticed and would clean them when she put the room back. She breathed out heavily, taking control once more and going to get some water to cool herself down. She could restore order here, she thought; it wasn't too late for that. She had a plan in place; it would just take some time.

"No one need know," she said aloud to the room, either to comfort herself or aimed at the being which had scuttled back into the shadows. Scuttled back into the beyond for good, she hoped.

She listened quietly for a moment, as if hearing Jason stir, perhaps unusually woken by her outbursts.

No sound came, only the wind once more which had hurried outside her window with more force than before, colder than normal.

-7-

She woke late following the early morning incident. She could hear the wind howling still and could tell it must be cloudy as little light came through the cracks in the curtains. Jason was still in bed next to her, dead to the world still. Numerous medication pots littering his bedside table. She got out of bed, noticing it was nearly ten. Her stomach rumbled, aching for breakfast. She decided to make some pancakes for them both and hurried to the bathroom before going downstairs to get them started.

Olivia had cleaned the room before going to bed earlier. Aside for some lingering and overlooked patches of chalk, you would be hard pressed to believe anything had happened there.

She busied herself with the breakfast, putting the lavish spread on the table for them both along with the array of pills and medication for Jason. Different ones for the day than the night. She went to wake him, helping him down to breakfast. She thought he must be in a lot of pain today, though he didn't mention it.

"Halloween tomorrow, then," he said, sitting at the table.

"Oh, yeah, I guess. Nearly forgot, to be honest," Olivia said, sitting down herself.

"Always a fun time when you're a kid, getting to dress up and roam the neighborhood. I never was allowed to go." Jason eyed the stacks of pancakes that Olivia had topped with blueberries.

"Oh really. I figured everyone went at least once. I never really was bothered. Happy to just carve the lanterns and eat popcorn in front of the tv," she said, pouring the syrup sparingly.

"I did go one year, but only the once."

"Good, glad you didn't miss out. What did you go as?" Olivia asked.

"An Indian... no, sorry, an indigenous person. Steven went as a cowboy," he said, grinning at her.

"Stop. That's not funny," Olivia said, putting her fork down.

"Wasn't meant to be funny. It's what happened. I went as Tonto, and Steve was the Lone Ranger," he replied but Olivia was shaking her head now, not wanting to listen.

"I said stop it!" she said, slamming her fists down on the table.

Just then, their doorbell rang out, chiming down the hallway like a tiny church bell.

Still dressed in her nightwear, Olivia peered down the hallway to see who it was. The house, with its blood red trim which ended in a splash at the giant red front door and its two glass panels which adorned the top half, made both looking in and looking out an easy task to see who was there.

Olivia could see the figure with their back to the door, perhaps enjoying the Halloween decorations that sported the street. 725 Hawthorne was devoid of any holiday trimmings, aside from the candy that Olivia had picked up for the following day. Olivia watched as the person turned around, Jane's profile framed in the glass like a Midwestern Mona Lisa.

"Damn it," Olivia whispered, and, as if hearing the tiny squeak, Jane pressed her face up to the glass to look within with more scrutiny. Olivia ducked back, but the bell chimed again, and she heard Jane calling in through the door.

Throwing on a hoody that hung over the back of a chair, Olivia made her way into the hallway and down towards the door. She opened up and was met by a fierce cool air that stung at her face, and she could understand Jane's impatience a little more.

"Hey, how are you?" Olivia said, greeting Jane with a smile. She held the door half closed, not offering the insides to Jane's eyes or intention.

"Olivia, sorry to pop by unannounced. I was driving Jake to his friend's house; they're having an early Halloween party this afternoon, and thought I would just stop by and see how Jason is doing." She had turned to indicate her son who sat in the back seat of her orange Tahoe, his face mangled and awash with bloody makeup. "He's a zombie," Jane added.

"With or without the phone?" Olivia added, noting the reflective glow from his phone on his face.

Jane laughed a little, the tiny sound muted slightly in the wind.

"Anyway. Any chance I can come in? I won't stay too long. I brought you guys a vegetable lasagna too," Jane implored, holding up a dish. The wind whipped up, blowing the autumn leaves that had fallen from the huge elm trees in the street up into the little porch, like tiny flecks of gold. It also carried with it a few tiny snowflakes, little flecks catching up on Jane's hair, melting on contact.

"I did say to call before, Jason being…" Olivia started, but Jane cut in.

"Oh, I know you did. And sorry, like I said; knew I'd be passing by today. But I did want to check with him about those Leader & Burke papers too," she said, hopefully.

"What's the problem with them?" Olivia asked, curtly.

"Oh, just a few anomalies on the account and I wanted to check with Jason before they went off." She smiled though she was shivering now as she had left her jacket in the car. It was becoming awkward that she was being kept on the porch.

"Maybe it's best to speak to Jason on Monday, when you're back in the office. They're not going over to the accountant till next week. And Jason had a pretty bad night last night; I don't think he's up for visitors today."

"Oh, really. That is a shame. How is he?" Jane asked, earnestly.

"Yeah, pretty bad. He's still in bed; it's such an effort to move some days," Olivia added, pulling the door a little bit more closed.

"I'm really sorry to hear that. He was always so active and in motion before. It must be awful for him to be so stuck and static."

"Well I'll tell him you stopped by," Olivia replied, hoping to conclude the visit. Even from the warmth of the doorway, the cold air and blowing snow was attacking her face now, and she didn't want the neighbors to see her lingering with someone in the doorway; it looked odd not to invite someone in in this weather.

"Thank you; but Olivia, I wanted to check if things are okay with you also. Must be a strain having to support Jason as much as you have been. A month already, it must have been quite an adjustment for you..." Jane said, clearly not wanting to conclude the conversation yet, snow or no snow.

"It is what it is I suppose. Has to be done," Olivia said, frowning a little. Behind her, she heard a knocking coming from the kitchen. She pushed the door closed even further, until there was barely space for her face to peak out. Jane seemed to notice this oddness and asked her again if things were okay.

"They're fine, Jane," Olivia snapped, the knocking slowly building to an incessive banging which was becoming harder to ignore.

"What is that noise?" Jane asked her, trying to peer over her to see down the hall.

"Just the television," Jane offered, lamely.

There then came a variety of sounds that could not be dismissed as the television. Bangs and hollers, thumps and the sound of breaking glass erupted from inside.

"Olivia!" Jane said, concerned as she watched Olivia leave the doorway and run down the hall towards noise.

Jane sped behind her, despite Olivia having tried to shut the door as she left. She came out of the hallway and into the room which was much how it had looked at 3am that morning. This time the windows had smashed, and the cold wind whipped in and around the room, dislodging papers, food off the table, and now broken glass. The scene was chaotic, the sound of the wind howled around them. Jane stood on the threshold of the room watching in shock as her eye went from one horror to the next. She dropped the lasagna dish to the ground.

Beside the chaos of the wind and the dislodged contents of the room, she saw Olivia screaming at a portrait on the far wall. She was yelling in a manic state, pulling at her hair and demanding for things to stop. Jane's stare then moved on to the table where Jason sat, and though a shambolic mess, he sat motionless as if nothing was happening. His corpse propped up with a huge broom handle which went down the back of his shirt. His head slumped forward, and his eyes rolled back in his head. Of all the images that met her that day, Jane would always remember that bit of pancake sticking to his bloated lip, holding on with the help of the sticky syrup as the wind swirled all around.

Friday. October 30th.
(AFTER)

- 8 -

As the snow began to pick up in earnest on the cul-de-sac of Hawthorne drive, two patrol cars sat nestled in the driveway of 725 next to Olivia's red Triumph.

Jane had asked her partner to come and pick up Jake, and Sherry had arrived quickly onto the scene to spirit Jane's son away; who insisted on going to his friend's still; ignorant to what had occurred inside the house.

Olivia had sat there with the police officers and watched the coroner take her husband away. She may have watched, but she was barely lucid at that stage and merely sat nodding as they officers tried to get more information from her. Fortunately, Jane was able to fill in the blanks, and they were able to piece the situation together.

It had been a month since Jason was involved in his accident, returning home a little damaged and shaken, but much better than Olivia had made out. It seems they had quarreled, over something Olivia would not say; though the truth be known it was the fact that he had argued over the state of the motorcycle, Jason opting to downplay it. The simple things can sometimes have the most terrible results. It hadn't been deliberate, but Olivia had launched a cup at him, knocking him squarely on the side of his head. Under normal circumstances this would have done little harm, but after his accident Jason had underlying damage to his skull and the impact of the mug hemorrhaged this when it hit him. He was dead by the time he hit the ground.

Distraught, unhinged or guilt ridden, Olivia had not called anyone. The emergency services were not raised, and instead she had gone about as if nothing had happened. She had proceeded to proclaim a story that Jason was recovering and was taking it easy. This was attested to by Jane who said she had received this information from Olivia herself, who had called her not long after this accident.

As the days rolled on, and Olivia fell further into her mental collapse, she had realized that she would have to keep up the appearance of Jason in certain areas. She called people pretending to be him, muffling her voice, and acting out scenarios which would pacify anyone's interest. This overflowed into the times when no-one was around and she began to act out situations with her husband, moving him around the house and dressing him for bed and for work. It transpired that Olivia had even gone full blown Norman Bates and dressed up as him herself to throw off the neighbors. The plumber and his assistant had also been and unwitting audience to her performances as she had pretended to be him when they had come over, exercising some character duality which had become present in her mind.

As Jason had slowly decayed there at number 725 Hawthorne Drive, his wife slipped further and further into insanity. Plagued by her guilt and driven mad by a need to continue the cover up, no matter what the cost.

Jane sat quietly, listening and adding when needed to those questions posed by the officers. They eventually took Olivia away, putting her in the back of the patrol car.

Jane was left to see to the house, eventually contacting Olivia's sister Rachel, informing her what had happened and explaining she would lock up and have the keys for her to collect when she was ready. Giving her details for her to come up from Chicago. She tidied up as best she could, blocking up the smashed windows with boarding from the basement and sweeping much of the mess into garbage bags which she left propped by the backdoor.

She hastily locked up the house, with Sherry returning to give her a hand as she didn't want to be there alone. As she turned off the lights in the den, her eyes stole momentarily to the painting that hung on the wall, the one Olivia had maniacally shouted at. Never knowing why Olivia had been so enraged with it, she wandered now what had so angered her about a small painting, beautifully done, of a sunset desert scene.

THE WOMAN IN THE WINDOW
456 W. HAWTHORNE DRIVE
by Mark Towse

Wednesday. October 28th.

The roar from what seemed to be the loudest lawnmower in the world escalated the intensity of the blood pounding in Chris's ears. Morning light seeped through the threadbare curtains, spilling across his eyes like acid. Quickly, he turned away, a burst of pain exploding across his forehead as he connected with the wooden leg of the couch. His stomach churned then, accompanied by a bolt of fiery reflux that eventually exploded in his throat, providing an unholy concoction of tobacco and garlic. *Fuck this!* Chris stayed completely still, staring at the ceiling, waiting for the world to stop. In the background, in a well-practiced morose tone, the reporter on the television spoke of a neighborhood dispute, resulting in one man getting a crossbow bolt lodged in his neck.

It was all too much for him. "Fuck suburbia," he said under his breath as he finally began pushing himself up, unwittingly slipping his fingers into the soft gooey leftovers of last night's pizza.

Carnage surrounded him; empty beer bottles, greasy pizza boxes, ashtrays spilling over like volcanoes, and on the coffee table next to him, a plastic bag containing four mushrooms. The dampness of his right leg brought the night flooding back, and at that moment, he wanted nothing more than to be back at home in the comfort of his bedroom where everything was safe and familiar. He'd been missing home a lot of late, but events last night had given the yearning a physical ache in the pit of his stomach.

The urgency for headache tablets overturned the temporary melancholy, and Chris began stepping over the bodies sprawled across the carpet, two of which he didn't even recognize. Adam was asleep on the couch, fingers still wrapped around a bong, a slice of half-eaten pizza resting on his already considerable belly.

"Adam," he hissed. Nothing. "Adam!" he repeated. There were a couple of moans from behind, but no sign of life from his friend on the couch. Only when he intentionally collided with his friend's feet hanging over the edge did Adam let out a snort and open his eyes.

"Sorry, bud," Chris said.

"What time is it? What day is it?" Adam croaked.

"Tablets?"

"Yeah. Second drawer down," Adam said, closing his eyes again.

"I know where they are," Chris said, stepping over Jon, noting the peaceful look on his face. He pushed the kitchen door open, sighing as the carnage confronted him. "You've got to be kidding," he said under his breath.

The first year at university was hard for him; a farm boy, out of his comfort zone, sat as far away from the other students as the seating would allow, not feeling worthy. Adam took him under his wing, though, and they soon became best friends, opting to share a house for year two. It seemed like a good idea at the time, but of late, his friend had lost interest, choosing the company of the scruffy reprobates that currently littered the floor of the house. He knew them all, but other than Becky, he wasn't particularly fond of any of them.

Trying to ignore the mess, he filled two glasses with water. Only six pills left. He made a mental note — the same one as last week — to get more from the supermarket. He washed two of them down. The water didn't taste like home; it was harsher.

"I had a weird one last night," he said to Adam, handing him the other glass and more pills.

"Oh man, me too!" Adam replied, pushing himself up and grimacing as the pain took hold. "Pills first, though," he said, reaching for the glass.

Chris sat down on the arm of the adjacent chair, being careful not to disturb Becky. "Those mushrooms, man; who brought them? Strong stuff, and — real dark. I mean, d-a-r-k."

"Tell me about it! That's why I started on the bong, just to try and take the edge off."

"I remember going upstairs to the bathroom," Chris started. "I kept thinking someone was behind me, and I thought I could hear whispering. But it wasn't normal whispering; it was like, in my head. I turned, but there was nobody there."

"Can you talk quietly?" Becky hissed, prodding him with one of her ankles.

"Anyway," Chris continued regardless. "I just put it down to the wind whistling through the cheap-ass door that the landlord installed. Even when I got upstairs, I could feel it, though — a presence — you know, a vibe that something wasn't right."

"Oh man, you thought that was bad, just — "

"Hey, I'm not finished!" Chris snapped. "I looked down to unzip, and then I heard someone whisper again, or at least I heard it in my head. It was a man's voice, Adam. He said my *name*."

Becky, now awake, suddenly boosted herself up, eyes wide with interest. "Then what happened?"

"Well, I thought it might be one of you lot playing a prank at first, but when I looked down the landing, I couldn't see anyone. Anyway, I shut the door and tried to take a piss. Another whisper—my name again. No way was I going to be able to go, so I zipped up and threw some water on my face. When I reached for the towel, I saw him—in the mirror, standing behind me. He was—"

"An insurance salesman?" Becky offered, following up with a little cackle.

"Faceless," Adam offered solemnly, his suddenly pale face exposing the dark circles under his bloodshot eyes.

"How the hell did you know?" Chris spat.

"I saw him, too," Adam said.

"This is a wind-up, guys, right?" Becky said, no longer laughing. "Elaborately planned, I'll give you that, but I wasn't born yesterday."

"Yes, faceless," Chris continued. "Grey flannel shirt, brown tie, and beige pants. I turned around—nobody there. But when I faced the mirror again, there he was, finger poised over the light switch. There was movement under the skin; subtle, but visible. Christ, I was petrified. I put it down to the drugs—a bad trip."

Mouth slightly ajar, Adam stared at his friend.

"And I swear to God, the light went out. I was in darkness. Couldn't move, Ads. My legs were like jelly. I felt dizzy, disoriented, and I'm ashamed to say, I finally managed to piss—all down my right leg."

"What then?" Becky said, screwing her face up and making a point of moving as far away from Chris as the chair would allow.

"A hand on my shoulder. Even through my sweater, it felt like a block of ice. And then his voice—in my head again."

"What did he say?" Becky asked urgently.

"He said—"

"She made me do it," Adam finished.

Chris eyed his friend, fear notching up again. "What the fuck?"

"I told you. He visited me, too."

"This is nuts, Becky," chirped. "Then what?"

"This is fucked up," Chris said, more to himself than the others. "He disappeared after that. I was shaking when I got back downstairs. I felt so stupid, Adam; thought I'd imagined the whole thing. You know, the drug playing with my head. I had this silly fear of mirrors as a kid, you see, but—"

"My turn now," Adam interrupted, patience with his friend wearing thin. "You lot were already gone. Flat out. You're right—those mushrooms were wicked. Anyhow, as I said before, I was taking a couple of hits from the bong just to curb the adrenaline when I saw something moving in the corner. At first, I assumed it was someone getting up or adjusting their position. Perhaps even a trick of the light. I didn't think much of it, so I closed my eyes and put my head back—you know—to let the good vibes flow. And then I heard someone whisper my name. Just like you said, it felt like it was in my head rather than external. But when I opened my eyes, our faceless friend was—"

He let out a shudder. He could feel his heart racing again.

"Shit. I thought I was going to have a bloody heart attack. Bong water went flying everywhere. The face—Jeez—kept drifting in and out of focus, but I swear it was smooth like a pebble. Hairless, featureless, terrifying. I tried to scream, but then he put a hand across my mouth. It was ice fucking cold, I tell you. I thought it was over; that I was going to die. And then, with his other hand, he put a finger to his non-existent mouth, and then vanished."

"Fuck me," Becky said. "What does it all mean?"

"I think it means no more mushrooms," Chris said frantically.

"But for you to both see the same thing? That's intense. Impossible," Becky offered, her face twisted in concern, but her voice expressing undeniable excitement.

"This isn't cool, Chris," Adam offered. "This is fucked." He found himself thinking back to his days as a kid, back in his old bedroom staring into the unlit corners—all those times biting his lip, praying for morning to come quickly. His parents wouldn't hear about it, said he had nothing to fear and that God was watching over him. That was a decade ago, though. It was one of the few plusses of getting older—no more nightmares. Yet, that faceless man had emerged from the dark corner of their living room and put a hand over his mouth. No, that wasn't part of the deal.

"We've been hitting it too hard of late, man. Maybe we should knock it on the head for a bit," Chris offered.

Adam let out a deep sigh. "You might be right. This has freaked me out for sure."

"I reckon a few early nights; strictly beers and Netflix for the next few days. Let's take it easy, get our heads straight, Ads."

Adam nodded. "I'm scared, man."

"Shit. I just remembered something!" Becky straightened herself up, eyes wide with the excitement of whatever she was about to deliver. "It must be the ghost!"

"Not the right time, Becks," Chris said dismissively.

"No, wait. I forgot all about this." She took a deep breath, milking the moment, building the suspense. "When I mentioned to my friend Jenny where you lived, she told me about a rumor that went around a few years ago. Her mom used to rent the house next to the one with all the crap in the front yard—always been the same shithole that place. Anyway, three police cars woke her up—somewhere near the end of the cul-de-sac. They found a guy hanging from the garage roof. He'd tried to cut his own face off."

"Bullshit," Chris spat.

"Hey, don't shoot the messenger, babe. Anyhow, rumor was that his missus caught him playing away from home. It wasn't long after they found him swinging."

"That's twice you've said the word rumor, Becks. I honestly don't think we need to hear this," Chris told her.

"Jenny said that some of the residents could sometimes hear a choking sound coming from the garage," Becky continued regardless.

"You're not helping, Becky," Adam commented, shaking his head.

"Look, it's probably nothing. You know what gossip is like, but I thought I'd mention it."

"Yep, thanks for your input, Becks," Adam said. "Just out of curiosity, which house was it?"

"I'm not sure. I'll ask Jenny tonight."

"Okay. Do me a favor, and get rid of this lot, B," Chris said. I want all reminders of last night gone. Adam, flush the rest of the stuff. Look, my hand — it's still shaking," Chris said, holding up his trembling fingers. "I need some air."

"I'll come with you," Becky said hopefully.

"Is it okay if you don't?" he replied, knowing she'd want to continue the discussion. "I'll call you later on today, okay?"

"Sure. Okay. Take it easy, though, Chris. You look tired," she said, trying to hide the disappointment.

The cool breeze immediately wrapped around him as he opened the front door, bringing with it the pleasant smell of freshly cut grass and reminding him of the farm once more. Using the top of the wooden door frame to stretch, he breathed in as much of it as he could. The old woman across the way was standing in the window, looking directly at him. He waved, but there was no acknowledgement. There never was. Ducking back inside momentarily, he grabbed his jacket from the hook and then began making his way down the street.

Reaching the bottom of the path, he spotted a woman on rollerblades in the distance, spitting out rapid clouds of dewy air. Head bopping up and down and her arms pumping in such an exaggerated way. As she approached, he recognized her as the woman next door — the one that Adam often ogled over. She waved as she turned into her driveway, and he waved back and smiled. A thought popped in his head that he might go for a jog later, but it didn't stay for long.

He took a moment to survey the cul-de-sac. It was as quiet and nondescript as any other, lined with well-established trees — some oak and maple. Chris thought the others might have been elm but wasn't sure. His dad would know. Some of the oaks were huge, and he guessed they'd been there for decades, perhaps even before the houses went up. According to their next-door neighbor, the place was named after the creepy lady opposite — Hawthorne, so God knows how old she was.

As he continued toward the end of the street, he noticed a van sitting in a driveway behind a red motorcycle, the gaudy purple logo across its side announcing to the neighborhood: *We Won't Drain Your Bank Account* and *Our Technicians Aren't Drips, Guaranteed*, complete with plumber's tools, pipes, and a local phone number. Chris rolled his eyes.

When he got to the bottom of the cul-de-sac, he rested against the fire hydrant and lit a cigarette. *This is suburbia,* he thought; *this was what I had to look forward to.* For a while, he focused on nothing but the disappearing wisps of air, but then his mind pulled him back to the events of the previous night. The clearer his head became, the less it made sense, and another wave of anxiety washed over him. He lifted his hand in a half-assed gesture as the two familiar rusty cars left the street. *Good job, Beck!* She waved from the back seat of the second.

Things had to change. He didn't want to let anyone down, particularly his parents, who had backed him from day one. His coursework had undeniably suffered of late, taking second place to the exploits of Adam and his friends. It annoyed the hell out of him sometimes, the way Adam could just breeze through the work, often without studying. For him, it came much harder. He had to really put the work in. He smoked another two cigarettes before heading back, pausing briefly to see if he could hear the sound of the choking ghost carrying on the wind. "What are you doing, Chris?" he whispered, shaking his head and setting off again.

"What the hell have you done with Adam?"

"Funny, Chris, real funny," Adam replied, spraying more apple disinfectant onto the dining table. "I might play the idiot, but this has really shaken me. I detest things that can't be explained; that's why I've always liked maths. For every problem, there's a solution. But this? Man, this is Twilight Zone stuff."

"Keep this up, Adam, and you'll get 'roommate of the year'."

"I'm serious, Chris. Whatever went down last night was some bad shit. Far too weird for me. We've got to get our shit together."

Chris wondered how long the new and improved Adam would be around, but for now, he was relieved to feel some control coming back into his life.

Two hours later, the house was unrecognizable. Clean, organized, and without an ashtray in sight. They spent the rest of the evening watching television and sipping bottles of light beer, hoping the faceless man wouldn't return.

He didn't.

Thursday. October 29th.

Adam woke languidly, but without a hangover for the first time in a while. He turned off the bedside lamp, mocking himself for being twenty years old and having to sleep with a light on. Recent events were still with him, though, and it seemed entirely plausible that the smooth faceless man that had recently stepped out of the dark could pay another visit. He knew it had unsettled Chris just as much. They'd sat in silence last night—neither prepared to discuss their implausible theories.

He pulled the sheets from his bed, taking them downstairs to the laundry, noting the time on the living room clock as six fifty-five. That was a first, being up and about before nine o'clock. He closed the door with a satisfying click, taking some comfort in the smell of laundry powder and the monotonous whir of the machine as it kicked into action.

"Morning, mate!"

"Jesus, Chris – don't sneak up on people like that!"

"I didn't. Coffee?"

"Just put it in a bucket, will you?" Adam replied.

Chris opened the pantry door, moved the guest coffee out the way, and reached for the good stuff. "Sounds like you had a rough night."

Adam considered lying. "Are we going to talk about what happened?"

"I think we have to," Chris replied. "Cigarette?" The thought of discussing it without a secondary distraction didn't appeal.

Adam expected the air outside to be fresh and invigorating; instead, it had an ominous heaviness that carried over from the house. "I might study at the library today. Do you fancy it? We could meet up with Becky and Suzy and perhaps get pizza on the way home."

"That's a great idea. No distractions, no – "

"Faceless visitors," Adam finished with a half-hearted smirk.

"There's no explanation, though, is there, Adam? Yes, we were off our faces, and yes, that might account for a hallucination, but for us to both see the same faceless apparition and for the same five words to be whispered by the man with no mouth – well, that's just something else."

Adam blew a smoke ring and turned to his friend. He'd been thinking about it in bed, trying to rationalize events, looking for a solution in a way he might approach a maths equation. "The subconscious is a powerful tool, Chris. The movie we were watching the other night—it's possible those exact words were uttered by one of those lousy actors—you know, when we were half in, half-out. Perhaps they just embedded in our brain at a crucial point."

Chris studied his friend to assess if the theory was delivered with any conviction or if it was just to self-soothe. "But I was up and about—fully conscious, Adam. That doesn't explain—"

"You were up, but in a drug-induced state, Chris! That stuff was powerful. Nothing we can recount from that night can be relied on."

"But to see the same faceless man?" Chris said, furrowing his brow to express disapproval at his friend's bullshit theory. "The same clothes. The same words."

"Just one of those things, Chris. An unfinished projection of our imagination."

"Have you heard yourself, Adam? You're supposed to be a fucking mathematician for Christ's sake, but right now, you sound like a really shit psychologist."

"And what have you got, bud? What's your offering?"

"Shit, I truly don't know. All I know is this place gives me the jitters," Chris replied, lifting his hand to show off his newly developed tremor. "Look, I'm thinking of going home for the weekend—leaving late tomorrow and getting back lunchtime on Monday. Do you fancy it? I could show you around the farm. We could make a real weekend of it. We could even see if Becky and Suzy fancy it."

"You know what, my friend? Why not? Let's do it."

"Awesome. I'll let my folks know. I'm sure the girls will be up for it." Already, he felt better, as though a weight was lifting. "Come on; I've got a ton of work to do before then."

"Are you sure your parents won't mind me tagging along, Chris?" Becky asked.

"Stop it. They're fine; very liberal," Chris reassured as he reread the same page for the fifth time. "They'll love you."

"So why has it taken over a year for me to meet them?"

"You never asked."

"Fair point. Is Suzy coming, too?"

"I'm not sure. She just doesn't know where she stands with Adam. They're on, and then they're off. I think she's a bit wary, that's all," Becky replied.

"Ah, yes, I get that. One minute you're flavor of the month, and the next, someone else takes your place. But I tell you, he's turned over a new leaf. He cleaned the entire house yesterday top to bottom, even the oven—and you know how bad that was."

"Adam? Nah, you're pulling my leg. It must have been another hallucination?"

"Funny, Becks. No, I'm serious. I don't want to tempt fate by using words like *maturity*, but he's got a different aura about him."

"Wow. This whole thing has shaken him up more than I thought. What about you? Have you talked about it?"

"I think he wants to put it behind him. I guess I do, too, but easier said than done. It all felt so real. Still does, Becks. The face—flawlessly smooth — but the tiny ripples underneath the flesh, as though the skin was concealing something underneath. And those words, 'She made me do it' — they just rattle in my head. I can't get them out."

"What are you going to do?" she asked, reaching for his hand.

"The manly thing. Run," he laughed nervously. "To tell you the truth, I can't wait to get away from Hawthorne Drive, even if it's just for a couple of days."

"Oh yeah," Becky said, leaning in towards him as though she had top-secret information. "Jenny asked her mom about the house where the accident happened." She emphasized the word 'accident' with air quotes, making Chris like her just a little bit less. "She didn't know the number, but she said it was the old beige one. I think that's the one opposite yours, yeah? Anyway, she said the woman was well known to be batshit crazy — always was — thought that she owned the street and nobody else was good enough. Paranoid as hell, too, apparently, always thinking people were talking about her, which they were. Now, get this. Jenny's mom also heard from someone else that the woman had spent time in a mental institution; claimed she was a witch. Can you believe that?"

"Come on, Becks. What am I supposed to do with this information? Chinese whispers — defamatory rumors about some poor old woman that can't defend herself."

Becky shrugged. "Jenny's mom said that one day the old bag stood at the end of her driveway, screaming at the entire street. Something about them all getting what's coming to them, one way or the other. I guess her husband's affair didn't help with her anger management."

"Fuck's sake, B. Can we just leave it?

"Last thing. One day her white dog got busted up pretty badly — on the road—one of the residents apparently. The next day someone saw her cradling the dog in her bedroom window. Not a mark on it."

"B!"

"Sorry, just saying," Becky said. "And she only wore black after the accident and never left the house."

Chris raised his eyebrows and gave her an intense look of disapproval that prompted her to giggle.

"I'm looking forward to seeing where you grew up," she said, changing the subject.

"Me too," he replied. "Now, I guess we better do what we came here to do."

"Do you want me to stay over tonight?" she added.

"It's all good. I think Adam has a movie marathon lined up—some mindless Schwarzenegger flicks, I believe. There's nothing like a series of explosions and extended scenes of violence to calm the nerves. Hey, do me a favor, will you?"

"Not mention anything of this to Adam?"

Chris nodded.

Adam was bored rigid. Getting out of the house seemed like a great idea at the time, but he regretted suggesting the library. There were half a dozen books to his right, all of them unopened. Across the table, Suzy was scribbling away, humming an unrecognizable tune, and tapping her feet annoyingly against the table.

"Suzy," he hissed sternly.

There was no acknowledgement. He gave her a gentle tap under the table and pointed to his ears.

"Yup?"

"Sorry. It's just—"

"What?" she asked.

Over her right shoulder and standing by the water dispenser—the faceless man was running his finger across one of the bookshelves.

"What? What is it, Adam?"

Her words seemed distant. He tried to speak, but it was as though he had forgotten how. Everything was beginning to blur; only the blank fleshy canvas of the man's face was in focus.

"—scaring me, Adam—"

The man grabbed his tie and wrapped around his neck like a makeshift noose. He gave a single tug—and then vanished.

"What is it?"

"Nothing," he replied, mouth dry, heart thumping. That was a lie. It was a lot. It was too much. "I'm getting hungry. We'll call it a day, yes?" he said, not phrasing it as a question.

He suddenly wanted a hit so bad, something to take the edge off. What he'd fed to Chris before was hopeful conjecture to try and make himself feel better, but there was no bullshitting the latest sighting.

He scanned the library, moving his stare from one face to the next. Chris's offer had come just at the right time. He'd even considered going home himself, facing his God-fearing parents and their inevitable disapproval. "Just need some water," he croaked.

There on the bookshelf closest to the water dispenser, he saw the book. It was poking an inch out from the rest and impossible to ignore. 'The Thinnest Veil' was written down the book's spine in intricate golden calligraphy, the delicate weaving of the letters suggesting heavy importance. He gulped back the water in the plastic cup and carefully eased the book from the shelf. In bolder writing across the front cover was the word, 'Samhain,' and beneath, in smaller italics, were three words: 'The Dark Truth.'

Adam turned to do a sweep of the library again—hairs standing erect on the back of his neck. The large plastic 'E' that was crudely attached to the bookshelf leant further weight that something unnatural was at play. All the other books were properly alphabetized—this one was an anomaly. The wrong place, the right time, he thought.

He never said anything as he drove to the pizza shop. He never said anything when they got home, or even to Chris after the girls had gone. The television did it's best to distract, but its limitations became apparent between explosions when the more muted light failed to adequately illuminate the dark recesses of the living room and the origin of his worries. He sat anxiously in his chair, occasionally taking part in ineffectual conversation forced by his friend, but his mind wouldn't let him forget the faceless man.

As midnight approached, Chris thought about relaying what Becky had told him, if only to end the stunted conversation. He opened his mouth, ready to say something but then thought better of it. There was a fragility about Adam, and he wasn't the only one that had noticed. Suzy had left early in a huff, feeling once again as though she was a fair-weather girlfriend, which she was.

It wasn't easy for Chris, either. Even going to the bathroom had become an ordeal. When he could no longer hold it, he'd run upstairs, relieve himself as quickly as possible, and wash his hands as though he'd just spilled acid all over them. Not so much as a glance in the mirror, even though there'd been no repeated sightings.

"I'm turning in, Adam," he said.

"Wait. Me too."

Friday. October 30th.

Chris woke up feeling good. Today was the mini-road trip, and the thought excited him more than expected. He had no doubt his mom would cook them up a storm — pastries, stews — and her cherry pie was to die for.

There was a lot to do before they left, but stuff that could only happen after coffee. He yanked the cord on the blinds, squinting as dull light filtered through low and ominous clouds. As he was about to walk away, his peripheral vision caught something; his eyes drawn to the upstairs window across the road. Dressed in her familiar black dress, the old lady was gazing right at him. Slightly behind her right shoulder stood the man with no face, adorned in the same bland shirt and tie. Chris had no idea how long the sinister standoff lasted before the faceless man eventually turned and walked away, followed shortly by the old lady. He let out a deep breath and slowly backed away from the window, heart pounding, suddenly aware that his fingernails were digging into his palm.

Dropping onto the bed, head in his hands, he knew his half-hearted attempts to pass the visitor off as over-indulgence had come to an end. That was always a stretch anyway — the identical accounts, the same clothes, the same whispered words. The same stretched skin.

From the bathroom, he heard Adam flush the toilet and wanted nothing more than to rush over and tell his friend about what he'd just seen but was well aware of the impact it would likely have. Besides, they would be on their way soon, sticking their heads out the window and breathing some proper country air. Suburbia could go fuck itself for a while, he thought.

"Morning!" Adam said, towel-drying his hair.

Chris thought his friend looked tired. "Hey, mate. You all set to be a country bumpkin for the weekend?"

"Sure am," he replied. "Can't wait, to be honest. We could leave a little earlier if you wanted?"

"I would, but I think Becky's got some classes this afternoon. We'll be on our way by seven, though."

"Fair enough," Adam replied.

Chris saw disappointment creep across his friend's face. "Believe me, we'd have been well on our way if it was down to me," he offered.

Adam smiled and nodded. "What are your plans for the day?"

"I've got some coursework to finish and a few loose ends to tie. Fancy heading down to the library again?"

The hairs on the back of Adam's neck made their presence known immediately. He felt his left eye give out a single nervous twitch. "No," he said urgently. "Do you mind if we don't? I mean, you can, if you like."

"Nah, it's fine. I don't think I can be bothered. I'll get the coffee on."

The day dragged. Each hour seemed to take an eternity as Chris and

Adam restlessly waited for evening to come. They drank copious amounts of coffee and distracted themselves as best they could. But it wasn't an easy task. The air felt heavier than usual to Adam, the way it often felt before a storm. And Chris felt it, too, an ominous feeling that something terrible was going to happen. Neither of them said anything, though. Outside, birds sang, dogs barked, vehicles came and went—all the usual sounds of suburbia, but even the normalcy didn't shift their settling unease.

"I've just remembered," Chris said. "It's Halloween tomorrow."

Samhain. The thought sent a shiver down Adam's spine.

Soon after, the wind picked up and snowfall started.

Adam stood at the window solemnly watching the street turn to white. Shit," he whispered under his breath.

"Shit indeed," Chris said, joining him at the window.

"What time is it?" Adam asked.

Chris looked down at this watch and then across to the clock on the mantelpiece. "That can't be right."

"What?"

"I looked at that clock only a few minutes ago, and it read just after five, now it says six minutes past seven, and so does my watch. And look, the second hand has stopped."

Adam shook his head. "It's nowhere near seven; it's still light—"

It didn't take a maths genius to work it out. 6:66. Adam swallowed, producing a noise that would be comical under different circumstances.

"Adam," Chris hissed sharply through clenched teeth, nodding towards the window.

From house 637's second-floor window, the old lady gazed towards them, the faceless man standing faithfully beside her. The old woman smiled and clicked her fingers, sending the boys' home into complete darkness as all their electric turned off, only the light from the room across the circle drive remaining. Not even a sliver of a moon through the snowfall. Terrified, they watched as the faceless man turned and walked away. The old woman followed, taking a final look back, before switching out the light and leaving both homes in near complete darkness. Only a faint purple light from the clouds overhead.

"This is fucked," Adam shouted as he ran to the doorway, flicking the light switch numerous times. "Shit." The only source of illumination came from the mobile phone on the table. Adam snapped it up quickly. No signal, no internet, and the time — six minutes past seven. He shook his head at Chris, who was looking towards him hopefully.

"What the fuck is going on?" Chris uttered.

"I saw him, Chris. At the library. That's why I didn't want to go back. This is him — them — I know it."

Chris shook his head. "Fuck! I saw him, too — this morning, from my window. But what does it mean? It makes no goddamn sense."

Adam switched his mobile to torch. "Where's yours?" he asked.

"Upstairs, I think. Don't we own a flashlight — something bigger?"

"What do you think?" Adam replied. "Fuck this! Let's go to the bar down Savoy Street. Drink some beers, play some pool. Get out of here for a bit."

"What about Becky? If it really is six minutes past seven, she'll be waiting for us."

"Chris, that's the least of our fucking worries right now. We need to get out of here!"

"Okay, Okay. Give me a sec. I'll need my phone and cash from upstairs. Can I borrow that?"

As Chris made his way up the stairs using the light from Adam's phone, he felt the heaviness of the air once more, but it was the silence that was even more overwhelming. It was as though time had stopped — no signs of suburbia and all its comforting annoyances. He made it halfway up before his friend cried out.

Chris turned and rushed downstairs, almost tripping over his feet in the process. He jumped the last three steps and swung himself into the living room, casting stark white light across the face of his friend.

"He's here, Chris. In this fucking room! He spoke to me."

"Where?"

"In the corner, over there," he whispered nervously, gesturing with his head.

Chris aimed the phone's light. "There's nothing there, Adam."

"I saw him, Chris. He came out of the darkness. Told me the old lady made him peel his face off with a knife." Adam's breathing was sharp and shallow, his head snapping left to right. "And then she made him wrap his tie around the joist."

"You're really fucking scaring me, Adam," Chris said, frantically sweeping the light across the room.

"He's coming. Quick, over there. Can't you see him?"

"I can't see anything!"

"Oh, fuck, Chris. He's got his hand on my shoulder," Adam hissed. He tried to move, but his legs wouldn't budge. "Fuck!"

"There's nobody there, Adam! Calm down for Christ's sake."

"I can feel him. So cold. He's in my head again. 'She tried to fit in; be normal. People only disappointed her, though.' Oh Christ, make him go away, Chris!"

"Tell me what to do! There's nobody there!" The purple haze seemed brighter now.

Adam felt the iciness begin to shift, slowly making its way towards his neck. "Help!" he screamed.

"Stop it, Adam!" Chris blurted, close to tears.

Adam reached out, wincing as his fingers connected with the cold and smooth skin of the man that was found hanging at 637. He tried to scream, but only a garbled croak emerged. As the pressure around his neck increased, he began to claw desperately at the featureless face.

Chris continued to watch Adam struggle with the seemingly invisible force. His friend's face was turning red, and his eyes appeared even wider than before. He was about to rush over, but something else began to happen. Something even more macabre.

It was Adam's mouth that first started to close, not in the normal way, but with a thick layer of skin that began to extend across it. The muffled cries gradually became even more muted until the mouth was fully concealed under new skin.

Chris stood, frozen, watching in fear at the continued metamorphosis of his best friend. He felt disoriented, and momentarily, as though he might pass out, reaching his arm out to the couch to steady himself. Adam's nose was next; skin gradually creeping from the nostrils to the bridge. A horrific cracking followed that sent shivers down Chris's spine. Unable to watch, he turned, pointing the phone directly ahead towards the front door. Immediately, though, his stomach dropped. The perfect reflection of the faceless man in the lounge room window, hands molding his friend's face as though it was pottery, was too much.

What the – ?

He turned round again, only to see Adam with his hands clawing at his eyes, but unable to prevent the skin from creeping across them. Sounds of suffocation emerged from beneath the newly formed skin.

"She made me do it. That's the dark truth," the man's voice said in his head. "If your friend is lucky, he'll find his way through the veil – to peace. But he'll have to move quickly." Everything seemed lit up in the purple light now.

Chris winced at the soft thud as Adam collapsed to the floor, hands raking at his smooth face, squirming in the final throes of death. Urgently looking back at the window, Chris saw the ghostly man making his way towards him.

Finally, he found the use of his legs and bolted for the door, adrenaline coursing through him. His fingers wrapped around the door handle, relishing the prospect of getting away from 456, back to the farm. He yanked it open, and –

"She plays with your fears, you see. You – the mirror. Your friend – the darkness. Mine was commitment, and I've been damned to be by her side since death. But you're my successor. She's been watching you. You're the one that will finally set me free."

Chris stood in the doorway, observing what lay ahead; the same green carpet, the same spider plant next to the coffee table, the same cheap coffee-stained wallpaper. The mirror image of their hallway. Now completely lit in the strange purple hue that came from everywhere and nowhere.

Impossible.

He watched, frozen to the spot, as the man with no face emerged from the living room doorway ahead and began making his way towards him.

Images of his parents, of the farm, and Becky, flashed in his head.

"She won't take your memories," the man said, reaching his hands out towards him. "But she will take your soul. And then she'll make you do things you will never—"

The voice in his head faded as the iciness began to take him. Hallway carpet gave way to the ever-thickening snow outside that swirled under the streetlights. He knew then that Hawthorne Drive would be his forever home.

Chris felt his skin begin to crawl.

VOICES IN THE FLAMES
637 W. HAWTHORNE DRIVE

by Joshua Marsella

A shrill, resounding bark accompanied by the smell of searing meat snapped Priscilla out of her daydream. She leapt up from her seat at the kitchen table as fast as her old legs would allow. Her nightgown barely moved as the soles of her slippers shuffled along the linoleum floor. Elvis continued to yip at her ankles, herding her to the stove.

"Oh, be quiet, you. I have everything under control," she scoffed, shooing the Bolognese away.

Elvis did as he was told. He tucked his fluffy tail between his legs, then sat down in front of his food dish. She had forgotten to feed him again. Not intentionally, of course, but her memory was getting worse by the day. Sometimes a little bark was enough to remind his forgetful master that he was still around.

Priscilla turned the knob on the stove, switching off the burner. The leftover ham was blackened on one side and dry as a sponge. There was no way she'd be able to eat it now. Letting out a sigh of disappointment at her mistake and the realization that she was likely to go hungry this morning, she looked down at her little white dog and smiled. His tail wagging excitedly.

"Well buddy, looks like you're eating like a king today," she picked up the hunk of meat with a fork and dropped it into Elvis's bowl. He immediately sunk his teeth into the ham steak without hesitation. "May as well get you some water while I'm down here." She picked up the empty dish and straightened back up. Her spine let out a few pops and crackles. With her free hand cupping the small of her back, her stomach growled as she made her way to the sink.

Letting the water run for a minute to get cold, she gazed out the window into the front yard. A shimmering frost coated the grass and dead copper-colored leaves that had fallen overnight from her beloved sugar maple. She had planted that tree shortly after the house was built. This was before the cul-de-sac had been constructed then named after her husband, before the other houses were built, but several years after the massive fire.

A light was on at the house across the street. The men who lived there seemed to always wake up early which she saw as admirable. She had never spoken to them, so she had no idea what they did for a living. She couldn't decide whether they were snobs or whether her demeanor was too cold and uninviting. Didn't matter either way. She enjoyed being alone most of the time. Besides, she had her Elvis.

Autumn was in full swing. She recognized the amber glaze of the late October sunrise which meant only one thing—Halloween was coming up.

Setting the bowl down, Elvis immediately took several gulps of the cool tap water to wash down his dry, yet sumptuous breakfast. Priscilla stroked the curls on his back a few times before going about her day.

Leaning over the kitchen sink, she grabbed the bottle of medication off the windowsill, popped it open, and removed the cotton ball. Tapping the bottle, she dropped two blue pills into her palm and chased them with a glass of lukewarm water. She was behind on her weekly cleaning and preferred sticking to her routine.

Two cups of black coffee later and she'd perked up enough to get the floors swept and mopped and the curtains pulled down for a washing. She always loved the way the house felt after a good tidying up. It was so welcoming and cozy. A record was spinning on the turntable, filling the old house with the familiar sounds of The Everly Brothers, then The Duprees, followed up by Elvis Presley, of course. Her musical tastes had never evolved beyond the days of doowop and who put the bomp in the bomp bah bomp bah bomp. To her recollection, those were the best of times.

After picking at it for most of the morning, Elvis had had his fill of the ham steak and skittered through the living room to the front door to be let outside. He let out a *yip* that startled Priscilla who was emptying the dustpan into the garbage can.

"Dang it, Elvis! You know that scares me every time. I'm coming, boy, just hold your horses," she said, giving the dustpan one last shake before clipping it to the broom handle. Walking to meet Elvis at the door, she retrieved the leash from the wall hook and clipped it to his collar.

"Just let me grab my coat." Elvis barked once more, pacing anxiously in a circle. As she slung her coat over her shoulders, a hard knock came at the front door. She gasped and slid her back against the wall. Elvis retreated to the living room, dragging the leash behind him. "Some guard dog you are," Priscilla scoffed in a loud whisper. "*Coward.*"

She stood still, waiting to see if the person would leave after no one answered the door. She could feel her heart pounding. *A few more kicks to the old ticker might just do me in for good one of these days*, she thought, holding her hand to her chest.

Another hard knock sounded at the door. Priscilla inhaled deeply, trying to build up the courage to peek out the window. For as long as she could remember, she suffered from an extreme case of social anxiety and did not appreciate uninvited visitors, especially solicitors. She had nothing to offer anyone and appreciated being left well enough alone.

She stepped in front of the door and positioned her good eye in front of the peephole. Letting her sight adjust to the tiny fisheye lens, she was surprised to see there was nobody standing on the other side the door. Moving her head around trying to get a better look, she couldn't see anyone. *Was this a prank?* Even more than uninvited visitors and solicitors, she loathed pranksters. She turned and glanced at the calendar on her wall. *October 30. Of course.* This was nothing more than a pre-Halloween prank being played by one of the handful of children that lived on Hawthorne.

Still, she couldn't shake her timidness over the thought that it might be something else. Mustering up some courage, she decided to take a chance and open the door. She unlocked the deadbolt, then waited with her hand gripping the knob for just a moment before swinging open the door. A rush of refreshing autumn air met her as she stepped forward and looked around the yard. Still not a soul in sight.

"Hm. Come on ya big chicken," she called to Elvis. "Let's go potty."

Elvis scurried back to the front door and paused at Priscilla's feet, allowing her to grab hold of the leash. They stepped out into the yard together and Elvis lead her onto the grass to relieve himself. Feeling anxious after leaving the safety of her house, she couldn't shake the feeling that she was being watched from all directions. The cul-de-sac was always quiet on Friday mornings. Some of her neighbors appeared to be home.

Elvis finished, then turned and scraped at the grass with his hind legs. This always made her chuckle. Looking around the yard, she noticed the frost had burned off in the mid-morning sunlight. The fresh air felt nice after cleaning all morning.

"Pssst," a noise sounded from behind her. She turned expecting to see one of the children that lived on Hawthorne peeking from around the corner but saw no one.

"Pssst," she heard again, from the opposite direction. This time it was followed by a childlike giggle. She turned towards the noise and again, seeing no one. A chill ran down her spine and she gently tugged on the leash to hurry Elvis along.

"Come on, boy. That's eno—" she froze as she felt a rush of warm air blow onto her neck and ear. The smell of sulfur and spoiled milk permeated her nostrils. She could sense a presence standing within inches of her, breathing down her neck. Snapping her head around, she screamed, "*Leave me alone!*" Swinging her hands up around her head, accidentally jerking Elvis forward in the process. He let out a pained *yip* and ran to her feet.

Turning to gaze around her empty front yard, the sun shone through the seasonally red leaves of the sugar maple casting a crimson hue on the grass. Her relief at finding no one behind her was short-lived. An unfamiliar face was watching her from a window of house number 456 across the street. She stared back attempting to reassure herself it was just one of the men that lived there just being nosey. The face—that she now saw was female—flashed her a malicious grin that made her uneasy. She smiled back and waved.

Another face peered out from the kitchen window of the same house. The facial features resembled that of an older man. The eyes were sunken back, almost hollow. It was then that she noticed both people weren't wearing any clothes, at least from the waist up. She grimaced at the thought of a bunch of naked weirdos watching her. *Who are these people were in her neighbor's house?*

She shifted her eyes to the second floor where she could see that every window was now occupied by a person staring out at her. All the faces were different, but they all had that malevolent expression, as if she didn't belong in her own front yard.

Jesus, did they throw a party last night? she thought.

Not knowing what else to do, she flipped the onlookers the bird. *If you can't beat em, join em.* Finally finished with his business, Elvis bolted towards the front door but stopped as he met the end of the leash. Priscilla shook her head and started to walk back to the house when she caught sight of more eerie onlookers. Every window of her neighbor's house—number 549—was occupied by the same peculiar-looking strangers. Every single window. This was unheard of. The owner was a bit of a loner, and extremely anal about his home. He'd rarely even allow a repairman in, let alone a bunch of creeps. It was the reason she trusted him to walk Elvis in the evenings for her, even if he *did* spoil the dog with expensive treats.

Elvis, feeding off her apprehension, was still tugging on the leash. She started back towards the house. Trying her best to keep her eyes focused straight ahead, her curiosity got the better of her. She looked over at her neighbor's house—number 725—and shivered as she saw similar people, except these faces were eerily misshapen. Like that of deteriorating mannequins at an abandoned department store. Even the basement windows had eyes peeking out of them, all locked onto her.

As if to test a theory, she turned and looked at the rest of the homes on Hawthorne. The windows of every house on the cul-de-sac were occupied by a person staring directly at her. Each face was different. Malformed in some way. Something felt very wrong about this and she no longer felt safe being outside.

Following Elvis's lead, she briskly walked back to the house, putting a pep in her step as if trying to outrun the sets of eyes watching her every move.

As she entered the front door, she bent down and unhooked the leash from Elvis' collar. Immediately he scurried off to his food dish to finish off the last few bites of ham steak.

Priscilla turned and took one final peek outside before shutting the door. Standing in the direct center of the cul-de-sac was a tall, brooding figure. Its body was drenched in shadow as if unaffected by the glaring, mid-morning sun. There was no shadow on the ground nor a face where one should have been, just bleak darkness. Its arm rose from its side and a long branchlike finger slid out from within its sleeve and pointed directly at her.

She slammed the door and locked the deadbolt.

What is going on?

The morning passed and the approaching evening brought with it dark clouds followed by an unexpected blanket of snow. It was common for snow to fall in October in Wisconsin, but rather unfortunate for it to happen the day before Halloween. It would surely dampen the spirits for people who planned on bringing their children trick-or-treating tomorrow.

Still uneasy from the events of mid-morning, she'd spent much of the day sitting at the kitchen table listening to her records, reminiscing on the past trying to distract herself. She'd considered calling up John Harris, the neighbor who walked Elvis, to see if he would confirm that he'd had guests this morning, but she hadn't seen him leave his home all day nor she could she bear the thought of him laughing at her like she was some looney old lady that belonged in an asylum. It was bad enough there were rumors going around regarding the supposed "mysterious death" of her late-husband Jim. She knew there was nothing mysterious about a heart attack, but her reputation as the recluse of Hawthorne wasn't helping anything.

It hadn't been her idea to build their home on the grounds of the former Greenfield Asylum, but Jim had an eye for cheap property and felt it was a worthy investment. The city paid for the demolition and removal after the hospital burnt down so there were few risks involved. Little did she know that all these years later she'd be living alone amongst all these homes filled with people and their families. Well, she wasn't alone exactly. She had her Elvis and her music.

Finally breaking free from her trance, she decided to look out the window to see if the snow was sticking to the ground. She'd planned on grabbing a few groceries this evening but was afraid to drive in the snow without snow tires. She slid back the curtain and peeked out. *Phew.* It was still snowing, but she was relieved to see the figure was no longer standing in the center of the cul-de-sac. Hopefully, that would be the last of that.

To her surprise, an ambulance was pulling onto Hawthorne making its way around the cul-de-sac before stopping directly in front of her house. This was no Greenfield ambulance. It looked almost antique. *How odd,* she thought. The backup lights kicked on and the ambulance backed into her driveway. Elvis — who was usually riled up by vehicles — lay still in his bed completely oblivious.

A man in a white orderly-looking outfit climbed out of the passenger side holding a clipboard. He walked up to her front steps appearing unbothered by the snow.

"What the heck is this all about?" she asked herself.

A knock came at the door and she approached with a healthy dose of curiosity. Again, she looked out the peephole and saw the same man. With a furrowed brow of concern, she opened the door and greeted him with an apprehensive *hello.*

"Good evening, Ma'am. We're here from C-13 with another body," the orderly said, reading off his clipboard. "It says here he was found in his cell shortly after lunch. Attempted to sever his own head with a butter knife he'd snuck out of the chow hall. A straight-forward suicide. Crazy bastard likely would have done it too if he hadn't hit his neck bone and bled to death," he scoffed. "Should we bring it to the morgue or directly to the crematory for you?"

"Excuse me?" she asked with a puzzled expression. Looking out at the ambulance she noticed a second orderly was opening the double doors at the back of the ambulance. "There must be some kind of mistake. This is my home, not a morgue."

"With all due respect Ma'am, I believe it is you who are mistaken. We make this run almost daily. This is most certainly the Greenfield Asylum morgue. Always has been," the orderly responded with a hint of contention in his tone.

She saw the second man starting to remove the stretcher from the ambulance. "Hey, wait — wait just a minute now. You have it all wrong. Please, put that back inside your ambulance and get off my property." The sound of her raised voice woke Elvis from his sleep and he quickly hustled to be at her side. "This is a sick joke you're playing."

"But Ma'am..." the orderly said, consulting his clipboard once more.

"Young man, this is my home. You better check your map one more time. Now get out of here and have yourself a good day."

She forcefully closed the door without letting him respond. The prank (although impressive in its execution) had gone too far. She certainly didn't appreciate being the butt of any joke, let alone one that was so tasteless.

With Elvis at her heels, she walked back to the window to make sure the men were actually leaving. *Where on Earth had they found such an old ambulance?* Sure enough, as the backdoors were shut, she noticed the **Greenfield Asylum - Emergency Services** decal. The driver climbed back in and before the first orderly followed suit, he turned back and looked at Priscilla through the window. He paused and stared at her before lifting his arm then pointing at her in a similar fashion as the figure had done earlier in the day. This sent a shiver down her spine. Then, he shot her a mischievous smile, his face becoming malformed like the people from earlier before turning and climbing back into the ambulance to join his partner.

She pulled the curtains shut, almost ripping the rod off the wall. This sudden movement startled Elvis and he skittered away to his bed.

"I'm sorry, buddy. Some people have nothing better to do than to play jokes on —"

A sudden hard thumping on the floor above her head cut her off. It sounded as if someone were running around upstairs. She stopped and listened. Elvis jumped out of his bed and scurried back over to her feet again. Priscilla bent down and picked him up, never taking her eyes off the ceiling.

"Did you hear that buddy? I think someone's in our house," turning back to the window, she peeked out from behind the curtain and saw the ambulance was gone. What was more surprising was the lack of tire tracks or footprints that should have been in the freshly fallen snow.

Again, a heavy thumping from above startled her and this time Elvis let out a nervous *yip* as if attempting to scare off the intruders.

"It's okay, Buddy. I'm calling the police." Still carrying Elvis, she walked over to the telephone on the wall. Picking up the receiver, she wasn't met with a dial tone but instead, a woman's voice spoke to her.

"This is the Greenfield Asylum operator; how may I direct your call?" the woman asked in a monotone voice. "Hello?"

Priscilla was dumbfounded. This had all gone too far. She slammed the phone back on the receiver and tried one more time. The same woman was on the other end repeating the same rehearsed line.

"Stop this right now!" Priscilla shouted into the phone before slamming it down for the last time.

At the sound of her abrupt shouting another series of pounding footsteps scampered across the floor above her head. This time it sounded as though there were several people up there. Elvis tried burying his face into her bosom as she squeezed him tight for comfort.

"I guess we're on our own." She walked over to the countertop, pulled open a drawer, and removed a meat cleaver from amongst the mess of utensils.

THUMP

Another loud bang sounded above, and she flinched, nearly dropping the blade.

She walked back into the living room and set Elvis down in his bed. "You stay here, my friend. You'll be safe if you remain quiet."

Elvis let out a pleading whimper as she covered him with his favorite plaid blankie.

"I'll be back in a few minutes. I'm sure it's just the house settling from the cold," she said, sounding unconvinced. "Stay here, Buddy."

Gripping tightly to the cleaver, she approached the stairs and slowly began her ascent. One hand on the railing, the other on the cleaver, she felt ridiculous.

THUMP THUMP

HAHAHAHA!

She paused halfway up as a maniacal laugh reverberated down the stairwell. She was not alone. On the wall across from her, she noticed the words *HE'S COMING FOR YOU* scratched into the plaster. The paint on the wall was cracked and peeling way. A shiver crept over her flesh and she continued up.

Reaching the second floor, she didn't recognize anything. This was not her house. The picture of Jim and herself on their twentieth anniversary was missing from the end of the hallway. The doors had changed from the heavy oak they'd always been to rusted steel with small sliding windows at eye level.

Her instincts told her to turn around and run like hell, but she was no longer feeling like herself. In fact, she'd been feeling off since breakfast. *That's it!* she thought. She hadn't eaten a damn thing all day. Her blood sugar must be all screwed up.

Her heart was steady as a kick drum in her chest. Beads of sweat collected on her brow. Looking down at the cleaver in her feeble grasp, she realized how insane she must look. She started towards the first door at the end of the hall. The floor itself had transformed into aged cement with cracks running through it in all directions.

She reached the first door — her spare bedroom — and hesitantly raised her hand to the small sliding window. She slid it open and leaned in for a look. The room was a dank, cold-looking cell with a metal bedframe chained to the wall. A single lightbulb hung from the ceiling was swaying causing disorienting shadows. Then she noticed a figure hunched over in the dark corner. It looked like a man wearing a hospital gown. The seam was open along his back barely held together by thin knotted strings. His exposed flesh was covered with burst blisters and seeping gangrenous wounds staining the gown with splotches of red and brown.

Priscilla looked on in terror. Unable to turn away, she let out a reactionary gasp. At this, the man snapped his head around and stared at her through the small window. One of his eyes was a dark hole dripping with aqueous humor that trickled down his cheek bone. He shot her a toothless grin and in an instant, was charging the door. The gown was flowing loosely at his side exposing his distorted genitals. Priscilla nearly stumbled backwards in an attempt to shut the small window. He let out a banshee-like scream as he dove headfirst into the solid steel door just as she managed to slide the window shut. Her back slammed into the cement wall behind her and the screaming in the cell stopped. She watched as a puddle of blood started seeping beneath the door into the hallway. She jerked back around being careful not to slip in the gore that had found its way into one of the deep cracks.

Continuing down the hallway toward her bedroom she saw that the door to her bathroom had changed as well. It resembled the other doorways except for the twelve-by-twelve fiberglass window. She looked in but could barely see through the coating of steam that accumulated on the glass. She could just make out the silhouettes of nude figures that were standing on both sides of the room, apparently showering where no showerheads had been before. The bathroom had completely transformed. Temptation pulled at her and she fought hard to resist opening the door to see who was in there, but under the circumstances, she felt it wise to move on without further investigation. Before she could move, the figure closest to her turned and started hobbling toward the door. A wet, wrinkled hand swiped clear the steam from the glass and the onyx eyes of an old man came into focus. He ogled Priscilla up and down, then slowly slipping his tongue out, he licked the full length of the window. She could hear his lascivious grunting before he broke out in a cackle. This caught the attention of the others in the room who started to run up behind him to glance at the goods. Priscilla, disgusted and mortified, had seen enough.

Why is this happening? Am I dreaming? This is my home, but it isn't. It's like I'm in some sort of prison. Or... an asylum. Her thoughts were becoming panicked, her judgement distorted. She knew she should have already taken Elvis and run to the nearest neighbor's house, but after her encounter with the ambulance and the telephone operator, she knew this misrepresentation of reality had reached beyond the walls of her home. Was there anywhere she could go to escape this madness?

Then she remembered the people she'd seen that morning. The strangers that were watching her from the other homes on Hawthorne. *The figure.* That figure in black had pointed directly at her. But why? Was she the catalyst in this hellscape? None of this was making sense. This was not some elaborate Halloween prank played at her expense. Something was very wrong here.

Moving on from the shower room, the hallway seemed to stretch on much farther than should have been possible. She passed by the stairwell wanting more than anything to go back downstairs, grab Elvis and just run away. The walls around her appeared to become more decrepit the further she went. Covered with fungi and moss, water dripped from the ceiling and chunks of concrete broke off onto the floor as if she'd found her way into some long-abandoned dungeon deep underground.

As she trudged on toward what had formerly been her bedroom, a familiar voice called out to her. "Prissy? Prissy, is that you?"

She gasped. Only one person had ever called her Prissy. The sound of Jim's voice made her heart flutter. He put emphasis on the esses in her name giving it a snake-like quality. It had been over 35 years since she'd last heard his voice. 35 years since he'd died.

"Jimmy?" her voice rose. "Jimmy, is that really you? How is this happening?"

"Oh Prissy, it's so good to hear your voice. I'm down here."

Her footsteps sped up. "But you're dead..." It hurt her to state the obvious even after he'd died so many years ago. "I'm coming, Jimmy. Please don't leave me. I've no idea what's going on and I'm scared," she said, her voice sounding exasperated with desperate confusion. How was she talking to her dead husband? Was she herself dead?

"We're being punished, Prissy. This is our punishment for what I did. Our purgatory."

"Punished? What do you mean? What did you do, Jim?" Having truly no idea what he was talking about, she continued walking towards his voice. The hallway continued its transformation. Rusted chains were hanging from the ceiling. Nonsensical scrawling covered the walls; *there's no escape. They're watching us. Kill me now. You're next!* A battered wheelchair with bent wheels appeared to have been somehow melted into the floor.

She'd walked directly into a nightmare.

She finally made it to the bedroom door. In the dim lighting she could just make out that it was the same type of door as the first room she'd encountered at the first cell.

"Hawthorne. Our namesake. How do you think we got this land for so cheap?"

"Jim, stop this. Where are you? I can't see you."

"The fire, Prissy. The fire. Why do you think I got such a good deal? No one was going to buy this land after all those deaths."

She looked back and noticed the light in the hallway was dimming as if the darkness was swallowing up the environment.

"What on Earth are you talking about? You're dead, Jimmy. How are you here and why would you be punished for the fire?"

"You know why, you've always known. You just tried to play dumb, like you didn't know what was going on," he said, sounding less than remorseful. She slid the small window open and looked in at her dead husband. He was sitting on the suspended bed, his head lowered.

"I'm the one that set the fire," he looked up at her through the window, a wide grin formed on his face. She noticed his arms were restrained in a beige straight jacket that was tarnished with age. "I burned down the asylum. I worked out a deal with the mayor to make it look like an accident. This place and these people were a burden on our small town. I took care of the problem; we got the land. *We.*"

"No! No Jim, that can't be true," she said with disbelief in her voice.

"Of course, it's true. I did this town a favor. Why do you think all this is happening? Everything worth having comes at a cost. Our chickens are coming home to roost, sweetheart." He stood up from the bed and walked to the door. His face contorted under the light of the incandescent. Nearly pressing himself against the cold steel of the door, he stared out at her; their faces almost close enough to kiss. She hadn't seen this face since the day of his funeral when he was lying in his open casket. It still had the unfortunate waxy complexion it had during the viewing. This made her feel uneasy. "You can play dumb with yourself, but he knows the truth, Prissy. And now he's coming for you."

With a harsh malevolence in his tone, he whispered, "I can still smell all those bodies burning. They smelled so sweet." His exaggerated enunciation pushed his putrid breath onto her face, reminding her of the odors that sometimes wafted out of her kitchen sink during a rainstorm. "I watched the whole thing from up on the hill. The same spot where we used to go to make love under the stars. Although it wasn't your screams of pleasure that I heard. It was the anguished screams of hundreds of people waking up to find they were burning alive."

Tears were forming as her heart sank.

"Aww...don't be sad, my love. My...Venus. Remember our song, Prissy? *Hey Venus*," he did his best to sing but his voice sounded like he was gargling mud.

A crackling sound came from behind her in the hallway. Startled, she jerked around and spotted an old announcement speaker suspended in the upper corner of the wall. The static cleared and the voice of Frankie Avalon crooned out over the airwaves.

Hey, Venus. . .

Oh, Venus. . .

She closed her eyes. The music was nostalgic. A gateway that pulled her from this nightmare and carried her to a safe place in the back of her mind. To better times. But those times weren't real, were they? They were just a facade that was now overshadowed by the violent deaths of hundreds of innocent lives. She had always known Jim was a monster. Did that make her a monster too?

From somewhere far off, Priscilla heard Elvis let out a shrill bark, followed by another.

She opened her eyes.

"Let me out, Prissy. Unlock the door. We can get out of this place. Together again," Jim pleaded.

"No, Jim," she said, slowly backing away from the door.

"What did you say?" he replied through gritted teeth. "Open the goddamn door, Priscilla!"

BARK, Elvis was trying hard to get her attention.

Backing away more, she told him, "You're where you belong. You're a murderer. Rot in your purgatory."

"PRISSY! He's coming for you too, HE'S COMING!" he screamed, banging his head hard against the door.

Venus, if you will. . .

"Goodbye, Jim," she said before turning and heading back down the hallway.

"You can't escape, Priscilla. There's no way out for any of us!"

She continued on, ignoring his calls. His voice reverberating off the cement walls.

"PRISCILLA!"

The voices of Jim and Frankie Avalon faded into the distance. Elvis' barking got louder as she made her way back down the hallway towards the stairs. She passed by the wheelchair, the chains, the scribbled words of madmen. Finally, she was back at the stairwell. Puffs of steam were seeping out through the jamb of the bathroom door and several sets of eyes peered out through the glass doing their best to catch a glimpse of her as she turned to go back down the stairs.

"I'm coming, Elvis!" she called down the stairs, sounding out of breath. Her heart was beating uncontrollably in her chest, and her surroundings made her feel disoriented.

As she reached the bottom of the stairs, she was glad to see her house was back to normal. Elvis had burrowed his way out from under his blanket and was standing just outside the cellar door. His tail was wagging excitedly as if trying to get Priscilla's attention.

"I'm here, boy. I'm here," she said, joining him. He stood up on his hind legs as she bent to pick him up. He greeted her with wet kisses on the face as she rubbed his curly scruff. The reunion was short-lived as she noticed smoke pouring out from the gap under the basement door.

"Oh no, buddy. A fire?" she asked, knowing the dog had no idea.

She tapped the doorknob to see if it was hot. It was cool, so she turned the knob and opened the door. Smoke escaped and rolled up to the ceiling. The smell reminded her of the burning ham steak from that morning. Once again, ignoring her instinct to run out the front door, she started down the basement steps. This was her home. She didn't want it burning down leaving her and Elvis homeless.

With each step she took, the smell got stronger. Peering down she could see a flickering orange light and the sound of clanging metal.

Is this another part of the nightmare?

As her feet hit the bottom step, she wasn't in any way prepared for what she saw. The two orderlies from earlier were standing in front of a large furnace getting ready to lift a corpse into it. The neck was split in half and the head was bent exposing the bone and raw meat beneath.

She gasped, unintentionally drawing their attention.

That was no furnace; it was a crematory.

She stood and stared. Sensing her fear, Elvis once again buried his face into her bosom.

"Wha — what are you —"

"Ma'am, we told you we had a body to dispose of. We can't just drive around all day with this guy in the ambulance," the man who'd met her at the door earlier explained. "We have a job to do."

"What is this? You need to get out of my house!"

Both men—indifferent to her agitation—turned away, completely ignoring her demands. Lifting up on both side of the body pan, they pushed it and the corpse of the patient into the furnace. The heat from the flames pressed against Priscilla's exposed skin.

"Alright, who's next on our list?" the orderly asked his silent partner who handed him the clipboard.

"Let's see... *Priscilla M. Hawthorne.* Well, that's odd," he said, rubbing his clean-shaven chin. "That's you, correct?" he asked, pointing at her.

"That can't be! I'm alive, you buffoon. I'm standing right here," she tried her best to disguise the trembling in her voice but failed miserably.

"That's not our problem, Ma'am. We just go by what the clipboard says," he said, sounding annoyed. "Come on down and we'll get you set up as soon as this guy is dust."

The second orderly laughed at this. Priscilla, gripped with fear, hugged Elvis tighter, anticipating her escape up the stairs. She could feel her heart trying to escape the confines of her ribcage.

The orderlies began to walk towards her. Starting off with a normal walk, then their feet began to drag as if the soles of their shoes were sticking to the concrete. As they slugged forward, their faces began to transform into the malformations she'd seen on the strangers earlier in the day. It was like their faces were melting in the immense heat of the furnace that was ablaze behind them.

The fire!

"There's no escape from Greenfield, Priscilla. Just ask Jim," the first orderly said through his loosening slack jaw. "You want out; this is your only chance."

Priscilla had seen and heard enough. They won. She wanted out of this house.

She turned and started back up the stairs, tripping herself up on the narrow wooden steps and nearly dropping Elvis. Instead, she turned her body and she took the brunt of the fall on her right shoulder, shielding the dog from the collision. Upon impact, her teeth slammed together, chipping her top incisor. The pain was immense, and it took her a moment to recover. A moment she couldn't spare as the orderlies continued their approach, now starting up the stairs.

"You can't escape, Priscilla. He's coming for you. You can't run from him."

Elvis let out a *yip* and Priscilla slowly but surely made it back up onto her feet.

Back on her feet, she pounded up the stairs; she took a quick glance down at the men chasing her. By this point, they were barely distinguishable as the men she'd seen a few moments ago. Their clothes had burned completely off; the skin had melted off like mozzarella cheese and was left behind on the floor in wet piles like dirty laundry. Their muscles had begun to liquify on their skeletons and their jaws were chattering up and down as if they were trying to speak. The smell wafting up the stairs was nauseating, again reminding her of the burnt ham steak.

She and Elvis finally made it to the top of the stairs, and she slammed the door behind her so hard, she was sure she almost knocked it off its hinges. Resting her back against the door to catch her breath, she closed her eyes and held Elvis tightly against her chest and chin. He was warm and comforting. He was the only thing she had left in this world besides this old house and Hawthorne Drive. With the recent revelation, those two things that had been such an intricate part of her life were now tainted. The very ground itself had been spoiled with the blood of hundreds of innocent people. All in the name of a cul-de-sac. *How was this possible? Did she actually believe that what she'd seen today was really happening?* These questions circled around in her head as she swiftly contemplated what the next step was. *Where could she go from here?*

Opening her eyes, she knew she needed fresh air. Whether what she'd seen was real or not, she couldn't stand to be in this house for one more second without some sort of palate cleanser for the mind.

The house looked like things were back to normal. The smells of freshly clean curtains and Pine-Sol were most welcome. Elvis, sensing her calm demeanor, licked her fiercely on her chin and cheek. His soft whimper and kisses set Priscilla's mind at ease.

"Come on, Boy. Let's get some fresh air. This has been a bizarre day."

Elvis let out an enthusiastic *yip* as they walked to the front door. She squeezed her companion tightly one more time before pulling open the front door and stepping onto the front steps.

The sight before her would be the last thing Priscilla Hawthorne would ever see. A crowd of what looked to be at least one hundred severely burnt faces and bodies surrounded her and Elvis on all sides. The smell was that of seared flesh and hair. Smoke rose from the crowd as though they were all simmering steaks or embers at the bottom of a fireplace.

Straight ahead of them standing on the sidewalk was the same figure from earlier who was cloaked in shadow. She could sense he was not of this Earth and his malevolent presence triggered something inside Priscilla. A purple hazy glow shown down from the night sky which intensified when he raised his hand and his extended finger pointed directly at her. A sinister laugh reverberated inside her head and there was nothing she could do to stop it.

Gasping at the sight before her, she was overwhelmed with an unfathomable terror. A razor-sharp pain shot up from her chest to her shoulder and she could no longer shelter Elvis. Her arms dropped and Elvis fell to the snow-covered ground landing safely on his paws. The same could not be said about Priscilla who winced in excruciating pain. She clutched her hand to her chest as she lost control of her legs. Bending at the knees, she tumbled forward off the front steps face first with no way of stopping herself. The thundering crack of her skull smashing onto the cement walkway was the last thing she would ever hear.

Elvis, devastated at the sight of his master laying lifeless in the snow, ran to her side and began licking her face to wake her up, letting out a random *yip* as if trying to get her attention. His efforts were fruitless. Priscilla was already dead.

The massive crowd of the deceased in-patients vanished. The front yard was empty save for Elvis who continued desperately attempting to resuscitate his master with kisses to no avail.

Having seen the entire tragic scene unfold, a figure wearing a grey suit jogged up the sidewalk and approached the old woman that had collapsed in the snow. Elvis spotted the man and took up a defensive stance in front of Priscilla's body.

"Hello, Ma'am? Are you okay? Ma'am?" the man asked as he knelt down beside her.

Elvis ran to him and set his front paws on the man's thigh letting out a *yip* to explain what happened. The man saw the snow was stained crimson around her head and he knew this was serious.

"Ma'am, I'm going to run inside and use your telephone to call 9-1-1. I'll be right back. Hang in there," he directed the dead woman.

Elvis stood beside his dead master and watched as the man hastily jogged past them and into 637 Hawthorne to use the phone.

Hello, I have an emergency at number 637...

Elvis could hear the man's voice coming from inside the kitchen as a dark figure peeked out around the front door from inside the house. The figure raised a boney finger up to his nonexistent face as if to tell the dog to shush.

Elvis' head cocked curiously to the side as the shadow man closed the front door.

A moment after the deadbolt was locked, a blood-curdling scream was heard coming from inside the house.

Elvis watched from the front yard and after a moment of silence, let out a concerned *yip*.

549 W. HAWTHORNE DRIVE

549 W. HAWTHORNE DRIVE

by Darren Diarmuid

That damn dog hasn't stopped barking ever since Gladys died.

I still remember that day rather vividly. It was an exquisite Saturday afternoon and I had decided to treat myself to a gander at the collection of paintings and antiquities in the Chazen Museum of Art in the University of Wisconsin. I remember looking at 'The Adoration of the Shepherds' by Giorgio Vasari and thinking about how wonderful it is to be alive and how nice it is to finally take a little break from my busy schedule. I remember the peculiar taste of the bratwurst sandwich as I gazed at the glacial waterways. I remember standing on the observation deck of the State Capitol, glancing at its majestic Roman-Renaissance dome, admiring the views of the city and the lakes. I remember stopping my car on the way home to take pictures of the purple wood violet flowers in the meadows during that beautiful day in June.

And then as soon as I made it back home, I saw my neighbor, the elderly Mrs. Hawthorne rushing about her front yard, squinted, horrified eyes, calling for her Gladys. I rushed inside and pulled the curtains. I didn't want to deal with it, and I still had some work to do, but I decided right then and there that I would take care of Mrs. Hawthorne in any way that I could. In a way, I felt responsible for her loss, but I couldn't deal with what was happening right now.

I knew that it would have a dire impact on my mental health and affect my work performance. I think the neighbors might have got the wrong impression and thought I was disrespectful and rude, but they don't understand that I have my own way of dealing with things, and they can think whatever they like because they don't owe her like I do.

Nowadays, I repay her quietly in my own way, walking her little Bolognese Elvis each evening, so she doesn't need bother leaving the house as often. My small penance. Even buying him expensive treats and such occasionally. It's been over a year and none of the other neighbors have even checked in on her, or asked how they could help after such a loss, which is just as well. *If they did, then perhaps they would discover some things that they probably wouldn't like to know.*

But a lot has changed since then. In my personal life, at least. I'm not quite sure about the other neighbors; I don't talk to them much. I've always been quite the worker, but this year I've decided to devote my life to it, sometimes working up to sixteen or eighteen hours a day.

Although I wish I hadn't done this, because outside disturbances are proving this to be rather difficult, I've decided to assign myself the rigorous task of completing three thousand words this hour towards my upcoming data analysis project for work. Twenty minutes in and not even a quarter of the way completed that yet, the initial sounds of laughter from the neighbors to the right is testing my patience. Students. Adam and Chris, as I recall. Two roaring imbeciles in their mid-twenties who rent the house next to me. Adam doesn't seem to leave the house very often, but Chris is restless. Together, they're something wretched. Every day is another noise disturbance.

I've left the window on the latch to distract me from the ticking of the pendulum counting down the time I have left to complete this challenge, but I certainly wish I hadn't. I can already smell the exhalation clouds of marijuana smoke filtering out past my window. Talks of smut. Laughs. Giggles. Then the crunching of an empty can of beer is casually disposed in the center of their lawn. I suspect that the loud music will start in precisely an hour and a half, and the syncopated dance beats will commence, with the same old booming bass thumping at the same rhythm for hours on end. And I'll be tossing and turning praying that I can get a decent night sleep, so I have the confidence and intellectual finesse to approach my boss about this new system in the workplace. I have grand ideas that may give me a raise.

The little dog starts barking again, and although he's probably snapping at the students or a squirrel, from a safe distance, it reminds me that I haven't walked him yet this evening. As soon as I finish my word count for this project, I scoop out a few high-end dog treats, leave the house, and avoid making eye contact with the students at all costs. I turn into the Hawthorne's lawn at as fast a pace as my legs can muster, open her side gate, and toss a pumpkin and peanut-butter treat to Elvis, who deftly snatches it from the air. His tail starts wagging and the barking stops. Perhaps he's happy to be fed, but I'd like to believe that we've somewhat bonded. As soon as he's finished eating, I give him belly rubs for a few minutes. Then I get the harness and leash and we go for a walk around the road. I hum the tune of 'That's Life' by Frank Sinatra as we start to walk, and just like usual, I keep my head tilted down towards the ground and avoid looking at the pesky students as they create little havocs and deplete their brain cells.

"Mr. Harris!" a woman calls as the other guests begin to arrive to their house, abandoning their cars all over the boys' lawn.

Don't look. Do not look at her.

"Mr. Harris!" she calls again, louder this time.

I look up and force a smile, realizing that there's no way that I wouldn't have heard her. She's an attractive brunette with beautiful, sun-kissed skin. Loose, white shirt with a purple bra underneath and an open, black button-up shirt on her shoulders. Endearing smile. She's holding a transparent glass with black cola in it. As I get closer, I can smell the vodka.

"Cute dog you've got there, Mr. Harris. What's her name?"

"His," I respond, gulping down saliva, nervously. "It's a 'he'; his name is Elvis."

She walks right up to Elvis, kneels, and starts rubbing his head. As I look down, uncomfortably, wanting to leave and carry on with my walk, my eyes accidently glance at her cleavage, so I look away as quickly as possible, hoping that no one saw me or get the wrong impression. Elvis sniffs at her drink and then starts barking at her. She backs away.

"Sorry, buddy," she says, with a sense of sass.

"He gets like that. I'm sorry. He's not my dog. Just walking him... Sorry."

"Whose dog is it?"

"Mrs. Hawthorne," I say, pointing at her house.

"You're so sweet," she says in a voice that I can't tell if it's sincere or condescending. "I've heard some things about her, but everything is different. She's so mysterious. She's almost like something of folklore now at this stage."

"I suppose. Really, she's a lovely lady. She lives a life of solitude ever since her husband passed, so I made a vow to take care of her."

Her eyes light up, endearingly. "Mr. Harris, that's so noble of you. Oh my god. What an amazing thing to do for someone. None of these assholes would ever do something like that for someone," she says, glancing back at the boys on the lawn chugging beers and doing bong rips. "It really makes me think, you know?"

"I, uh... Yeah. What does it make you think of?"

"It makes me think that I'd like to hang out with you sometime. You seem cool."

I feel bouts of anxiety travelling through my body. I think about the gardening I must do later, plus the write-up for my boss, dust down the living room, clean the cutlery, study the real estate market, and then write another five thousand words towards my upcoming edition of financial literacy, which has a deadline of this day next week. After that, I must call up my mother, Celia, and listen to her complain about her neighbor, Geraldine, for approximately forty-five minutes until the sleeping pills kick in and she passes out abruptly. I also wanted to get a little bit of study in on Egyptian mythology, perhaps only twenty minutes or so, but worse-case scenario, I can always save that until tomorrow. I feel my body language moving away from her, nervously. I still have so much to do today, and this young lady is probably mocking me. I can't take any chances.

"I, uh... Yeah. I don't know. Why?"

"Excuse me?" she says, taking another swig of the drink.

"I, uh... Why would you like to hang out with me?" I continue, tripping over my words.

She starts laughing and playfully slaps my chest. "You're funny, Mr. Harris." She glances down at the ground and looks at me, flirtatiously. "And I probably shouldn't be saying this, but I think you're really hot."

I feel my eyes opening wide like I just took a flight abroad and remembered that I left the oven on. *How am I supposed to respond to this information?*

"Well, eh… I, uh… I think you're quite the, uh… I think you're quite attractive too…" I say, as my eyes neurotically dart towards the ground.

"And not just looks, but personality too. These men can lift all the weights and hook up with all the women in the world, but they'll never be the man that you are. Noble. Compassionate. Dedicated."

I begin to blush and feel ecstatic, simultaneously. Nobody has complimented me like that in years. "I, uh… That means a lot. Thank you, pretty lady. I don't know what to say."

"Can you say that you'd like to hang out with me?"

"I would certainly like to hang out with you," I respond, both truthfully and anxiously.

I don't know what her intentions are, and I have so much work to do. Where is this going? What will happen? Will this counteract my vow of celibacy?

"Great! Would you like to come over and we can talk some more once you're finished walking Elvis? Maybe we can get *all shook up?*" she says, batting her eyelids flirtatiously.

"Suzy, why are you talking to this suit?" Adam shouts over, walking out the front door in a red bubble jacket and a can of Bud Light. He tilts his baseball cap sideways, obnoxiously coughs up a ball of phlegm, pierces a hole in the side of the beer can with a compass and skulls back the drink in one go. I tap my feet and want to leave, immediately, but can't find any social signs where it wouldn't feel rude to do so.

"Shut up, Adam! Why you gotta be such an asshole?"

"Why you gotta be such a yuppie sympathizer?" he retorts.

"He's cooler than you! Look at him! Nice, ironed shirt. Combed hair. Clear skin. Clean garden. You don't have to be jealous!"

"Jealous?! Ha! Jealous?!! Baby, don't be foolish!"

"Don't call me 'baby', jerk!"

"I'm so sorry about this, Mr. Harris," she says, consoling me, sincerely. "He just gets this way."

"I, uh… That's okay, Suzy."

She smiles, takes another swig of vodka, and brushes her hand against my shoulder. "Let's hang out later, please. I'll let you carry on with Elvis."

"Yeah. I, uh… Yeah. Cool. Okay, I'll see you later," I smile.

Turning around as quickly as possible, I suck down a gracious deep breath of fresh air that I finally get to leave. As I look at the manicured hedges and fences and the beautiful oak and elm trees shedding their colors, it suddenly occurs to me that my skin is quite clear, in fact, and my hair is nice and sophisticated when it's combed. I suppose she was right about that. Sure, I mightn't be the best-looking gentleman, but I present myself well. And, as for these obnoxious men, I may feel dazzled and unconfident around them, but at least they don't have anything on me, in that regard. I feel a little bit of guilt that I have no intention of talking to her again, but at least I can rest easy tonight that someone would talk about me that kindly. What a nice young lady.

When we get around the corner, Elvis drops some fresh steaming feces against the sugar maple tree outside the Terrance's house. I pick it up with a green bag and consider throwing it into the boys' unkempt yard. Perhaps that will teach them a lesson. But then reality reminds me that I don't want or need any altercations. Suzy was right; he is a jerk.

When we finish our loop, I cross my fingers and hope that no one from the students' house are out on the lawn. I couldn't deal with another conversation. Luckily enough, no one is. They've all returned into the house. I leave Elvis in his back garden, knocking on Mrs. Hawthorne's back door to let her know he's back, then hurry back to my own house, shut the door, and turn on the television to the History Channel. The background noise keeps me occupied as I work because my thoughts shift around too sporadically to work in silence. It appears that I've made it just in time for the weather report. My heart sinks a little bit when the weatherman warns us that it's due to snow in a few nights. Snow for all of Wisconsin. Temperatures to drop. *Just my luck*, I think to myself, *more work for me!* Oh well, I'll do it in the morning. I can't worry about it now. I must undertake these five thousand words towards my financial literacy project. Essential work. A priority.

Suddenly, the doorbell rings. It sends a shock throughout my nervous system. I don't know who it could be. I don't have visitors. Reluctantly, I get up and open the door.

Suzy.

"You said you would call," she says, leaning against the doorframe, with another drink in her hand.

"Oh... Suzy. Hi. I, uh... Yes, I most certainly would have, but I still have a little bit of work to do."

"That's okay. What is it?"

"It's, eh… Egyptians. Egyptian mythology.

Her eyes light up like city lights. "Oh my god, really?"

"Of course. I, uh… I work as an Egyptian mythologist."

"Mr. Harris," she says, impressed and wide-eyed. "I thought you might be fascinating, but, oh my god. I'm speechless. That's so cool."

"Yes, I suppose it is," I smile from ear to ear, looking at the ground, clumsily.

"Do you have much more work to do?"

"I, uh…"

"Can I come in?"

"Excuse me?"

"I'd love to come in if that's okay. You seem cool. I don't want to talk to those dipshits anymore. I want to bring that party over to you," she smiles.

"I'm sorry Suzy, but I don't party."

"Mr. Harris!" she teases, gently tapping his chest with her fingers. "Of course, you do. We all do!"

"Unless you, uh… Unless you can call Egyptian study a party, then I really don't think I do…"

"Sounds like my type of party!" she claims. "If I run back and get some more alcohol, will you promise to let me back in?" she asks with her beautiful brown eyes, widening.

"I should really be--"

"Please? Promise me?" she says with a smile that melts me.

"I, uh... Yes. Of course, I will."

She struts out the door and I look at the fluidity of her walk as she leaves. I take a seat on the couch and try to sit in a position that is both comfortable and confident, but it appears that I've sadly mistaken how unnatural something so trivial feels. Cross-legged? No. Left leg up on knee? No. Legs spread apart with feet firmly rooted to the ground? Oh, how I long to acquire some natural swagger.

"What's up with you?" I hear Adam shout from outside.

"Fuck you!" Suzy snaps back.

"You better not be giving my liquor to that guy over there!"

"Or what, Adam? Or what? We're gonna have a great time tonight."

I suddenly get nervous wondering what that could mean. I don't want any trouble between Adam and I for various reasons, most notably the fact that he's my next-door neighbor and appears rather sporadic and volatile.

Suzy walks in and closes the door behind her with her elbow. She has half of a bottle of vodka in one hand, and a big bottle of cola in the other. She takes a seat beside me in the living room, and the scent of her perfume, her feminine energy, the endorphins, makes my entire body tingle. She places the drinks on the table, whips her hair back over her shoulder, and faces me on the couch, reaching her hands out to lock with mine. We hold hands and lock eye contact, and I try with every ounce of my being not to glance around the room in a fidgety manner, but my woodpecker is stiff and twitching out of control and I haven't been this intimately close with a stranger in years.

"Sorry if you heard that. He's such a jerk. I can't believe I fell for him before."

"It's, uh... It happens. Happens to all of us..." I say not wanting to let go of her hands but also to fix my nether regions, hoping she doesn't notice.

"I should've known better. He's so immature. Seriously. Like, we hooked up once, and he has the nerve, the audacity, to call me 'baby' and treat me like something he can just use whenever he wants to. What kind of bullshit is that?"

"You're quite right. That truly sounds like a little bit of bullshit, alright."

"I need to find a good man. They're hard to find. You strike me as a good man."

"I suppose! If you insist," I laugh, nervously, appreciating the compliment and not knowing what to say to that.

"See, and you're humble too. That's what a man should be. All these fake-ass boys walking around trying to be over-confident and cocky, it's bullshit. It's so obvious. It's a mask. A real man has a silent confidence about him. He's not over-compensating that he's morally bankrupt. A real man takes care of himself. A real man studies Egyptian mythology!"

I glance around, dumbfounded, and we both burst into laughter.

"You're funny, Suzy."

"Oh my god, you think so?"

"I, uh… I know so. And you strike me as an intelligent woman, too. You, eh… You know what you want, and you have standards, and I think that's great."

"Thank you, Mr. Harris! I'll drink to that!"

"Please, you don't have to call me Mr. Harris. You can call me 'John.'"

"I'd rather call you 'Mr.' I think it sounds sexy."

She picks up the bottle of vodka and realizes that there are no glasses. I insist that she should relax, and I'll get them myself. I walk into the kitchen, finally getting the opportunity to adjust myself, and then I grab two tall glasses that I purchased in a souvenir shop in Estonia and place them down on the table.

"One for me and one for the beautiful lady."

She glances at me, wide-eyed and respectfully. "Those other guys don't call me beautiful… or a lady. Thank you. I'm impressed."

"Honesty is the best policy, I've been told."

She smiles. "You have a really nice place. So clean. Immaculate!"

It's been quite a while since I've last had a drink. Two years, in fact. So, every time we go match to match on more vodka, I try my best to mask the initial face-scrunch every time I take a sip of it. I don't enjoy it at all, but I enjoy her company, and if that's the compromise I must pay to be in her presence, then that's alright with me. Outside, the music starts blaring. Every few minutes there's another slamming of a car door and someone revving the engine. The chaos is about to commence, but at least I don't have to worry too much about the work. *Oh my god, the work...*

Suddenly, there's a booming, aggressive knock on the door. Suzy and I glance at each other suspiciously and then she rolls her eyes and sighs when she registers who it is.

"Let me get this," she sighs. "I can take a wild guess who it is."

She opens the door and there's Adam, looking angry. Pinned pupils. Scouring face. He has a marijuana joint curled between his fingers and the smoke lingers through the hallway. The musty smell overpowers the cherry and lilac scented candles that I purchased recently, and I'm not too happy about that, but I wish I had the audacity to show it.

"What are you doing here, babe? Enough is enough, already."

"No, it's not. I'm done with you and your bullshit. Go away."

"The fuck do you see in this stuffed shirt anyway? Look at him!"

"Yeah, I look at him and I see more of a man than you'll ever be."

Adam sneers and scoffs and pivots his body from side to side like an aggravated pitbull that wants to smash and obliterate everything and anything in its way. My legs tense up just seeing the unfiltered rage building up inside of him.

"You've gotta be kidding me! If I flicked this prick in the forehead, he'd drop dead. Look at him! Made of twigs. He ain't shit!"

"Why are you here? What do you even want, anyway?"

"You, babe. I want you."

"No, you don't. Stop pretending that you care about me."

"If I didn't, then why would I be here?"

"Because your fragile little ego can't be told 'no.' You didn't care about me like this yesterday."

"Of course, I did!" he says, trying to appear thoughtful and sympathetic.

"And that's why you sent Jenny a picture of your chode? Word gets around, moron."

"Look, are you leaving here or what? Enough is enough," he snaps.

"Adam, I've already told you this, but fuck off."

And with that she closes the door on his face and locks the door. She sits down on the couch and curls her legs up beside me where her magnificent booty is beside my palm, and even though I'm quite nervous, it is undoubtedly exciting too.

"I'm so sorry about that," she whispers in my ear.

And all I can think of is how I feel somewhat shell-shocked by this whole scenario that I don't want to be in. I'm supposed to be working towards my financial literacy assignment, and cleaning the cutlery, and yet, I find myself in the middle of a debacle with an immature *boy*. Good grief. Perhaps this is what the Roman gladiators felt.

"…But he's harmless, darling," she continues. "He's all talk. He'll have forgotten me by morning."

Oh my god, she called me darling.

"Want to play truth or dare?" she asks.

"I, uh… Mmm… Yes, I suppose" I respond, reluctantly, not wanting to know how dull I am at this game, hoping that she doesn't ask for 'truth'. If she asks for 'truth' she's not going to get any information that the younger generation would describe as particularly 'juicy.' "You ask first."

"Okay," she laughs and leans in towards me with a suggestive stare. "I dare you to kiss me."

I pounce on her like a Persian leopard.

I wake up to the sound of some ungodly thumping noise coming from downstairs. The digital alarm clock on my bedside dresser reads 3:33am. I feel something beside me, and I look over and see that beautiful woman tossing over to one side of the mattress with her long hair parted in every direction across the pillow. And it suddenly registers to me what happened. Despite the oncoming thump of an excruciating hangover, I grin from ear to ear, as snippets of memories reveal themselves back to me and I notice the ecstatic tingles in my nether region. And then I remember my vow of celibacy and all the work I was supposed to do, and compulsively, I feel slightly ashamed and conflicted.

But the noise continues. It sounds like its coming from downstairs. It sounds like someone is walking around. And when I listen in closer, it's unmistakable. There's an intruder.

It's just as well and rather peculiar that I took my father's advice of keeping a baseball bat underneath my bed. It's something I never wanted to possess, and I always considered it bad luck, but for the first time in my life, it may indeed prove itself to be convenient. I reach under the bed and clutch it with the sliver of might that I possess because lord knows I can't protect myself adequately.

Suzy tosses and mutters something to herself. I realize that this is the worst-case scenario of something to wake up to, so I hope in my heart that she doesn't wake up. Thankfully, she turns over and grips the pillow, proving to be still asleep.

I pick up the baseball bat and grip it like I'm in a stadium about to hit a cracker of a shot that will score me a home run. I suppose in this scenario it would be thumping this trespasser over their dumb little noggin.

I tip-toe out of the room, considerate of not waking Suzy. It sounds like whoever it is, is in the kitchen. Some cutlery falls and shatters on the ground. Followed by more, and more, and more. Glasses. Jars. And, strangely enough, it's the careless shattering of my precious expensive mugs and plates that concerns me more than the thought of someone, potentially harmful, breaking in my house. They were all so expensive.

I get to the bottom step, grip the handle of the baseball bat as tightly as possible. My heartbeat escalates, and in my heart of hearts I want to turn around and cower, but I know that I need to stand up for myself, for my house, for my pride, for my dignity, for my wellbeing, for once in my life. And if Suzy thinks I'm a man, I've got to be one.

And so, I open the door. All I see is the silhouette of someone, some strange, faceless being, or a masked man with a big build, obscured by the darkness of the night sky with a strange faint purple glow to it peering through the window. He quickly backs up and gets rigid in his posture. He gasps, pulls the sliding door at the back of the house, and runs out into the night. I follow him out to my quiet neighborhood street. I glance down and observe he's left a trail of footprints right through my prized Juliet rose bed. I know that he has something in his hand, but I can't tell for the life of me what it could be. But intuition tells me that it's valuable.

He climbs and jumps over the back gate. I unlock it and follow him out onto the road, and I see the shape of someone jumping the gate into the back garden of Mrs. Hawthorne's house. Suddenly, I'm conflicted. I don't want to break into her house but she's vulnerable and needs to be protected. So, I choose the latter.

But why isn't Elvis making any noise?

I follow him into Mrs. Hawthorne's home and glance around. Elvis is nowhere to be found. There's nothing happening. Nothing. Not a peep. I remain still just for another moment, just to be certain. Lord knows that I couldn't live with myself if anything was to happen to Mrs. Hawthorne. She needs to be safe and protected. I walk through her house, clutching the bat, quietly shuffling from room to room. The living room, the kitchen, the bathroom, and everywhere downstairs are clear.

I tip-toe up the stairs and enter Mrs. Hawthorne's room. She's safe, still sleeping, apparently her pills allowing her to sleep through everything. Elvis lifts his head inquisitively but doesn't make a sound. I give him a treat, but I don't question how it came to be in my hand.

If anyone were to ever hurt her, I would not be able to live with myself. Not to mention the money. Without her assistance, I wouldn't be the man I am today. The mortgage. The career. Everything. I'm forever in debt to her grace and generosity, and I will do everything I can to protect her.

I stay as still as possible just to be positive that I can't hear anything. Not a sound. Nothing. I quietly stroll into the back bedroom and glance out the window at the patch of land beside the garden shed. I'm still certain that no one would ever know. I did a good job of that, I think. *Her precious Gladys never stood a chance that morning. The little female bitch, companion to Elvis, had dug under the hedge and into my yard one too many times. I only meant to scare her off. I remember carrying her lifeless body under cover of night. I remember the dark soil beneath my fingernails. I remember telling Mrs. Hawthorne, no, I had not seen her little dog since the morning prior. And now, I owe her everything...*

I walk back out onto the street and drop my guard down and carry the baseball bat limp-like by my legs as I walk.

Of course, Adam is standing out on the front lawn smoking a cigarette. He notices me.

"Mr. Harris! What the fuck are you doing with that?!"

"I, uh..."

I sprint into my own house and slam the door behind me as loudly as possible. I take a deep breath, quickly remember that Suzy is upstairs and then I run up the steps and into the room. As I shut the door and lean my back against it, gasping, she sits up, switches on the lamp, sees the baseball bat in my hand, and screams.

"What is wrong with you?! What are you doing?!"

"Suzy, I can explain!"

She grunts and throws the empty bottle of vodka beside the bed at me, which shatters against the wall into a million little fragments and cuts my arm. Still mostly naked, with nothing on other that her underwear, she grabs her phone and jumps off the bed and locks herself in the bathroom.

"Suzy, please!"

"Fuck off!" she retorts.

I place the baseball bat back underneath the bed where it belongs, and sit on the mattress, helpless and mortified.

"Hello?" I hear her say from inside. "Officer, I'm in house five-four-nine west Hawthorne Drive. I'm locked inside the upstairs bathroom. There's a man outside the door with a baseball bat and I don't know what he's going to do but I'm scared!"

I sigh to myself and realize that there's no backing out of this one now. I'm screwed.

"Okay, thank you," she says. "Please hurry."

"Suzy?" I start as she finishes the call.

No response.

I place my ear against the door, and I can hear her panting out of breath. I'm almost certain I can hear her heartbeat.

"Suzy?" I call a second time, but once again, no response.

I collapse back on the bed in a spread-eagle position. After some time, which could've been anywhere between twenty seconds to twenty minutes, I hear a car pull up at my driveway, followed by two doors slamming and knocking on my door.

I get up off the bed, walk downstairs, and open the front door with an escalating pulse. Sure enough, it's two police officers.

"Mr. Harris, we're with the Greenfield Police," one of them says, holding up his badge. "We received several calls about you in the space of five minutes or less. May we come in?"

"Of course!" I say, extending my arm to let them in, trying to be as courteous as possible.

"There's a woman who called us from your bathroom. Is she still here?"

"Yeah, she is."

"Okay, Martin, you stay right here with this guy and make sure he doesn't get up to any funny business," one of them says to the other officer. "I'm going to go up and check on her."

Officer Martin nods his head, and we stand across from one another as the other officer walks up the stairs. We don't say a word to each other the entire time. He slowly paces around the kitchen, looking for potential pieces of evidence or threat. Amongst the silence, I can hear the officer consoling Suzy and telling her that everything is going to be alright. I hear the distinctive squeak of the bathroom door opening and the rumblings and whisperings of everything going on up there. After a few moments, from the opened hallway door, I see Suzy, now fully clothed, stepping outside the front door with my favorite coat and lighting a cigarette and shaking. The other officer walks back into the room.

"Mr. Harris, you're under arrest."

"This is unjust, officer! I was merely protecting myself and my home. I thought there was an intruder."

"Sir, we received a call of you being a possible threat to your neighborhood, with allegation of home invasion with intention of potential battery and assault. The other was from the terrified young woman who locked herself in your bathroom."

"It wasn't home invasion, officer! I take care of Mrs. Hawthorne. She needs me. Someone broke into her home, and I was merely protecting her."

"Which house does Mrs. Hawthorne live in?"

"The next one. 637. The beige house with the blue trim."

The one police officer whispers something to the other one, who nods his head, firmly and righteously.

"We're going to have to ask Mrs. Hawthorne about the matter. We need her verdict."

My throat dries up and I feel my body begin to tremble. "I don't think that's a good idea, officer."

"Why not?"

"Mrs. Hawthorne is umm... very unwell. She's a widower and she doesn't like to speak to people she doesn't know. She's ah, well, a sick lady. Bedridden."

"Mr. Harris, if we don't speak to her, it's not going to be looking good for you."

"But I'm innocent, officer!"

"Mr. Harris, the Wisconsin law states that if you provoke an attack, you can't claim self-defense unless you've exhausted every other means to escape the situation. You must reasonably believe that the force of a threat is necessary to prevent imminent death or great bodily harm."

"But I was! There was an intruder in my home! He was breaking things in my kitchen, and then ran into the Hawthorne's house. I had to protect her!"

"What did he look like?"

"I'm not sure. It was dark."

"And what time was this at?"

"I'm not quite sure. It's all been such a blur, officer. Thirty to forty minutes ago, I would have to say if I were to guess."

"And what things did this intruder smash in your kitchen?"

"Glass jars, bottles. Things of that nature."

The officer sighs. "Mr. Harris," he begins, locking eyes with me intensely and fixing his posture. "You're telling me that this intruder broke into your house and smashed up your kitchen. He then ran into your neighbor's house, so you followed him in with a baseball bat. You have no idea what this man looked like, and when you followed him into her house, he was no longer there. Correct?"

"...Correct."

"And in that space of time, with everything going on, you thought it would be necessary to sweep the broken glass off your kitchen floor and scrub down any mess made by this intruder. Correct?"

I dart my eyes back and forth between both police officers anxiously, and realize they've figured out something that I didn't even think of. I didn't clean the kitchen. Of course, I would have if there was a mess, but there was no mess. The intruder smashed things in my kitchen. I'm certain of that. But there's no evidence to suggest that. Perhaps this is what Nikola Tesla felt when he experienced hallucinations after watching his brother getting trampled by a horse.

"I, uh… I don't quite remember doing that, but I'm certain I must have, officer. I have nervous ticks, you see. I wash my hands compulsively and clean everything around me. I clean places that aren't even particularly dirty. I need to keep things in order. I can't help myself. But, uh… Everything that has happened since then feels like such a blur, you see. A rather intense blur at that."

They both nod their heads, understandably. "Mr. Harris, will you walk with us to the front door and have a look outside?"

"Of course."

They walk into the hallway and look outside the front door where Suzy is finishing off her cigarette and looking petrified. "This intruder also ran into your neighbor's house, you say. To protect yourself and herself you followed him into her home with a baseball bat. Correct?"

I nod my head. "Correct."

"We noticed your flowerbed here is trampled down. Someone broke right through these roses. I'm sure that you're aware of that already, Mr. Harris."

I squint my eyes, unsure of where he's going with this. "Indeed, I'm aware of that."

"But there's only one set of footprints through it, only one trail of dirty footprints leading to and from Mrs. Hawthorne's house."

Suddenly, I feel my heart slowly sinking. It's rather evident that I'm in the wrong. I notice fresh scratches on my arms from the thorns.

But that means I must have imagined everything happening. Am I going insane? Am I going prison? Oh Lord, I'm going to prison. I must be. There's nothing I can say to climb out of this hole.

I subtly nod my head, sheepishly and reluctantly.

"I want to contact a criminal defense lawyer. I want to protect my rights."

"You can do that, Mr. Harris, but as of now, the evidence isn't stacking up in your favor and I'm afraid we're going to bring you into the police station for some answers to some hard questions: home invasion, possible kidnapping, public disorder, and threat of battery or assault to name a few. This isn't to be taken lightly. I hope you understand that."

"...Kidnapping?" I respond, confused and fearful.

"According to Wisconsin law, a person committing the crime of kidnapping is a 'Class C' felony. It's when the threat of imminent force carries a person from one place to another without their consent, or deceitfully induces someone to go from one place to another with intent to cause them to secretly confine or imprison or hold to service against their will. In this case, Suzy has stated that she didn't want to be here."

"You've got to be kidding me!"

"As an officer of the law, I can assure you that I'm not kidding you, Mr.

Harris. Now, please, if you will, can you make this easy for us and follow us out to the car?"

Once again, I nod my head, reluctantly.

I feel the cold handcuffs clamp around my wrist, and they put me in the back of the police car. Suddenly, I'm in the center of some terrible, terrible scenario that I never could've imagined that I ever would've been in, and all I can seem to think about is this is how Frank Sinatra must've felt when he was arrested in Bergen County in 1938 for having a sexual relationship with a married woman. *Good grief. How awful.* I glance around the police car not really seeing anything at all with a feeling of deep melancholy and intense adrenaline.

I look out the window at the Hawthorne's house and I see the shadowy man, he's faceless, I can see that now, wearing a crisp, tailored suit and that purple glow in the sky deepened.

His presence follows me as the car takes off.

IN THE SHADOW OF THE SEAM

392 W. HAWTHORNE DRIVE

by Robert Birkhofer

Sunday. October 25th.

—*Sketching*—

Esther sat outside the Milwaukee Art Museum, perched on a bench along the shore of Lake Michigan. Marigold skies above reflected in unperturbed waters below, and between the two sat Esther, eating her dinner and watching the day die.

Esther had visited the museum to see a special exhibition featuring the woodblock prints of Hokusai, the Japanese artist. Specifically, she had wanted to see *The Great Wave off Kanagawa*, Hokusai's most famous work, in person. She had spent all afternoon standing in front of the image, lost in its every detail.

In the print, a blue behemoth of a wave towered over three fishing boats. The wave reared its foamy crest and spat briny spray at the sailors below it. The men on the boats were resolute, but surely doomed, because the wave was poised to crash down on them with all the fury of the sea.

On her bench outside the museum, Esther ate a few berries and listened to the gentle undulations of Lake Michigan. She took a sip from her green smoothie and tried to imagine what the *Great Wave* must have sounded like as it engulfed the fishermen and their boats, claiming them all for the deep.

"Nice pants."

Esther choked on her mouthful of smoothie. She hadn't even noticed the stranger approach her bench. "I—I'm sorry?"

"Those are nice pants," the woman repeated. "Where'd you get them?"

"Oh, um." Esther cleared her throat. "I made them, actually. I'm a clothing designer. I have a shop just around the corner."

The newcomer was a handful of years older than Esther—late thirties, maybe—and from her jacket to her boots, she was dressed completely in gray.

"Tore my favorite pair of pants at work the other day," the woman said. "Was a real bitch."

Esther smiled apologetically. "Life's a bitch, right?"

The woman snorted. "Life is bullshit, is what it is." And then, without asking for or waiting for an invitation, she sat down beside Esther and gazed out at the water. "Don't mind if I smoke, do you?"

Esther did mind, but she didn't say anything. Instead, she ate another berry and studied the stranger on her bench out of the corner of her eye. Like Esther, the woman was slender and had short hair. Unlike Esther's neat buzz, however, the older woman had more of an unkempt pixie, and it was a lighter shade than Esther's raven. Her all-gray look wasn't an entirely unpleasing aesthetic, but she would have benefited from a splash of color in there somewhere.

"What, um, kind of work do you do?" Esther ventured, for lack of a better thing to say.

The stranger sighed out a smoky cloud, looked at Esther, and with more than a little pride, said, "I kill ghosts. Send the fucking cunts straight back to wherever the hell."

Esther opened her mouth to reply, could think of nothing to say, and closed it again.

"Most ghosts are harmless, but there are some murderous ones out there, just like there are murderers among us here in life. Stalkers and psychos that prey on the helpless. My team and I track those ghosts down, and then we *put* them down."

Esther took a drink from her smoothie.

"Most people don't even know they're being haunted until it's too late," the woman went on. "There are lots of early warning signs, but people usually don't recognize them for what they are. Pictures that won't hang straight, mirrors that don't reflect right, lights that flicker. Haven't noticed anything like that at your place, have you?"

"Um, no."

"Well, like I said," the lady in gray went on, "life is bullshit. But I figure that if I can bring a little bit of order to all the chaos in this messy world...then maybe it will all be worth it in the end. Life, I mean. Killing ghosts is my way of bringing order."

Light had been steadily fleeing the sky above the two women. Esther made a show of looking at her watch and making an *oh-is-that-what-time-it-is?* noise. "I should, um, probably get going."

"Yeah. Good talk. Hey, I'm Dimeter by the way."

"Esther," Esther replied, extending her hand. After they shook, Esther discovered that Dimeter had pressed a small card into her palm.

"If you notice anything weird," Dimeter said, nodding at the card, "call me."

Esther nodded.

After Dimeter had walked away, Esther looked down at the business card she held. It was creased in the middle, and one of the corners was folded over. It said:

THE WATCHERS
Experts in paranormal activity
Experienced ghost exterminators

On the back, there was a phone number. Because Esther didn't want Dimeter to see her tossing it in the trash, she slipped the card into her purse.

As Esther finished her supper, the sky above her faded to black. The reflections in the water surrendered their glittering luster to the night, until all that remained were murmuring waves in the darkness.

Monday. October 26th.
— Selecting Fabric —

West Hawthorne Drive was not without its quirks, but to Esther, it was home. Gliding down the short street and around the cul-de-sac on her rollerblades, she thought about what the stranger in gray had said the evening before.

The truth was, many of Esther's neighbors *did* believe in ghosts. Many of them claimed to have experienced things on Hawthorne Drive that could only be attributed to supernatural activity. Esther hadn't lived on the street very long, but had never seen or heard anything out of the ordinary for herself. She had never believed in ghost stories, and she wasn't about to start.

As she breezed into her driveway, Esther clutched her arms across her chest to guard against the gathering chill of the autumn afternoon. The house at 392 West Hawthorne Drive, nestled right at the base of the cul-de-sac, was a pale sandy color. The red trim needed to be repainted, but it didn't bother Esther — it gave the home a weathered, lived-in look.

Halfway to her front porch, Esther noticed a white, fluffy something prowling around her bushes. Looking closer, she saw that it was one of her next-door neighbors' cats. Esther often saw him sitting in the window, but had never seen him outside before. Esther called out, which resulted in the animal promptly disappearing into the greenery.

With a sigh, Esther kicked off her rollerblades and got down on her hands and knees beside the bushes. She racked her brain for the name of the cat, because she knew her neighbors had told her once. Was it Brandon? No. *Bentley.*

"Come on, Bentley! It's okay! Are you in there?"

It wasn't until Esther dangled her sweatshirt's drawstring back and forth near the ground that Bentley finally slunk out, belly low and eyes wide. He was a handsome animal — all white except for his blond tail. He reached out a paw to bat the string, and Esther gingerly picked him up.

Clutching Bentley in her arms, Esther walked across the lawn in her socks to her neighbors' front door. She had always liked the couple who lived in the yellow house next to hers. They had done their best to make her feel welcome on Hawthorne Drive, and they were cat people, which was usually a good thing.

After returning Bentley to his owners and graciously refusing the two men's invitation to join them inside for a cup of coffee, Esther hurried back to her own porch to collect her rollerblades. Her feet were cold, and she was anxious for a hot shower.

Just as she was reaching for her doorknob, the light around Esther suddenly dimmed. Confused, she looked up and gasped.

Something was falling out of the sky. Rather, *nothing* was falling out of the sky, but the extent to which it was nothing had made it something. A spot of intense blackness was descending directly toward her, sucking up all the light around it as it fell, the way a sponge absorbs water.

Esther didn't have time to react. As the thing plummeted down on her, she was suddenly enveloped in perfect, absolute darkness. She felt the falling object brush past her arm, touching her briefly and sending a piercing electric shock through her body. Esther cried out, took a step, and lost her balance in the arrant blackness.

As she fell, Esther couldn't see a thing, but squeezed her eyes shut anyway and slammed into the concrete surface of the porch. Pain shot through her wrist, tears exploded from beneath her eyelids, and all the air left her lungs in a great *whoosh*. Rolling onto her back, Esther grasped her arm and found that it was slippery.

She opened her eyes.

Late afternoon sun shone down. Blood from her arm seeped through her fingers. She looked around for the thing that had fallen, but there was nothing on her porch apart from the rollerblades she had dropped.

Next door, Bentley was sitting in his window, swishing his blond tail and watching her with wide eyes. No one else had seen her fall.

Esther pushed herself to her feet, stumbled into her house, and picked her way upstairs to the bathroom. As she waited for the shower to heat up, she cradled her arm and watched the blood soak into her shirt. She felt lightheaded, and had to make an effort to remain standing. Finally, she peeled off her clothes and stepped into the hot flow of water.

The whole of her lower arm was skinned badly, and Esther lathered it with soap as gently as she could. Strangely, it was her upper arm that hurt the most, even though there wasn't a single bruise or scratch above her elbow. Esther was sure that it was her upper arm that had been shocked by the falling shadow-object. Struck by another sudden wave of dizziness, Esther leaned against the wall of the shower, and suddenly froze.

The smallest of sounds had come from outside the bathroom. It had almost sounded like the house making its house noises — creaking and shifting and sighing. Almost.

Esther whispered a terrified curse to herself and shut off the water, trying desperately to remember if she had locked the front door.

Stepping out of the shower, Esther wrapped a towel around her still-bleeding arm. She again heard the low noise that sounded like the house but was not the house. It seemed to be coming from the opposite side of the hallway, from inside her sewing room.

Esther's heart was in her throat as she crept across the carpeted hall and slowly turned the doorknob. She opened the door to the sewing room just a crack, and peered through to see someone inside.

Esther clapped a hand over her mouth to keep from screaming. She could tell that the person in the sewing room was a woman, even though her face was turned away. The intruder was crouched under a table, almost as if hiding from something.

Abruptly, the woman darted from under the table and rushed toward the door. Panicked, Esther backed away, acutely aware that the only thing she was wearing was a towel wrapped around her arm.

The almost-house noise came again, louder and more drawn out, a lengthy series of creaks and pops and groans. A feeling of extreme terror hit Esther like a physical thing. The intruder bolted straight past her and off down the hallway, and Esther knew that she was running from whatever was making the sound. Esther turned to run after her, but caught her foot on the doorframe and for the second time that night, crashed gracelessly to the ground.

The noise was close now — so close — unbearably loud. Esther scuttled backward, crab-like, desperate to get away. She drew her knees up to her chest, pressed her palms over her ears, and screamed as loud as she could.

And then the noise was gone.

Esther lay there in the hallway, breathing. The towel had fallen off her arm, and water and blood pervaded the carpet. Silence reigned.

Esther played back the image of the intruder rushing past her. The woman who had been hiding in the sewing room had not had a face. It wasn't that that Esther hadn't *seen* her face, for she had looked directly into the woman's eyes as she had run past. Only, there had been no eyes. There had been no features at all. In place of a face, there had just been a dark pall, as if a shadow had run by.

Furthermore, the door to the sewing room was still open just a crack. How had the woman managed to get out without throwing the door wide?

And what had made that noise?

Tuesday. October 27th.
— *Draping* —

Esther frowned as she backed from her driveway in the early hours of the morning, because the van was parked across the street again. It was a big van that had swing-open doors in the rear, the type supposedly driven by serial killers. The van always appeared after dark and left before sunrise, and there was no pattern to the nights it was present. It had first shown up several weeks ago, and Esther had never once seen anyone get into or out of it. It simply sat on the curb all night, directly across from her driveway.

As Esther drove the short distance to the mouth of Hawthorne Drive, she eyed the van in her rearview mirror. Parked as it was in the shadows, she could never be sure of its exact color, but it was a dark and dreary shade that matched its nocturnal tendencies.

Shaking her head, Esther rubbed her arm and turned the corner.

She hadn't slept much after the episode in her sewing room. She had gone through the house and checked all her doors and windows several times, but they had all been locked. There was simply no way a trespasser could have gotten in. By the time Esther had finally drifted off, she had half-convinced herself that there had been no intruder, and that the whole thing had been a hallucination brought on by trauma and loss of blood.

Headlights blurred together on the 94 as Esther drove toward downtown Milwaukee. The pain in her upper arm was making it difficult to concentrate, and she kept having to guide her car back into the center of her lane.

As she so often did when tired or confused, Esther thought of her mom.

Why did you leave?

For the most part, Esther's early childhood had been happy. She had spent it drawing dresses with her crayons and hand-stitching baggy outfits for her dolls. Her mom had always taken the time to inspect and praise each of Esther's creations. Fashion had been something Esther could share with her mother, even before Esther knew what fashion was.

Was I not enough?

It was no surprise to anyone that, when Esther grew up, she became a fashion designer. She bought a little boutique in downtown Milwaukee, called it Threads, and launched her first line of streetwear. She wondered then, as she still did, if her mom would be proud of her.

How will I know, if you're not here to tell me?

One evening, when Esther had been six, she had heard her parents fighting—something that had been completely foreign to her. It was scary. They threw things against the walls and shouted words at each other that Esther didn't understand. She was in her room, coloring with her crayons. She didn't know what to do, so she just listened and cried.

Eventually, Esther's mom stomped out of the house, screaming the whole time that she was never coming back. Her dad slammed the door so hard behind her that a doll on Esther's dresser fell over.

Her mom took the car and drove less than five miles when a drunk driver swerved into her lane and hit her head-on.

At the funeral, Esther had cried, of course, but for a different reason than everyone else. Everyone knew that her mother had left the living world, but Esther also knew that her mom had left *her*.

Who am I, without you?

Esther pulled into the gravel parking lot of her boutique and turned the car off. Threads was small, and it was wedged between a tattoo parlor and a florist. The building was old and finicky, but it was Esther's space to do with as she wanted, to fill with all her own creations.

Hokusai did woodblock prints—Esther did clothes. Each was an art form all its own. Another thing that Esther would never forget about her mom was that the woman had loved *The Great Wave off Kanagawa*.

Esther had grown up surrounded by dish towels, notebooks, and coffee mugs adorned with the image of the towering wave. Esther supposed that when she visited the art museum on Sunday to see Hokusai's print in person, she had really just been trying to feel close to her mom.

Midmorning, Esther was refolding a stack of shirts. The little bell above the door had been jingling steadily as people came and went, and Esther was pleased with the sales so far. She paused to rub at her arm. There were still no marks on her skin where the falling object had touched her, but the pain was only getting worse.

"What's up with your arm?"

Esther jumped, but she recognized the voice, especially since it was accompanied by a faint smoky smell. The woman from the park bench stood behind her, dressed again in gray, holding a small mountain of clothing in her arms.

"Oh, um, hi Dimeter." Esther did her best to smile.

The other woman nodded, indicating her armload. "Found some new pants. Other things too. Look like good clothes."

"Yeah, I, um…thanks." Esther eyed the heap of garments Dimeter held. It looked as though she had gone through the store and picked out every gray piece of clothing in the place. "Let me help you with those," Esther said, leading Dimeter to the register.

As Esther was ringing up her purchases, Dimeter said, "I liked watching the sunset with you."

Esther itched at her arm. Like so much of what came out of Dimeter's mouth, she simply wasn't sure how to respond.

Dimeter was undeterred. "You know, when I was little, we had this window that faced the west. I used to sit there every evening, making up names for all the different colors I saw in the sky."

"That's nice." Esther smiled.

"Yeah, it was." A pause, and then, "When I was eleven, everyone in my family died. Parents, brothers, all of them, just..." She snapped her fingers. "Everyone but me."

"Oh," Esther stammered. "I—"

"You don't have to say sorry," Dimeter cut in. "It's implied."

"Well...I lost my mom," Esther supplied. "When I was six. Car crash."

Dimeter shook her head. "Damned travesty, isn't it? Life, I mean. So...fucking cold. Utter bullshit, you know?"

Esther rubbed her arm.

"So," Dimeter asked again, "what's up with your arm?"

Esther dropped her hands to the register and mumbled something about how the Wisconsin winters dried her skin out.

Dimeter gave her a searching look, made a *huh* sound in her throat, and finally said, "Damned right about that. So, think about what I said? Notice anything weird back home you want me to check out?"

Esther frowned and met the woman's eyes for a moment. "Um, no."

"Okay. Cool. Well, call me if anything comes up, okay?"

Esther nodded.

"Hey, thanks for the clothes. I needed these, you know?"

Esther managed a smile. "Thanks for coming in, Dimeter."

That evening, after Esther had drunk a green smoothie and eaten a handful of nuts for dinner, she ventured upstairs to her sewing room. She wasn't keen on going inside, but she was determined to find some evidence that there *had* been a trespasser in her home the evening before. Esther pushed open the sewing room door and flicked on the light.

Everything was in its place. Her table was there, with her machine and her patterns and her samples. Her dress form was there, wearing a draped and pinned bit of muslin. Her tools were all there, her tech packs were there, her fabric was there. Even her poster of the Versaces — wait. Her poster.

On the wall, Esther had hung a black and white poster of Gianni and Donatella smiling on the runway ahead of a train of models. Only, the poster was no longer black and white. It was purple. Blinking, Esther realized she wasn't seeing the poster itself, but a reflection in the glass of the frame. She saw jagged spars of wood that looked like rafters, and through them, a deep violet sky.

Esther took a step forward, and the reflection vanished.

Retreating to where she had stood before, she tried to position her head at exactly the same angle it had been. Her arm was in agony, as if there were something beneath her skin trying to get out.

The reflection of the purple sky came back into focus, but this time it showed more than just beams of wood in the foreground. It showed a person standing right behind Esther, looming over her. Esther yelled and whirled around, but there was no one there.

When she turned back to the poster, the reflection was again gone, and try as she might, Esther could not reconjure it. The only thing in the frame was the image of the smiling Versaces—a captured moment, frozen in time.

Wednesday. October 28th.
—Pattern-Making—

Esther stared at the creased business card lying on the counter. The day had dragged, and sales had been slow. Esther's last customer had left thirty minutes ago, and in another thirty, she would be able to close for the night. Threads was quiet as a half-forgotten thought.

Esther had decided that she wasn't going home. She couldn't endure another sleepless night, tossing on her bed while being haunted by visions of shadowy figures and velvet skies. She had a little cot in her workroom at the back of the store. She would arm the security system, cover herself with a blanket, and hopefully, pass out until the morning.

But what then? What about the next night? Esther ran a hand over her buzzed scalp. It was greasy—she could really use a shower.

Esther flipped the business card over, where the Watchers' phone number was printed on the back. Maybe her neighbors were right. Maybe Hawthorne Drive *was* haunted.

Esther's phone was in her hand. She was actually dialing the area code of the number on the card when the bell above the store's door jingled, startling her so badly that she swore out loud.

The biggest man Esther had ever seen was entering her boutique. Was she imagining it, or did he actually have to duck to get through the door? His suit jacket was buttoned in the front and well-tailored. He looked about as sturdy as the sugar maple tree that grew in her front yard back home.

Esther greeted the man in the cheeriest voice she could muster, but he didn't seem to have heard her.

"Um, can I help you find anything?" Esther tried again.

The man's eyes flicked over to hers for the barest of moments. They were shiny and sharp as sewing shears. Still, he said nothing.

"You'll 'ave to 'scuse 'im," said a dry and dusty voice. "My friend, 'e doesn't say much."

Esther hadn't even seen the second man enter the store, insignificant as he seemed next to his companion. He was infinitely older and smaller than the first.

Esther glanced at the time. "Are you gentlemen shopping for yourselves today, or looking for gifts?"

Like the big fellow's, the second man's suit was impeccably tailored, and the navy-blue fabric was the perfect shade to complement their dark skin. But Esther could see a few threadbare edges, now that she was looking, a few worn and faded spots. If the two men were hoping to buy new formalwear, they had come to the wrong place.

"I s'pose you could say we're shopping for th' world," the old man answered in his gravelly voice. "And for th' space beyond th' world. And for th' poor souls who've lost their way there'bouts."

"Oh." Esther closed her mouth. Opened and closed it again. "Oh."

"But I'm getting ahead of myself." The man ran a wrinkled hand over a rack of garments. "I must say, Miss Esther, these are fine clothes."

Esther smiled and muttered a thank you.

"Folks call me Buddy," the old man rasped, "and this is Barima. Came as soon as we could, but we 'ad such a very long way to travel. We know you've 'ad a rough couple of days, 'aven't you, Miss Esther?"

"Um." Esther cleared her throat. "How do you know?"

"Well, when certain things 'appen, there are signs. We d'cipher th' signs and follow where they lead. In this case, they led us to you."

"I've been…" Esther took a deep breath. "Seeing things. Hearing things. Feeling things." The words were out of her mouth before she could stop them.

The old man nodded his head knowingly.

"Can you tell me what is happening to me?" Esther asked, hopeful and afraid.

Buddy smiled then, and it was a sad, Indian summer sort of smile, a smile that was warm despite being well-acquainted with the icy sting of pain.

"I can do my best," the old man began. "You see, those of us who inhabit this earth — living our lives, going about our business — do so in our bodies. Our bodies are th' shells that carry th' essence of who we are. When we face death, our shell crumbles, but our essence passes on."

"Passes on to where?" Esther asked.

Buddy spread his arms, smiled again, and simply said, "Beyond."

Esther blinked and nodded.

"Now, sometimes," Buddy went on, "when a shell crumbles, th' essence doesn't make it to where it needs to go. Unable to reach th' beyond, but also unable to inhabit th' living world without a shell, th' poor souls become trapped somewhere in between. They become ghosts."

Esther nodded again, more hesitantly this time. All the while Buddy had been talking, his companion, Barima, had stood perfectly still, staring at her with those glittering eyes.

"Most of th' time, we can't perceive ghosts," Buddy said, "nor they, us. But in some areas, areas that 'ave been witness to great amounts of pain or despair, th' bound'ries between our world and theirs 'ave been worn thin. Th' street you live on, Miss Esther, is one such place."

"So, um, you're saying that on Hawthorne Drive, ghosts can come into our world?"

"No," Buddy replied. "They will never be able to cross back into th' living world, but they can interact with it. Interact with *us*."

"Um," Esther asked, "what is this place called? This place where people get trapped after they die and turn into ghosts?"

"It's more of a place *between* places, Miss Esther, not so much of a place itself."

"Well," Esther replied, "a place has got to have a name, doesn't it? Even if it's just, um, a place between places."

"I s'pose you're right, and I s'pose it does," Buddy conceded in his gritty voice. "But such things are beyond our knowledge. Beyond even what we ought to consider. These are dangerous and mysterious subjects that we dabble in, Miss Esther."

"It's the shadow of a seam," Esther said, almost cheerily, because she could finally relate all that Buddy was saying to something she knew very well.

"Come again?" Buddy asked.

"Follow me." Esther locked the front door of the boutique, turned off the lighted sign, and led the two men through the store and into her workroom.

Esther rummaged through her half-completed projects, shoving aside scraps of muslin and tulle, until she found a sample of a green dress that she had begun sewing a black waistband to.

"Okay," she said, holding the garment-in-progress up so that Buddy and Barima could see the thin line of stitching that was holding the waistband in place. "A seam is where two pieces of material are joined together. It's essentially the space between the two pieces of fabric."

Buddy leaned in close to look. "It's not much of a space, is it Barima?" he asked. Barima, of course, said nothing.

"The green fabric," Esther continued, "is where we are now, the living world. The black fabric is the beyond. Between the two, the seam, is the place inhabited by the ghosts."

Esther lay the material on her worktable, folded the black waistband over itself, and pressed it into the seamline. "When you stitch in the shadow of the seam, you secure your piece of fabric by sewing it directly into the existing stitching. It's a finishing touch that, when done properly, will hide the seam from view. Most people call it stitching in the ditch, but stitching in the shadow of the seam always sounded more artistic to me."

Esther glanced up at Buddy and Barima, who were looking at her intently. "That's what you're describing, isn't it? A place that is normally hidden from view. In areas like Hawthorne Drive, the seam has become visible." Esther unfolded the waistband, revealing the stitches again.

The two men shared a look, and something imperceptible passed between them. "That was quite astute, Miss Esther," Buddy said.

Esther shrugged, looked down, and smiled.

Buddy drew in a deep, rattling breath, and said, "Now, Miss Esther, there was an object that fell onto your prop'rty somewhere — it's what led us to you. Your proximity to it 'as made you more sens'tive to th'…well, to th' seam. *That's* why you've been seeing things. *That's* why you've been 'earing things. You've been bearing witness to events 'appening in th' seam."

Esther reached up to touch the aching spot on her upper arm and winced.

"Miss Esther, are you quite a'right?"

"Well, um, when that thing fell on me —"

Buddy made a spluttering noise and had to grasp the edge of Esther's worktable for support. Even Barima's stony features took on a new intensity.

"Miss Esther…we…you…do you mean to say…it touched you? It actu'lly…"

"Um." Esther nodded. She was suddenly worried. "What does that mean? What was that thing?"

"That *thing* is th' key to ev'rything, and it's what Barima and I are after. It is a rare natural phenom'non found within th' seam." Buddy sat down in a nearby chair. "Th' fact that that it touched you, Miss Esther, means…well, it means that you now share a connection to th' seam, that you carry a part of th' seam within you. And it means, unless we are very much mistaken, that you can *enter* th' seam."

Esther remained silent.

"It is th' goal of Barima and myself to eventu'lly destroy th' seam. We want to 'elp th' essence of all those trapped there to pass on. Th' object—th' phenom'non—is th' means to doing that."

"Where did the seam come from?" Esther asked. "If it can be destroyed, it must have been created somehow, right?"

A darkness passed over Buddy's features. He hid it well, but Esther had seen it. Rather than answering, Buddy said, "We need your 'elp, Miss Esther. Would you do us th' great honor of lending us your aid?"

Esther thought about it, or at least, she thought about thinking about it. But the truth was, these two gentlemen had begun to give her answers, and in the process, had begun to give her hope. And, she couldn't say why, but she liked them.

"If you help me," Esther said, cupping a hand over her arm, "I'll help you."

Buddy's smile crinkled his whole face.

Thursday. October 29th.
—Sewing—

Standing over the bathroom sink in Threads, Esther turned off the water and dried her face. As planned, she had spent the night in the workroom. In a few minutes, she would be meeting Buddy and Barima, and they would return to Hawthorne Drive together.

Esther clutched her arm and squeezed as tightly as she could, trying to lessen the pain. For a few seconds, she allowed herself to wish that she had accepted her neighbors' invitation to join them for coffee after returning Bentley. If she would have had done that, if she would have just been a few minutes later getting back to her porch, she wouldn't have been touched by the falling phenomenon.

Cocking her head at herself in the bathroom mirror, Esther wondered what the world saw when it looked at her. She was just another misguided thirty-something—too edgy, too skinny, too pale. Badly in need of a shower and anything but normal. To make matters worse, she had a sliver of a supernatural realm stuck beneath her skin.

"To hell with it all," Esther finally said aloud. "Normal be damned, and wishes along with it."

She jammed a baseball hat on her head, swallowed a few ibuprofens, and left the bathroom.

After giving instructions to her assistant manager, Esther waited outside Threads for Buddy and Barima. Upon arrival, they were dressed exactly as the night before, in their navy-colored suits. Esther climbed into the back of the gentlemen's vehicle, leaving her car in the parking lot.

When they arrived at 392 West Hawthorne Drive, Esther glimpsed Bentley sitting in his window next door, swishing his blond tail and watching them. Esther instructed Barima to pull around and park instead in the back alley. She hardly ever parked in the alley, but she didn't want any neighbors to see her going through the front door with two strange men in tow. Esther still wasn't sure what the two strange men in question planned to do in the house, and a part of her still couldn't believe she had agreed to let them into her home.

As Esther showed Buddy and Barima inside, she was suddenly conscious of the dishes left in the sink, the clothes lying scattered about, and the place's general need for a good cleaning. She began to wonder if this had perhaps not been the best idea after all.

"So, um, what do we do?" Esther asked.

Buddy and Barima proceeded to survey the house. They measured the wall-to-wall distance of some rooms, the floor-to-ceiling height of others. They rapped on windows with their knuckles, bent over and put their ears against the kitchen countertops, and even cut out a tiny section of carpet from the living room. All the while, Esther hovered in the background, massaging her arm and watching the two men work, nervous and curious at the same time.

When morning had passed to afternoon, Buddy and Esther sat down.

"Miss Esther," he asked, "would you be willing to try and enter th' seam?"

Esther raised her eyebrows. "What? Now? Why?"

"Don't be alarmed! We just want to test your connection, that's all. If all goes well, maybe you can 'elp us gather some data later on."

"Um, how do I get there?" she asked.

"You should be able to flit between th' seam and th' living world at will, anywhere in th' 'ouse," Buddy said. "But your sens'tivity to th' seam will be th' greatest in th' places where you've already 'sperienced it. Maybe we could try in your sewing room?"

As Esther followed Buddy upstairs, he said, "Remember, we just want to test your connection. Once you get in, take a look around and come back out."

"Will you be able to see me? Speak to me?" Esther asked.

"So long as you stay close, yes," replied Buddy. "We'll be able to see a shadow form of you. And you should be able to see th' same of us."

"But what do I *do*? To get there?"

"Focus on th' spot where your arm 'urts, Miss Esther. That's where your connection resides. Conc'ntrate on it, feel it, and follow th' connection."

Esther stood in the middle of her sewing room and closed her eyes.

She directed all her thought to the area of her arm touched by the otherworldly phenomenon. This of course only made her more acutely aware of the throbbing pain. But to Esther's surprise, she also felt something else, a threadlike trickle of…energy…flowing into her. Esther focused on the tremulous link and followed it with her mind. As she did, a change came over the air around her.

Esther opened her eyes.

The bright colors of her sewing room faded away, to be replaced by murky darkness. Almost immediately, the murk began to resolve itself into shapes. Her sewing room faded back into focus all around her, but it was different. Esther looked down at her hands. *She* looked the same, but her sewing room did not. The walls were dilapidated, the floor was moldy, and through the rotted rafters, light from a violet sky shone down.

Esther was so shocked that she promptly lost her focus and faded back into the living world.

"You 'ad it, Miss Esther!" Buddy was practically bouncing with excitement. "You 'ad it!"

Esther closed her eyes, again following the strange energy with her mind, again feeling a change in the air as she faded from the living world. This time, when she opened her eyes, she was ready.

The seam mirrored the world she lived in, except that in the seam, everything was dead. Huge chunks of the walls, floors, and ceilings were missing from the ruined husk of her house.

Esther looked at where Buddy and Barima stood. She could still see them, but they appeared now as two shadows, one much larger than the other.

"I did it!" Esther shouted. "I'm here!"

"Now, take a look around th' room, Miss Esther, and come back out!" Buddy's voice was muffled, as if he was speaking in a separate room and Esther was hearing him through the wall.

Esther explored the parallel sewing room slowly at first, then with more curiosity. All her things were there, albeit in severe states of deterioration — she even found a twisted chunk of plastic and metal that she identified as her sewing machine. An entire world that only she had access to was at her fingertips. It was her world to discover. Esther called out, "I'm going downstairs now!"

"No, Miss Esther — best to stay close!"

But she was already in the hallway. She felt good, better than she had all week. Better, in fact, than she had in a while.

Esther descended the stairs, being careful to avoid the gaping holes in the floor. Once on ground level, Esther walked straight through one of the jagged tears in the wall. Outside, the velvet sky had no sun, but seemed to produce its own light, which cast everything in dim shadow. Esther's feet crunched over dried grass as she walked along the perimeter of the house. When she stepped around the corner and saw the front of the building, she stopped.

The front half of the porch was gone. Not gone in the way that sections of the walls and roof were gone — the outer rails of the porch had been swallowed by a darkness so absolute that it hurt Esther's eyes to look directly at it. As she approached the lightless area, Esther squinted. She knew that the thing sought by Buddy and Barima, the ethereal phenomenon that connected her to the seam, lay in the center of the shadow.

Esther got down on her hands and knees at the shadow's edge and reached inside it. She couldn't even see her own hand. She felt around, reaching farther and farther, until her fingers brushed against a small object. A wild, electric thrill surged through her body, and she jerked her hand back out.

From a far way off, Esther heard the almost-house noise, a long string of pops and groans.

She rolled back on her heels and adjusted her hat as she looked around. Cold tendrils of unease crept into the pit of her stomach. She realized for the first time that she couldn't actually see very far in the seam. Even the spot where she knew her neighbors' house was in the living world, the one owned by Oxford, Teddy, and their cats, was just an ambiguous shape at the edge of her vision.

Esther got to her feet. The sound came again, louder, and it almost seemed like the roar of an animal. In the violet-colored haze obscuring the house next-door, something huge was moving, *running*. Esther could sense it heaving and pitching like an indomitable wave — coming, coming, coming. Terror flooded through her. Every instinct in her body screamed at her to *get away*.

Esther turned and ran. "Help me! Help me!" she shouted, though she knew Buddy and Barima could not hear her.

Esther flew around the corner and through the hole in the wall, looking back as she did at the enormous creature barreling toward her, getting closer, bellowing with that horrible creaking-popping roar. She saw it for an instant, matted fur and snarling teeth and bulging yellow eyes.

Esther hurtled up the stairs and into the sewing room. She threw herself on the floor, closed her eyes, and desperately tried to isolate the sensation in her arm so that she could follow the connection back to the living world.

"Take me back, take me back, take me back," she whimpered.

Esther envisioned the table with her sewing machine, the dress form draped in muslin, the poster of Gianni and Donatella. She concentrated with all her being on her throbbing arm. The air began to change. The roar was deafening.

Something gripped Esther's shoulders with crushing strength. She thrashed and kicked, sure she was about to be ripped to pieces, still trying frantically to visualize the sewing room where she yearned to be.

"Miss Esther! Miss Esther!" croaked Buddy.

Esther opened her eyes. Barima was pinning her to the ground, trying to hold her still.

"Buddy, what the hell was —"

"Shh!" the old man cut her off. His eyes were wide. "There's someone in th' 'ouse!"

"Of course there is! In the seam, I just saw —"

"No, no." Buddy made placating gestures, trying to get her to be quiet. "Someone *alive* is in your 'ouse!"

Esther immediately lay still.

"Miss Esther, do you know these folks?" Buddy whispered, beckoning to her from beside the sewing room's window.

Esther crawled across the room and peered over the windowsill. The van from the street was parked in her driveway, as close as it could get to her house. Seeing it in the daylight for the first time, Esther could now tell that its color was gray. As she watched, Dimeter jumped out of the vehicle's rear double doors. She was dressed in her new clothes from Threads, and had a wide variety of satchels and packs strapped to her body. She glanced up at the house, and Esther quickly ducked down.

"They're some sort of ghost-hunting company," Esther whispered. "The Watchers, they're called."

She chanced another look outside. A new individual had gotten out of the van to join Dimeter. He too was clad in gray, and he wore a backpack with a long, flexible tube attached to a device held in his hand.

"Who do they think they are—the Ghostbusters?" Esther asked. And then she was struck with understanding. "We parked in the alley. And my car is still at the store. They don't know we're here!"

Buddy and Barima shared a long look. The two men seemed able to communicate without words, like best friends in a TV show.

Just then, a noise came from within the house downstairs, and Esther asked, "Did you say one of them is *inside*?"

Buddy nodded solemnly and Barima produced a very long pistol from somewhere in his jacket.

"Barima, what are you doing?" Esther hissed.

The giant man left the room in a half-crouch, making less noise than a cat on the prowl.

Esther looked at Buddy, who said in a low voice, "'E's going to tell these tresp'ssers to leave."

Esther very much doubted Barima planned on saying anything, but she remained huddled out of sight next to Buddy.

Several minutes dragged by, and then—sounds from downstairs. The erratic rhythm of shuffling feet. A loud thump and a shout of pain. A crash. Silence.

Through the window, Esther saw Dimeter motion to the man beside her. He made an adjustment to the hose on his backpack and rushed into the house, where his cry of surprise was abruptly cut short by the sound of thunder.

Esther tried to breathe. She peered outside to see Dimeter taking cover behind the van, staring up at her through the sewing room window. Their eyes met, and Esther saw shocked rage on the other woman's features. Esther ducked and heard the van's engine fire to life, followed by squealing tires. When she dared to look over the windowsill again, the van was speeding away down Hawthorne Drive.

Jumping to her feet, Esther rushed out of the sewing room and down the stairs.

She found Barima in the front hall, standing over an unmoving, gray-clothed form. Behind the unmoving form, little dark red droplets had been spattered along the walls. A second motionless figure could be seen lying in the living room off the hall. Esther screamed.

"What the hell, Barima! You killed them!" Esther didn't know what else to say. "You killed them!"

"Just shells." Buddy had followed her downstairs. He was wearing his sad, knowing smile, and his voice was even more gravelly than usual.

"I don't...I just..."

"There, there, Miss Esther. Why don't you come away from all...this."

"Don't touch me!" Esther recoiled from the hand Buddy offered, but allowed him to usher her into the kitchen, where she pulled a chair back from the table and collapsed into it.

"Don't mind if I make us a little something, do you?" Buddy asked.

Numb from what she had just witnessed, Esther simply shrugged. Buddy took her indifference as an invitation to start bustling about the kitchen. After what could have been several minutes or several hours, he set a steaming cup of tea before Esther. After placing a second cup on the table for himself, Buddy unbuttoned his jacket and sat down.

Esther stared at the tea in silence, dimly aware of Barima's hulking form moving slowly past the kitchen doorway. She didn't want to think about what he was doing, so she instead turned her attention to Buddy and said, "In the seam, something chased me."

The old man put down his cup and closed his eyes. "I 'eard it."

"What?" Esther spluttered. "You're telling me you know what that thing was?"

"It's why we didn't want you to stray too far from th' sewing room, Miss Esther." Buddy's shoulders slumped forward. "Th' creature will never be far from th' phenom'non."

"The *creature*?" Esther repeated. All the emotions of the past hour were finally catching up to her. "When were you planning on telling me about this *creature*?!"

"Th' creature is old as time itself," he said softly. "And even older, according to some. It…well, it created th' seam, you see. Th' creature created th' seam to snares souls as they pass from our world to th' next, so that it can feed on them."

"It *feeds* on them?"

"Yes. Th' creature 'unts ghosts through th' seam and feeds on their essence."

"Right." Esther tapped her finger on the table as she tried to wrap her mind around what Buddy was saying. "What's this creature called?"

Buddy opened his mouth, but somehow Esther knew by his expression exactly what he was about to say.

"Got it," she cut him off. "No name, right?"

"All things 'ave names, Miss Esther," Buddy said, almost apologetically, "but not all names should be known, and cert'nly not all names should be uttered aloud."

Esther shook her head. She was aware that Barima had paused his work and was standing just inside the kitchen. What was it with these two and names? She looked icily from one man to the other and asked, "Who are you? What have you gotten me into?"

"We told you that we dabble in dangerous and mysterious subjects, Miss Esther."

"You didn't tell me you were killers!" Esther exploded, slamming a fist onto the table. "I didn't sign up to be an accessory to murder, and I sure as hell didn't sign up to be part of a vendetta against a supernatural fucking monster!"

"But you did sign up to do th' right thing, did you not?"

"The right thing?! What is the right thing, Buddy? Tell me about this *right thing*."

Esther glared at Buddy, and he lowered his eyes.

"It takes a terrible power to destroy a soul," Buddy said slowly, "and this is the power possessed by th' creature. You see, if a ghost dies in th' seam — if th' creature gets them — their journey ends. They never reach th' beyond, and they never receive peace. That's why Barima and I are working to destroy th' seam — to give th' ghosts a chance at peace. Th' creature created th' seam, and therefore, th' seam's 'sistence is tied to that of th' creature. To destroy th' seam, we must kill th' creature."

"And how do you kill an ageless monster that feeds on souls?" Esther asked, almost sarcastically, because the entire situation was growing more absurd by the minute.

"Th' phenom'non contains a power equal to that of th' creature. Th' creature is drawn to th' object, but we don't think it is able to actu'lly touch it. We think th' phenom'non is so powerful that phys'cal contact with it would kill th' creature."

"But I touched it."

"And that may well be th' most miraculous part of all!" Buddy was looking at her with something like wonder. "Th' phenom'non will kill anything in th' seam it touches, ghost or creature. But you — you who are not a true inhabitant of th' seam — can touch it, pick it up, 'andle it."

"Um, okay." A plan had begun to take shape in Esther's mind, but she wasn't sure she liked where it led.

"Our intention was to study th' object," Buddy went on. "Observe it and try to find a way to use it against th' creature from 'ere in th' living world. We never intended to put you in 'arm's way, Miss Esther. But things 'ave esc'lated rather quickly. I 'spect that these...Watchers will surely be back."

"They were trespassing," Esther said as she picked up her phone. "We'll call the police on them."

"There are people who seek to 'sploit th' seam. They are very powerful, and their eyes and ears are ev'rywhere, including within th' police. If these people learn of this street, this 'ouse—if they learn of *you*, Miss Esther…" Buddy shook his head. "No, we cannot call th' police."

Esther set her phone beside her untouched tea. Barima strode across the kitchen and sat down, barely fitting his legs under the table.

"Miss Esther," Buddy asked after a pause, "I wonder if you could tell us what it looked like? Th' creature?"

"It looked like…" Esther trailed off. She realized that she could not form a mental image of the thing that had been chasing her, even though she was sure she had seen it clearly. It was odd—she could remember exactly what everything else looked like from the seam, but not the creature.

"Well…" Esther started again. She thought of the way Hokusai's *Great Wave* reared up, unrelenting and possessed of immeasurable power. She thought of how the three fishing boats under the wave were defenseless against the water's strength. She thought about how the foaming edges of the wave in Hokusai's print looked almost like hundreds of little claws, reaching for the men onboard the boats.

"It looked like a wave," Esther said finally.

Buddy nodded, as if Esther's description was the most logical thing in the world.

"Look," Esther said, "when I'm working on a collection of clothing, I put everything into my garments—every bit of inspiration and every ounce of passion I have. It's tempting to hold back, to save some of it for the next project. But you get into trouble when you do that. If you want your collection to be the best it can be, you have to design and sew and revise like it's the last collection you'll ever make. You have to trust that, when the time comes to start the next one, you'll find new inspiration, have new ideas."

"What are you saying, Miss Esther?" Buddy asked.

"I'm saying that I am in the habit of giving my all to the things I commit to. We have everything here in front of us — we know the monster is close, and we have the means to kill it." Esther looked from Buddy to Barima. "So, let's kill it. I'll enter the seam and grab the phenomenon. When the creature comes, I'll let it get close and then throw the phenomenon at it. The seam will go away, the ghosts will be free, and the Watchers — whatever they want — will have nothing left here. They'll have no choice but to leave. All our problems will be solved."

Barima's eyes glittered even brighter than usual, and Buddy was looking at her with a curious expression.

"Miss Esther, are you quite —"

"Yes," Esther cut him off. "I'm quite sure. We'll do it tomorrow."

Esther lay in her bed, staring at shadows on the ceiling. Buddy's soft, rattling snores came faintly from the guestroom across the hall, and every once in a while, Barima's footfalls were heard pacing past the door as he worked through his perpetual circuit of the house. All else was still.

The three of them had spent the evening in preparation. In the morning, Esther would face the Great Wave.

Unable to sleep, Esther rolled over and retrieved her phone from the nightstand. After searching a few different phrases in her web browser, she began to pull up results for the Watchers. They didn't have a website, but there were plenty of references to them from former customers and fellow paranormal specialists. Just a few days ago, Esther would have scoffed at every single one of them.

The more she read, the more unsettled Esther became. There were reports of accidents, ghost-hunting jobs gone wrong, property destroyed and people hurt. The word *fanatical* was mentioned more than once.

Eventually, Esther found what she was really looking for—information on Dimeter. There was a collection of newspaper articles dated twenty-eight years prior that described how a husband, wife, and three children had all died in their home on a single horrific night. The authorities had declared the cause of death asphyxiation from a gas leak, but the facts didn't all add up, and most journalists had pointed out several holes in the authorities' theory. No one, however, had been able to offer a more plausible explanation.

Esther stared at a grainy photograph scanned from one of the old newspapers. There had been a fourth child, one who had survived. In the picture, a knot of firemen stood around a young girl while lights flashed in the background. The article said Dimeter had been found sitting on the floor, mumbling the names of colors while staring out her bedroom window.

Esther continued her search to find that Dimeter had done an interview with a tabloid at some point during her teenage years. In the interview, Dimeter had claimed that her family was murdered by a ghost, and had insisted that she saw a spectral figure in her childhood home the night they died. The tabloid had discounted Dimeter entirely, sensationalizing her story and painting her as a poor, delusional orphan driven mad by grief.

Esther let her phone screen go dark and thought about what Dimeter had said to her on the park bench beside Lake Michigan. All her talk about tracking and exterminating killer ghosts, about bringing order to a chaotic and messy world, suddenly didn't seem so crazy. Lying awake in the darkness, Esther felt a thread of understanding, and even sympathy, for the lady in gray. But then she remembered the rage with which Dimeter had met her eyes earlier that very day, and shivered.

It was clear that the Watchers had been watching Esther, and perhaps the entire street, for some time. But what had brought them to 392 West Hawthorne Drive? They didn't seem to know about the phenomenon — they were only interested in what was inside the house. But what was inside?

In any event, even if Esther were successful in destroying the seam, Dimeter didn't seem like the type of person who would simply let go and leave them be.

In time, Esther fell into a troubled sleep. She dreamed of waves — beautiful, terrible, brave waves that condemned sailors to their deaths and crushed ships like origami figurines.

Friday. October 30th.
—Model Fitting—

When Buddy shook Esther awake, she had a few moments to wonder if it was very early or very late before a crash echoed through the house, causing her to sit bolt upright. It sounded like the front door had been thrown inward with such force that it had slammed into the opposite wall. Rushing footsteps flooded over the threshold downstairs.

Esther stumbled out of bed, half listening as Buddy told her that the van was back, along with a second, identical vehicle. By the time she followed him to where Barima was crouched at the top of the stairs, the shooting had started.

The Watchers' backpack weapons were nearly silent, but they emitted brilliant shafts of light that illumed the dark house in strobing flashes.

Their fire was directed at the second-floor landing, where Barima responded with single, deliberate shots from his pistol. Esther learned, in those few minutes of pure chaos, what gun smoke smelled like.

"Too loud!" Buddy expressed between blasts. "We'll draw th' author'ties if this keeps up!"

Barima nodded once, ceased firing, and tucked his gun back into his jacket. The Watchers' barrage intensified, blasting photos from the walls and blowing chunks out of Esther's banister.

"I'm going to go now," Esther announced, and both men looked at her. "Whatever's going to happen when the monster dies, it's the only way we have a chance of stopping this madness!"

In one of the dazzling flashes from the Watchers' weapons, Esther saw Buddy looking at his companion. "Barima, old friend, do you think you can escort Miss Esther downstairs?"

"I don't need an escort," Esther said. "I'll be in the seam, so they won't be able to shoot at me. I'll just walk past them."

"Those backpacks of theirs," Buddy replied, "are designed to 'urt ghosts. I'm afraid they'll be able to 'urt you too, even in th' seam."

Esther hadn't thought of that.

"Barima?" Buddy asked again.

The big man nodded without hesitation.

"Okay," Buddy said, turning to Esther. "Barima will clear a path for you in th' living world. Follow 'im in th' seam, but be careful."

Esther looked to Barima, and found that he was watching her with those bright, glittering eyes. She smiled, only a little, but enough to say *I trust you.* She could have sworn she saw his mouth twitch upward in response.

Esther felt the air around her change as she slipped into the seam. The massive shade that was Barima stepped in front of her, protecting her like a shield.

"Alright," Esther said. "I'm ready."

She wasn't ready for what happened next.

Barima launched himself down the stairs, taking them three at a time. He was on the ground floor before the Watchers had time to react. His shadow was a blur — lashing out, spinning, striking — always on the move. Esther hurried down the stairs after him.

The Watchers' cries of surprise and fear were muffled in the seam. Esther could hear Dimeter shouting orders, and finally the Watchers recovered enough to begin shooting again. The volleys from their backpacks resounded through the seam, ear-splittingly loud, much more physical than they had been in the living world.

Barima's shadow ducked and wove, flattened itself against walls, pirouetted like a dancer. More than once, Esther saw him lurch backward, as if taking a punch, only to shake his head and carry on.

At last, they were in the front hall. Barima stumbled out the door and onto the porch, where in the seam, the all-consuming darkness hid his shade from Esther's view. A single backpack was still frantically firing. There was a muffled scream, the shooting abruptly stopped, and then all was still.

"Esther."

Esther's heart leapt within her. The voice was clear, not muted like she was accustomed to hearing. It was a voice she hadn't heard in almost thirty years, yet one she recognized instantly. Hardly daring to believe it, Esther turned around.

Her mom looked exactly the same as she remembered. She was even wearing the same clothes, the ones she had on when she had stormed out of the house all those years ago.

"Oh, Esther." The ghost of Esther's mother stared at her in the way that only a parent can look at a child. "You've grown up."

Esther could only shake her head.

Her mom took a step forward. "I've been here a few weeks," she continued. "At least, I think it's been a few weeks. It's not easy to track time in this place. Not easy to find your way either. I've been trying to find you Esther, trying to come back to you, for a very long time."

Esther finally regained her voice. "It's you I've been seeing in my sewing room."

Her mom nodded. "There's not much joy to be found here, but...I've found some in watching you work."

Esther held her arms out to display the shirt she was wearing. For a second, she was a child again, proudly exhibiting her work to her mother. "Do you like it, Mom? I made this."

A smile brightened her mother's face. "I'm so proud of you, Esther. So proud. I remember when you made those clothes for your dolls, and I just knew that one day..."

Esther's mom stepped forward again, but suddenly stopped. Her countenance fell. "I need to tell you something, Esther."

Esther fidgeted with the hem of her shirt.

"I need to tell you that I'm sorry."

"Mom…"

"I am so, so sorry for what I put you through, for what I…what I…"

Esther shuffled her feet. Emotions were building inside her, and she didn't have time to unpack them. She looked at the lightless black pall that waited for her on the porch, just a few feet away. She was suddenly apprehensive of the object that lay within, now that she knew its true power.

"Mom, it doesn't matter right now, okay? There's something I have to do, but I don't know if I can do it. Will you stay close? Watch over me?"

"I won't leave you again."

And then Esther couldn't help herself. The question that had haunted her for nearly three decades tumbled out of her mouth before she even realized she was asking it. "Why did you leave in the first place?"

There was a long pause. "Life is complicated," Esther's mom said at last. "So is love. So is marriage."

"But what about *me*?! Was *I* so complicated?"

"Oh, Esther…"

Esther shook her head. "Mom, I have to go."

Esther walked onto the porch and dropped to her knees at the edge of the lightless void. Her hands were shaking and her concentration was slipping. Even as she fought against it, the air began to change and Esther felt herself fading back into the living world.

The violet-tinted murk of the seam was replaced by the warm glow of her porchlight, and that was when Esther saw Barima. He was lying on the concrete, his perfectly-tailored jacket marred with blood. He coughed, and his whole body shuddered, like a great ship running aground.

"Barima!"

Esther was beside him in an instant. Something moved in the periphery of her vision, startling her, but it was only Bentley, who looked like he had been in her hedge again. The cat slunk out of the bushes, tail held high, and padded up the porch steps. After rubbing against Esther's leg, Bentley hopped onto Barima. The big man raised a shaky hand to pet the animal, and Bentley settled into his chest.

When he spoke, Barima's voice was measured and surprisingly gentle.

"What is it that makes us strive so hard against one another?" he breathed, turning his head to stare into the unseeing eyes of the fallen Watcher sprawled beside him on the porch. "Furious and turbulent are these souls of ours. A pity we didn't stand shoulder to shoulder, that we didn't direct our fury at the true foe."

Esther lay a hand on Barima's massive shoulder. He didn't say anything else for a while, and Esther was afraid he had gone, but then she noticed a single finger stroking Bentley's chin, leaving traces of blood in the cat's milky-white fur.

"This animal has afforded me more peace, here at the end, than has a lifetime of zealous toil."

Esther had to lean in close to hear. Barima's voice was little more than rustling grass on a windless day.

"I wonder if that hasn't always been the answer to everything—if that isn't what makes this world worth inhabiting—if it hasn't...always just been..."

His eyes found her face, and Esther watched as they faded to black. The bright reflections in Barima's eyes surrendered their glittering luster to the night, until all that remained were murmuring memories in the darkness.

Esther reached up to brush something out of her own eyes, and her fingers came away wet. Even though she wasn't sure that he could hear her, Esther put her mouth right next to Barima's ear and whispered, "It's not the end."

Around Esther, a heaviness hung over the manicured, street-lit lawns of West Hawthorne Drive. It seemed as though the entire street were holding its breath, or perhaps being smothered. Esther couldn't help but notice that there were no faces peering around the drawn curtains and closed blinds of her neighbors' windows, and she got the feeling that every other house was up to its eaves in troubles of its own.

"Hey, Esther. You're a real cunt—you know that?"

It was Dimeter. She was sitting just inside the front door, slumped against the wall. Bits of plaster flecked her untidy hair. Her gray clothes were torn, covered in dust, and soaked in blood.

Esther stood up. "Well, you're full of shit—do you know *that*? All your righteous talk about order and the only thing I see is more chaos."

Dimeter snorted. "Every woman worth a damn is full of shit."

Esther stepped into the front hall, giving Dimeter a wide berth. "Why are you doing this to me?" she asked. "What do you want with my house?"

"There's a ghost here, and I aim to kill it."

"Why does it matter? Why this one? Aren't there others out there for you to chase?"

Dimeter put her head back against the wall and loosened the cinches of the backpack she wore. Esther found herself wondering, of all things, how many friends the lady in gray had just lost.

A pity we didn't stand shoulder to shoulder.

"I've been tracking the ghost that's moved in here for twenty-eight years," Dimeter said. "That's why it matters. Okay?"

Esther frowned. Dimeter's family had been killed twenty-eight years ago. Is that really what this was all about? "Dimeter, I've met the ghost living here. It's not the one who killed your family. It's my mom."

Dimeter tried to stand, grimaced, and sunk back to the floor. "What did you say?"

"The ghost is my mom," Esther repeated.

Dimeter stared at Esther, and then said, "You told me that your mom died in a car accident when you were six."

Esther nodded, and Dimeter continued. "She was killed in a car accident with a drunk driver, wasn't she?"

Esther hadn't told Dimeter that part. A chill descended on her.

"He drove off," Esther stated, "and they never found him. But witnesses said he was swerving all over the road, so we knew he was drunk."

"Fucking hell," Dimeter said. Her mouth worked wordlessly for a while before she finally managed, "I think that was my dad."

Esther shook her head. "What?"

"The evening before the haunting," Dimeter said, "my dad came home drunk as all hell, just like usual. The car was all smashed up though, which wasn't usual. Dad said he'd hit a deer, but he kept acting funny about it. I never found out what actually happened, because later that night..." Dimeter shook her head. "All of them but me."

"Are you saying..."

"I'm saying that my dad was the drunk driver who killed your mom," Dimeter continued. "When she died, your mom became one pissed off ghost, and followed my dad home. She killed him. She killed his wife. She killed his sons. And when she found me, she stopped."

"Because you reminded her of me," Esther finished.

"Fucking hell," Dimeter said again.

At long last, Esther moved close to Dimeter and offered her hand. The lady in gray looked at it for a moment before grasping it and hauling herself to her feet.

"Look," Esther said, "I know a way to make all of this stop, forever." It felt like all the weight of the world had just settled onto her shoulders.

"How?"

Too weary to answer, Esther closed her eyes, isolated the connection in her throbbing arm, and followed it back to the seam. When she opened them, rot and decay surrounded her, and a full-color version of Dimeter stood beside her.

"What the hell?" said Dimeter.

Esther realized with a sinking feeling that the other woman's hand was still clasped in her own, and that she must have somehow brought Dimeter with her.

Before Esther could think about taking Dimeter back to the living world, the smallest of sounds was heard. It almost sounded like the house making its house noises — creaking and shifting and sighing. Almost.

"The fuck was that?" Dimeter fumbled with the nozzle of her backpack hose.

"Listen to me." Esther looked Dimeter in the eyes. "There's something coming, and I have to kill it."

A sequence of creaking-popping noises made both women freeze.

"What's coming?" Dimeter asked, a hint of alarm in her voice.

"The Great Wave."

"Hokusai," said a voice at Esther's shoulder. "Do you know why I always liked that old picture?"

Esther's mom wore a haunted look. "It reminded me of you, Esther. You were always so strong, so sure of yourself, even as a child." She looked at her daughter with an expression full of regret. "Life is filled with both ugliness and beauty, and which one of the two you focus on determines your path. That night...I was too focused on the ugliness, both before and after I died."

There was a terrible silence, and then the Great Wave's roar shook the floorboards under Esther's feet. The monster surged through the front door, skirting the dark area on the porch. Filthy fur flew about its face as its maw stretched wide. Insatiable hunger and sinister intelligence shone out of its yellow eyes.

A blinding flash of light lit the hall, followed by a deafening blast, and the Great Wave recoiled. The flash came again, striking the creature and driving it back. At the far end of the hallway, Dimeter was firing her backpack weapon, leaning against the wall for support and screaming a string of curses that Esther couldn't hear.

The monster hunched down and coursed forward, flooding, flying. Just in time, Esther threw herself aside, feeling a rush of foul air as the thing hurtled past. Dimeter discharged a fresh volley, causing the creature to howl in agony and rage as it drew up short of her. But Dimeter was in trouble, and she knew it. She was resolute, but in the way Hokusai's fishermen were resolute as they sailed into the wave.

Esther felt something touch her arm. Her mother's fingers were delicate, just as she remembered from her childhood. Her mom smiled a full, beautiful smile, and was off, running up the hall after the Great Wave. Esther ran the opposite way, closing the distance to the phenomenon in a few short paces. She dove into the pool of perfect, absolute darkness and swept her hands back and forth. Her fingers found the phenomenon and she closed it in her fist.

The wild, electric thrill surged through her body. Her entire being quivered, from the tips of her toes to the hairs of her scalp. The darkness that surrounded the phenomenon grew smaller as it was drawn inward, as it was drawn into *her*.

Turning back to the hallway, Esther saw her mom pounding on the monster's side with her fists in an attempt to distract it from Dimeter. It worked. The Great Wave whirled around, teeth gleaming in the velvet glow of the place between places. The creature's jaws snapped shut, and the ghost of Esther's mother blinked out of existence.

Esther threw the phenomenon with all the strength she had. A long trail of shadows bridged the gap between Esther's hand and the flying object. It was pulling something out of her, and as it travelled farther and farther, it pulled more and more, until nothing of the seam remained within her. The throbbing ache that had plagued her all week was suddenly gone, and Esther knew that her connection to the seam had been severed. She knew that she would be able to *leave* the seam — she didn't belong there, after all. But she also knew that once she left, she would not be coming back.

The Great Wave looked at Esther, and she thought she saw it hesitate for a moment, as if confused by the thing flying toward it. Then the phenomenon made contact, and the creature collapsed into a writhing mass, flopping and thrashing, bellowing louder than Esther had ever heard. Dimeter poured more fire into it, blasting it again and again until at last, the Great Wave was still.

Esther waited, panting. A minute passed, then another. She and Dimeter stared at each other over the heap of tangled fur. They waited and waited, but nothing happened. Eventually, Esther walked to where the other woman stood, put a hand on her shoulder, and said, "Let's get out of here."

The air changed around the two women as they left the seam for the last time, and Esther found that she was already having trouble remembering what the Great Wave had looked like. As the desecrated features of the seam congealed and became a collection of murky shadows, Esther squinted to get one final look at the pile of dirty fur sprawling across the hall. Just before the seam faded completely from view, Esther saw a single yellow eye following her movements.

"It's alive! It's still alive!" Esther gasped as the shapes and colors of the living world came into focus.

Dimeter grabbed something with a tiny screen from one of her satchels and pointed it at the floor where the creature had lain. After peering at the screen, Dimeter declared, "It's not alive. There's nothing there."

"No, I saw it! It wasn't dead!"

Esther closed her eyes, but with the connection to the seam no longer inside her, she knew she would not be able to go back, no matter how hard she concentrated. She strained her ears, and thought she heard a creaking-popping noise retreating down the hall, out the front door, and away.

—Final Revisions—

Dimeter flicked a spent cigarette into the predawn darkness. "I've spent so many years filling buckets with water," she said. "And all this time, I should've been searching for the damned hole in the dike."

Esther, Dimeter, and Buddy stood together under the sugar maple in the front yard of 392 West Hawthorne Drive. Dimeter selected a new cigarette, looked at Buddy, and asked, "You ready to find that hole?"

Buddy nodded. "Do not make th' mistake of 'specting this to come easy, Miss Dimeter. I 'ave been searching, as you called it, for many long years, with almost no fruit to show for my labors."

"Well," Dimeter replied, "you didn't have *me* all those years, did you?"

Dimeter and her Watchers had worked for twenty-four hours straight to help Esther and Buddy clean up the collective mess they had made of the sandy-colored house at the base of the cul-de-sac. The earth, too, had seemingly done its part, depositing a thin layer of snow during the prior evening and into the night, a gilding of purity to cover over the griminess of life.

Dimeter brushed a snowflake from her gray jeans, disheveled and ripped from the day before. "Tore my favorite pair of pants at work yesterday," she said with a sideways glance at Esther. "Was a real bitch."

Esther smiled. "Bring them by Threads sometime. I'll mend them for you."

Dimeter bobbed her head and limped off. Before long, the sound of an engine split the air.

Buddy drew a rattling breath. "S'pose that's my cue."

It was odd, Esther thought, seeing Buddy without his partner. It was like discovering a sewing machine had lost its foot.

"I'm sorry about Barima," she said softly.

Buddy's sad, Indian summer smile spread across his face, and Esther's heart broke. "Just a shell," he said. "'E's not th' only one who made a sacr'fice. I'm sorry for your loss as well."

"I lost something, yes. But I also gained something, and I think Mom did too." Esther paused, and then asked, "How do you stay encouraged, after all these years? After giving so much, and still coming up short?"

Buddy looked at her. "Sometimes, Miss Esther, at th' end of th' day, it is simply enough to 'ave th' strength to say *I will try again tomorrow.* There is a quiet courage in that. And a quiet form of victory."

Buddy adjusted his navy-blue suit and said, "Thank you for ev'rything you 'ave done this week, Miss Esther. I s'pose I'll be seeing you around."

"I suppose you will. See you, Buddy."

Buddy climbed into the passenger seat of the gray van, and together with Dimeter, backed out of the driveway. Esther walked to the curb so she could watch them drive to the mouth of the street and turn the corner.

After the van had joined the flow of early-morning traffic heading toward Milwaukee, Esther remained outside, perched on her curb beside the road. Dawn was little more than a luminous smear across the eastern horizon—little more than a promise. The promise grew in strength above, and was reflected in the glass windows of West Hawthorne Drive below, and between the two stood Esther, watching the birth of a new day.

EPILOGUE
THE HAWTHORNE PROJECT

by Jeremiah Fox

"I told you: you weren't going to like knowing the truth, Colonel. The Hawthorne Project has been one on-going program since the early sixties. There's a lot of hush-hush, a lot of dirt, and more than enough bloodshed in this one. But it's all there; you can read it for yourself. I've left nothing out. Make your own conclusions."

It's a hefty file. Files. Well over three thousand pages, he estimates. It had sat on his desk initially for nearly a month after Patterson had left it sitting, bordering on insolent in his tone and stance. The colonel, a remarkable man in his own right with a history of shedding light onto the darker military and paramilitary "programs" over his career, had thought he'd seen just about everything. That was, until he opened the first of the many well-organized and carefully cross-indexed folders and began reading. That was nearly ninety days ago. Now he sits. Patterson is due any moment for an additional meeting and he's got to have some answers. *He must.*

A curt knock on the door and Nick Patterson enters, a string of man in his mid-forties, he's quick and almost bird-like in his movements, even down to the rapid eye-blinks and odd cocking of his head while in thought or intense conversation. Though appearing absent-minded, he is methodical and calculated in his work, for which the colonel is immensely grateful for. He salutes and takes the seat across the vast desk as indicated.

"Colonel."

"Patterson. Let's skip the pleasantries and get right to it." At this the colonel pushes a button on the desk, and a small red light blinks to life, a recording device, not only voice but several discreet cameras as well. This Project might have some dark secrets but he's not willing to lose an iota of information to be gleaned right from the man himself. Clearing his throat, he launches in. "Let's summarize a little, shall we? This... Hawthorne Project... it's almost unbelievable in its inception, in the conclusions. I began to wonder, reading through your notes, if I were reading science fiction or fact."

"If I hadn't seen it, witnessed events for myself, I, too, would struggle to believe it. But there it is. Proof positive: life after death."

"So, as I understand it, William H. Shaw, in 1937, comes up with a little idea, experiments on sanatorium patients. With approval, he opens Greenfield Asylum, outside Milwaukee city limits, in '41. It runs, quite successfully, for nearly twenty years. During which time, the town is growing up around them and questions are being asked. Funding is running low, patients are leaking questionable information, but word is spreading. Something diabolical is happening. Along comes a young physicist, with a side degree in human biology, with solutions for the city mayor. No questions asked, but he gets the land afterward as a sort of payment."

"Just so, Colonel. For two years this physicist, young Jim Hawthorne, has a verbal contract with both Shaw and the mayor, he gets both the grounds and the patients contained within to use for his own purposes. He claims he's part of a government agency, but in the sixties, no one asks and no one verifies. Then, he devises a method for removing the pesky problem. The fire. Problem solved." Nick spreads his hands wide, splays his fingers, suppressing the fire himself.

"Now that sums up the history. But the real interesting part, for me, is the Project itself." At this the colonel leans forward earnestly. "Is it real, Patterson? Does the veil really exist? Is there a hunter of ghosts? It's almost unfathomable."

"It is so, Colonel. No one knows who first discovered the veil. Of course it has always been a part of legends and speculation. But who discovered its actual existence?" Patterson shrugs and it almost looks like the ruffling of feathers. "What I can say is this: events have escalated in recent months. I noticed last autumn a huge shift and upped my surveillance of Hawthorne Drive. I marked on my maps the events as they occurred. Why, the week before Halloween is when it all changed. Of course Hawthorne's widow died in a strange way, with a man brutally murdered in her home that very night. Several strange instances all that week..." his voice trails off.

The colonel clears his voice at the pregnant pause. "Yes well... and did I read that one of the house owners, a, umm... Ted, I believe, in house 218 actually works under the same corporation umbrella as the late Jim Hawthorne? How can this be explained? Were thorough investigations done into this young man?"

Patterson cocks his head and rapidly taps his long fingertips on his bent knee, nods twice in quick succession. "Pure coincidence, I'm afraid. I could scarcely believe it myself. The young man has suffered several nervous breakdowns; the company dabbles in some shady business, human experiments, though they claim to only work with animals. It did not take a lot of digging or bribery to learn otherwise. That's a company to keep an eye on... after this mess gets under control, of course."

"Naturally." The elder man jots a quick note to himself and gestures for Patterson to continue.

Patterson, for his part, straightens a bit, smoothes his pants, tugs his button-down shirt a little, then launches back in. "Here's what I can tell you. At some point early in his career, Jim Hawthorne made a deal with the devil, as they say. Somehow getting his hands on information about the veil, this *in-between places*. Perhaps he discovered it himself, he *was* quite brilliant... either way, he aimed to control it. He sought for some way to travel from this realm to the next and back again. He and his team create a way. It's a "beast." A beast with an insatiable hunger. Problem is, being true to its other-realmly nature, they immediately lose control of it, once they release it. It tears its way through the veil. Instead of becoming a conduit, it becomes a monster, roaming the realm, devouring the dead. Due to the intense and violent mass murder of the Asylum brought on by Jim Hawthorne, and possibly because it is also ground zero, as it were, the creature doesn't wander far, and when it does, it returns often. The veil is thinner there, on the grounds.

"The dead from the asylum, somehow or another, are able to evade the monster. Theory is that because they were already there before the monster itself arrived, they have a different hold. They appear to have mastered the ability to travel from our realm to their shadow realm at will. And just like in the living world, there are some who are... nicer than others, shall we say. Some seem downright evil. Some wanting a body back to live in. Some sad and lonely. Some wanting revenge. But, I believe, in their own ways, they all just want peace. It is my belief that these "ghosts" were attempting to contact the various families on the street in order to right a wrong. To be noticed. Have their story told. And maybe even be rid of Jim Hawthorne's most terrible creation of all: the hunter of ghosts."

The colonel holds up his hands, stopping the younger man. "So these faceless people haunting the cul-de-sac..."

"The poor murdered patients of the Greenfield Asylum, yes."

The colonel shakes his head. Yes, he read it correctly then. A pause rests between the men for a minute or so, each in his own thoughts. Then, "the hunter still lives?"

Patterson nods sadly. "We tried to send through into the veil a talisman to draw the creature in, to annihilate it. Somehow or another, this talisman existed in both places at once, falling right into the yard of the young woman in number 392. Damn thing actually touched her last autumn. It's actually the event which changed everything and brought this whole damn project to your attention, sir. The street got in the news. That whole week the police were there nearly a dozen times. It was too much, some journalist got wind of it and they became a weekend sensation. Too much to pass up, really. Murders. Mysterious deaths. Attempted burglary. Breaking and entering. That family on the end. All of them. Frozen solid. Of course they blamed that freak storm coming through. But we know that wasn't the case. The college boys, both of them hallucinating, for weeks on end. The media spun it as drugs... all the attention Greenfield got last winter, I knew someone high up was going to notice.

"And here we are. And I'm answering questions for something I've been cataloging and studying for my entire adult life..." Nick trails off again.

"Tell me, Patterson..." the colonel whispers, "can it be stopped? It's tearing through the veil more and more frequently now. We can't keep up with it. That talisman trick... it's made the damn thing smarter, stronger. More hungry. The dead are breaking through. And it sure seems like there are more angry ones than friendly types. So: Can. It. Be. Stopped."

The young man hangs his head, unable to meet the colonel's piercing gaze. *The veil is thinning.* And sometimes when he closes his eyes, all he sees are yellow eyes and fangs and fur and blood and screams and the ever-present violet haze which covers the surrounding states glows even brighter.

The End.

Author Biographies

RIVER DIXON has unknowingly found himself trapped in the incessant heat and beauty of Arizona. It is here, along with his family, that he finds solace stringing together words in an attempt to find a structure or sequence that may one day makes sense of all this.

Blog: The Stories In Between at *thestoriesinbetween.com*
Website: *Potter's Grove Press at pottersgrovepress.com*
Goodreads: *goodreads.com/River_Dixon*

— — —

CHISTO HEALY has had over 200 stories published and several book series on the way. Much of his inspiration comes from the mind of his teenage, Ella. His other teen, Julia, has been published alongside him. He spends every day in North Carolina joyously watching his toddler, Boe, grow and evolve. He loves to hear from readers and authors alike.

Blog: *chistohealy.blogspot.com*
Instagram: *@ChistoHealy*

— — —

TRISTAN DRUE ROGERS has had his writing and poetry featured in literary magazines (such as Vamp Cat, OPEN: Journal of Arts & Letters, and Weird Mask) and horror anthologies (such as *Twenty Twenty* by Black Hare Press). Tristan lives with his lovely wife Sarah and their son Rhett in Texas.

Blog: *tristandrue.wordpress.com*

— — —

SARAH ANNE ROGERS is an artist and a writer. She lives in East Texas with her son, husband, and yeller dog.

Blog: *sarahrogersart.wordpress.com*

LOU RASMUS is a writer from Chicago. His short fiction has been published in print by Raw Earth Ink and Manic Raven Press, and his poetry has been featured online by various publications, including Silverleaf Poetry, UntwineMe USA, and The Grey Scene. His most recent novel, *Primrose Isle*, released on Amazon in early 2021, and his other two titles, *Grapefruit Juice* and *DEAD RED FISH*, are also available online.

Website: *lourasmus.com*
Instagram: *@lou_rasmus*

— — —

MARK RYAN was born in Oxford, growing up in the shadow of the dreaming spires. He studied film at London Metropolitan University, graduating to M.A in Film Theory. His work leans, bends, and sways to the metaphysical and supernatural, with a tendency to dabble in the macabre. Questioning questions and searching for answers in the eye of the storm, where there is always hope.

Blog: Havoc and Consequence at *havocandconsequence.wordpress.com*
Website: *markryanhavoc.com*
Instagram: *@havocandconsequence*
Goodreads: *goodreads.com/Mark_Ryan*

— — —

MARK TOWSE is an Englishman living in Australia. He would sell his soul to the devil or anyone buying if it meant he could write full-time. Alas, he left it very late to begin his journey, penning his first story since primary school at the ripe old age of 45. Since then, he's been published in the likes of Flash Fiction Magazine, Cosmic Horror, Suspense Magazine, ParABnormal, Raconteur, and over 30 anthologies. His work has also appeared three times on *The No Sleep Podcast* and many other excellent productions. His first collection, *Face the Music*, published by All Things That Matter Press, is available at various online retailers.

Blog: *marktowsedarkfiction.wordpress.com*
Twitter: *@marktowsey12*
Goodreads: *goodreads.com/Mark_Towse*

JOSHUA MARSELLA is a Maine native and stay-at-home dad. He is the author of *Scratches* and *Severed* and several short stories.

Linktr.ee: *linktr.ee/joshuamarsella*
Instagram: *@joshua_marsella*
Goodreads: *goodreads.com/Joshua_Marsella*

— — —

DARREN DIARMUID is a writer from Ireland. He is currently working on a novel and his collection of dark poetry, *Dream Sequence,* is due to release in 2021. His style blends raw emotion into surreal imagery.

Blog: *darrendiarmuid.com*
Instagram: *@darrendiarmuid*

— — —

ROBERT BIRKHOFER is a writer, a dreamer, and a coffee drinker. He lives in sunny Arizona with his wife and their two cats. Visit Robert's website to read more of his stories and for information on his other published works.

Blog: The Mad Puppeteer at *themadpuppeteer.com*
Instagram: *@the_madpuppeteer*

— — —

JEREMIAH FOX is a figment of your imagination. He never existed but remains to this day. Creativity flows from his fingertips and drenches everything he touches. When asked why he writes short fiction, he merely whispered, *A conduit: I am only a passage for the visions I see.* Mr. Fox has been published previously yet rarely seen.